Hyde & Zeke

Cutie and the Beast

JOSH LANGSTON

Hyde and Zeke

JOSH LANGSTON

Dedication

I'm delighted to dedicate this book to a great friend and neighbor, Jan Feese. Not only is she a welcoming, caring person, she's well-read, too. She volunteered her skills as a First Reader, and she came up with the subtitle for this story.

I couldn't be more pleased.

Thank you, Jan!

Acknowledgments

I am honored to claim membership in two amazing writer's groups: the **Verb Mongers** and the **Soleil Critters**. The members of these two gangs have gone out of their way to help me improve my work, an ongoing process for sure. So, hat's off to these marvelous Mongers: Doris Reidy, Pam Olinto, Betty Smith, Sonya Braverman Cooper, Don O'Briant, and Joe Kalcso.

Among the Critters, the following have been brutally helpful: Jack Bowie, Erika Passantino, Brad Ballish, Fred Cruser, Lou Knight, and Brian Paley.

Lastly, I want to thank the additional First Readers who waded through my manuscript and helped me turn it into a readable, and hopefully enjoyable tale. These folks are amazing, too: Don Wolf, Jan Feese, Karen Boyce, and my favorite, Annie Langston.

Chapter One

"I am fond of pigs. Dogs look up to us. Cats look down on us. Pigs treat us as equals." –Winston Churchill

Granville, Georgia. 1981 — It began during my senior year in high school....

Despite everything that's happened over the years, and that's saying a lot, Zeke is still my best friend. I couldn't have said that in the beginning, of course, because... Well, let's just say we got off to a weird start.

I remember it clearly. Malindi Moore had just announced we were through, and I was in a desperately rotten mood. She claimed it wasn't anything I said or did. She "just needed her space." She "needed to experience more of the world." I think what really happened is that she heard the school yearbook layout was done, and she no longer needed to spend time with the yearbook photographer, me.

I shouldn't have been surprised. Malindi made being shallow an art form. When I no longer proved useful, she discarded me like an old lens cloth. Zeke would have tried to warn me if we'd known each other back when Malindi and I first got together. But, of course, that didn't happen.

Sorry. I'm getting ahead of myself. I do that a lot, so rather than apologizing all the time, you'll just have to get used to it.

So, Zeke. He came into my life right about the time Malindi left it. And if she hadn't dumped me as cruelly as she did, he and I would never have met.

When Malindi dropped me, I headed straight for the woods. It was right next to my house, and I'd spent plenty of time there in the past experimenting with nature shots. But I didn't bring a camera then. I just needed some privacy. I figured if I shed a tear or two, nobody would see it and realize what a complete loser I am—well, was. See, Malindi was my first real girlfriend. She wasn't my first big crush; that was Miss Lovingood, my World History teacher. She wasn't a bad teacher for someone fresh out of college, but she'd have been an absolutely awesome swimsuit model.

Malindi wasn't in the same league as Miss Lovingood, but she was really cute, and that should have been a warning sign. Back then, really cute girls just didn't dig guys like me. It's not in their genes.

Zeke could have told me that. Not then, of course, but later, when he learned to communicate.

So anyway, there I was in the woods, sobbing and sniffling, and doing the love-sick moron thing. That's what you're supposed to do after a cataclysmic breakup, right? Weep. Moan. Eventually pour out your tale of woe in song lyrics. Constantly relive the misery in a ballad. With harmony. Make it sound really good. Get a recording contract. Achieve stardom, and then get revenge by marrying your former true love's best friend.

To be honest, I doubt Malindi had a best friend, and if she did, he or she would probably have been just as shallow. Birds of a feather, right? Probably vultures.

Whatever. Anyway, there I was, firmly embedded in nature and busy agonizing over the demise of my love life. I'd settled myself on the trunk of a fallen tree, head in hands, and figured I could bask in my wretchedness a while longer, though I needed to get back to civilization before dusk. Folks have seen bears in those woods. I'm not a fan of omnivorous critters bigger than gerbils, especially not after dark.

Which, when I think back on it, makes my introduction to Zeke even stranger.

He was a whole lot smaller than he is now, and not in the least bit intimidating. He looked as pitiful as I felt. I didn't know he was a "he" at the time, and I've got to admit, I'm still not sure that label is accurate. It probably doesn't apply to his species, whatever it is.

Way back then, he gave off a sad puppy vibe. We've all seen it—mournful eyes, trembling lip, soft fur. Okay, I may have imagined the trembling lip thing; I haven't seen him do it since. Anyway, just looking at him, I felt absolutely sure he'd been dumped, too. Abandoned. Probably by someone like Malindi. Kindred spirits, no?

"What are you doing out here?" I asked.

He didn't vocalize, but looked right at me. The eyes got me. They were... I dunno, soulful.

I reached out to him, slowly. Scaring him wouldn't do. But he didn't seem intimidated at all. He sniffed my hand and must have sensed I didn't intend to eat him because he wiggled close enough to rub himself against my knuckles.

He didn't look anything like a mink, probably because of the extra legs, but I imagined he felt like one—maybe on steroids. He wrapped himself around my outstretched hand like a mitten of stunningly soft, thick fluff.

And then he sighed.

"My name's Denver," I said. "Most folks call me Denny, 'cause I think they know I hate it."

And then he sighed again, and it sounded like he said, "Zeke" in a quiet, breathy kind of voice that dwelt on the vowel sound.

That clinched it; we were formally introduced.

He had a name, and he had me. No way could I leave him there, all alone in the woods. With the bears. Or worse. If Malindi found him, she'd have him skinned and turned into ear muffs or something. So, I took him home.

And that's how Zeke and I got started.

~*~

To keep this in perspective, I need to step back a few months. Bear with me; it'll all make sense eventually.

Miss Lovingood asked me, "How'd you like to join the *Gangway* staff?"

The question took me totally by surprise. I never thought Miss Lovingood would say two words to me outside of class. I had no idea she was the faculty advisor for the school yearbook.

I'm not much of a joiner, but the thought of working alongside Miss Lovingood had me all but drooling. "Uh, doing what?"

"Some of the kids say you're a whiz with a camera," she said. "We need someone with skills like that to create a photographic record of all the cool stuff that goes on here at Herbert Hoover High."

Cool stuff? I wasn't aware of anything like that. Mostly, I suspect, because the cool stuff was committed by the cool people, and I definitely wasn't one of them. The cool people did cool things and had cool nicknames for all of it. They never said Herbert Hoover High; it was always H3. So... *cool.*

"Well, what do you say?" she asked, all smiles. Dazzling smiles; narrow-waisted and D-cupped.

Dazzling smiles mind you; dazzling *me*. There wasn't a microscopic chance in hell that I'd pass up an opportunity to spend time with the most desirable female on planet Earth. "You bet," I said. "That'd be... Uhm. Cool."

I couldn't believe that was the best thing I could come up with. But then, I'd been ambushed. It wasn't like I had time to think of something clever.

"Excellent!" she said. "Our first staff meeting is at three this afternoon, in the library, right after school."

I watched her walk away, mesmerized by the sight of her retreating figure—a graduate-level course in celestial mechanics. Utterly awe inspiring. At that precise moment, Malindi Moore stepped between us, and my focus abruptly shifted back to the real world.

She actually batted her eyelashes at me, and she had the cupid lips thing going full throttle. "So," she said, her smile accentuated by bright lip gloss and perfect, brace-free teeth, "you're going to take pictures for *The Gangway*?"

"Yeah," I stammered. "I guess so." Master of the understatement, that's me.

"Do you know if they'll use pictures students provide? I've got some really good ones."

I could only imagine how good they were, and

suddenly I realized she was posing for me: pouty lips, hair "just so," one hand parked strategically on her hip. "Uh, maybe," I said. "I don't know how anything works yet. I just—"

"But you have a camera, right?"

"Sure! It's a Nikon with—"

"Great—you can take some pictures of me!" She fluffed her hair and did some kind of wiggle thing that left me distinctly short of words. And breath.

"Okay," I managed. "You wanna do it... here?"

She looked around, slowly, as if hoping to spot something interesting, a virtual impossibility on the ground-floor hallway of H3. "Here would work, I guess. Provided you can do some special effects stuff; you know, like make the hallway out of focus."

Finally, something I was good at. "I can do better than that! With a little planning, I can change the background completely. How does a beach in Hawaii sound?"

"With me dressed like *this?*" She waved the idea off, thought for a moment, then said, "Have you ever looked at a fashion magazine?"

I didn't want to admit that I hadn't. "I'm more into... you know... *Photography Today* or maybe—"

"I'm talking about fashion, Denver." She paused, thinking. "It *is* Denver, isn't it? Like, in Wyoming?"

"More like the one in Colorado," I said,

immediately wishing I'd said something cool instead, but she didn't seem to notice I'd corrected her.

"So, where's your camera? I'm ready."

"Uhm. Well... See, I don't usually bring it to school. The halls are always crowded, and if somebody knocked it outta my hands or something, I—"

"Well, bring it tomorrow, for sure. Okay?" She winked at me.

Oh, my God, she winked at me! "Uh, right. No problem."

"I'll meet you here," she said tapping on one of the five zillion identical metal doors that lined the hallway. "My locker. Right after classes."

I'd miss the bus, but I didn't care; I'd walked home before. Now however, I had a reason: Malindi Moore, locker number 1222, wanted to pose for me. Life was good.

Of course, back then, I was pretty stupid.

I figured out later that luscious Miss Lovingood got saddled with the faculty advisor job on *The Gangway* because she had less seniority than anyone else at H3. Barely four years older than me, she had no idea how to organize a yearbook. For some reason, the girls on the staff picked up on that before the guys did.

She stumbled through that first meeting

appointing students to various tasks based on—who knew? Maybe hair color or shoe size. And class, definitely class. Seniors got all the choice spots. Juniors got left-overs. Sophomores and freshmen need not have applied. "Come back next year," she told them. "We'll really need you then." Unless, of course, you still hadn't aged up to one of the privileged ranks.

It turns out I was the only person who knew how to operate a camera. Remember, this was back in the day before everyone had one buried inside a cell phone. And anyone who could actually develop their own film was considered some kind of wizard. Polaroids? Ha! For the first time in my life, I was in demand.

~*~

Most of the people on the staff were okay. None of us were in the cool crowd—make that "cool but cruel" crowd. We took pictures of them, and wrote about them, and some of us probably wished we *were* them. Not me.

And then there was Burt Boeheim. Most of us thought of him as Burt Bovine due to his size. The biggest guy on the H3 football team—"Go Explorers!"—he had an equally oversized ego. I think his plans for the future required proving to everyone what a badass he was. He got as far as proving what a dumbass he was, not that anyone had the nerve to tell him.

Miss Lovingood made him *The Gangway's*

liaison for sports. It took some effort to translate that into words Burt could handle. Single syllables seemed to work best for him. Sadly, the library had no English-Neanderthal dictionaries.

Anyway, between dodging Burt and taking photos of Malindi at every venue she could think of, I found myself hard pressed to shoot the stuff Miss Lovingood and the rest of the staff wanted me to shoot.

You're probably wondering what Zeke was doing all this time while I was running around taking pictures of cool people doing cool stuff. The best way I can think of to describe it is simply to say he was evolving—*from* what and *to what*, exactly, I'm not sure of. But I'll get into all that soon enough. Bear with me.

Chapter Two

"Strange how paranoia can link up with reality now and again." –Phillip K. Dick

At some point, one gets tired of being in demand, especially when the demand requires you to focus your attention on people who get way too much attention anyway. Constantly taking photos of them made me a little cranky. For the record, if you're relying on a photographer to get flattering shots of you, it's a good idea to avoid making him cranky. I turned in a truckload of photos featuring cool people in astonishingly uncool poses. I thought of it as revenge, well-chilled. And, yes, it tasted sweet.

Malindi figured it out in no time, and she thought it was pretty funny, too. That, I suspect, was her way of avoiding the same treatment. Besides, she gave me little rewards for my efforts on her behalf. She dated me. Exclusively, or so I thought.

Granted, I was required to bring my Nikon with me wherever we went. That was her requirement, not the *Gangway's*, although nobody there complained. Miss Lovingood even complimented me on my production. There were times when she actually asked my opinion about how things might be staged. I'd suggest angles, lighting options, and other technical stuff, and in return she treated me almost like an equal.

Okay, "almost" is a bit of an exaggeration, but at least she was nice to me. Burt Bovine absolutely hated that.

I took a ton of Burt photos, the best of which featured him bending away from the camera, showing his desk-wide backside. It wasn't my fault someone on staff used it for a dart board.

The photos of our stellar athlete fell into two distinct groups: Burt eating, and Burt trying to look like a Heisman candidate. The last lineman to win the Heisman Trophy was Leon Hart in 1950. I know; I looked it up. Burt didn't stand a chance of following in Leon's footsteps. The only way he'd ever get off the line and spend time in the backfield would be while grazing. I had no intention of telling him that, of course. I'm not a complete idiot. Burt made up for his bad temper and lack of intellect with a very short fuse.

With all those photos of him I'd taken, it's no surprise the local paper came to me a bit later and begged for a couple to go with the story they ran about Burt's disappearance.

~*~

It's funny how word gets around. At first, everyone just thought how pleasant it was without Burt harassing them. Kind of a communal vacation. Nobody expected foul play. Seriously, who in the world would be crazy enough to try and hurt someone that big? Heisman candidate or not, Burt would've been more than a double handful for anyone, including a gang of sumo wrestling hitmen. We all just assumed he suffered from a tsunami of indigestion.

Miss Lovingood told me the police called and said they wanted to interview me, though she assured me I wasn't a suspect. I could have my parents present if that would make me more comfortable. I didn't laugh at that, but I felt like it; *my* parents make *me* feel more comfortable?

She couldn't have been more wrong. I knew I hadn't done anything criminal, although some of the subjects in my photos might have disagreed. Fortunately, getting a snapshot of an in-crowder doing something stupid isn't a hangin' offense.

Granville isn't a huge place, nor is it a hotbed of criminal activity, so I was actually surprised to learn they had a detective on the local police force. I can't imagine how little detective work he was likely called upon to perform. Missing cats, maybe, but missing linemen? It didn't seem likely.

Detective Weiner—"That's Why-ner, not Wee-ner," according to Miss Lovingood—showed up that same afternoon and wanted to know why I'd taken so many photos of his missing person.

"It's kinda what I do," I replied. I could tell he thought I was trying to be cute. "No, really," I said, "I take lots of photos for the yearbook."

"And how'd the newspaper find out about you?"

He had me there, but not for long. Miss Lovingood came to the rescue with, "Excuse me, Detective?"

Apparently, cops are no more immune from first impressions than anyone else, and the impression Miss Lovingood provided, to males anyhow, was profound. Weiner swallowed hard, cleared his throat, and gave her his full attention. "Yes'm?"

"I was the one who contacted the *Granville Gazetter* and offered to provide photos of poor Burt. Have you any idea what happened to him?"

"It's still early. At this point, we're just gathering information." He cleared his throat again, unable to take his eyes off her, something I understood completely. "Do you know if the young man had any enemies?"

I couldn't help but chuckle, which earned me the stink eye from Weiner. "What's so funny?" he asked.

"You should've asked if Burt had any *friends*."

He gazed back at Miss Lovingood and jabbed his thumb over his shoulder at me. "So, he's the staff comedian?"

"Denver is our staff *photographer*," she said, giving me a frown, "and resident smart aleck."

That hurt. I couldn't believe she thought of me in those terms.

"Well," Weiner went on, "is he right? Didn't anyone like Mr. Boeheim?"

Mister Boeheim? I struggled to keep a straight face.

"Oh, gosh," she said, all fluttery. "I'm sure lots of people liked him. He was a star player on the football team."

"A regular tackling machine," I added. "Four hundred pounds of pure... Uhm... Boeheim."

Weiner was not amused. "I want a copy of every picture you took of him."

"Seriously? *All* of 'em?"

"Yeah."

"Are you looking for anything in particular?" I asked.

"Suspicious characters," he said, waving his hand in the general direction of the school.

I felt myself brighten. "You'll have a bunch to choose from."

Miss Lovingood frowned at me again, instantly killing the vibe.

Weiner continued, "I want eight-by-tens. In color. You got a problem with that?"

"Color might be a bit of a problem," I said.

Weiner's face went into scrunch mode. "Why's that?"

"Most of the stuff I shoot for the *Gangway* is in greyscale."

He stared at me as if suspecting I might morph into a Disney character. So, I opted to solve the mystery for him. "It means black and white."

"Yeah, right. I knew that."

"Listen," said Miss Lovingood. "I can drop the negatives off at the drug store, but you'll have to pay for the prints. The yearbook doesn't have much of a budget."

I couldn't resist making an offer. "Or I can do 'em for half the price."

His laugh sounded mean. "Just give the negatives—*all of them*—to Miss Lovegod here."

"It's Loving*good*," she said.

"Right. Sorry. I— N'mind."

I could've told him I thought of her the same way, but he clearly wasn't interested in my input. He dismissed me, probably so he could ask the Love Goddess for a date. Personally? I thought he was much too old for her. But like I said, my opinion wasn't requested. A pity.

Still and all, I found Burt's disappearance puzzling. So, evidently, did the H3 football coaches. The Explorers didn't win another game all season.

~*~

For the next few weeks, stories of all sorts floated around the school, each claiming to expose "the truth" behind the missing Bovine. The one I thought might actually contain a fact or two suggested that Burt's father ran afoul of the mob, and the family had to move away in the dead of night or their remains would turn up somewhere weird... and also in the dead of night.

A quick trip past the Boeheim double-wide confirmed that the rest of the herd still remained. That seemed a little disappointing. If the mob had ties to Granville, it suggested there might be something worth caring about around here. At that point, I hadn't found it yet. Remember, I wouldn't meet Zeke for a good while.

Malindi's reaction to the whole Burt thing surprised me, too. Normally, she wouldn't care about anything that didn't feature her front and center, but I seriously doubted her vanity could lead her to commit murder. She might swipe a lipstick, or something sparkly for her hair, but she'd never make Granville's "Most Wanted" list. Not the one in the police station, anyway.

Speaking of lists, Miss Lovingood tried to get the *Gangway* staff to devote a section of the annual to

"Senior Superlatives." The very thought made me gag. In the end we agreed to work up a list of "Most Likely" candidates. I had several categories in mind: Most Likely to Commit Tax Fraud, Most Likely to Contract a Venereal Disease, etc. Miss Lovingood tried not to laugh, I could tell, but in the end, she vetoed each of my carefully worded suggestions anyway.

"If you keep that up, Denver," she said, "you'll be voted Most Likely to Have a Camera Wrapped Around Your Head."

The most bizarre scenario floated around to explain what happened to Burt involved our very own uber-delectable yearbook advisor. Burt supposedly saw her in a compromising situation with Coach Doobin, the driving force behind H3's pathetic track and field team.

A spindly runner himself, the coach supposedly dispatched the 400-plus-pound lineman single-handedly. Coach Doobin weighed about as much as one of Burt's legs, so I doubt he would have survived a fistfight. He did, however, have a National Rifle Association decal on the rear window of his dinky, Italian car. That alone was enough for some of my classmates to want him indicted. Besides, I firmly believed Miss Lovingood had better taste. After all, she went to Auburn; he went to Alabama—a highly unstable combination.

I suppose it's possible a rival team might have ganged up on the Bovine, but if I'm being honest, the H3 student body had way more animosity for him than anyone else. More than likely, old Burt just pissed off the wrong person, probably someone with a front-end loader and a bit of land where no one would look for his body.

~*~

"Y'know, Denny, Burt's big brother is looking for you," Malindi advised, well before the infamous dumping.

"Oh?" I said, then added, "Burt has a brother? And by 'big' do you mean *also* big or big-*ger*?"

"Both," she said. "I guess he was some kinda super-stud here before he got kicked out. He's a couple years older than Burt."

"And a similar size?"

She nodded. "For sure. Like everyone else in that family, Buck is huge."

"Buck?"

"Yeah."

Great. "Do you know what he wants? According to Detective Weiner, I'm not a suspect."

Her face sort of squinched up on one side at that. "I doubt Buck sees it that way."

"Why? 'Cause I took pictures of Burt?"

"I don't know why, but I'm pretty sure he thinks you killed him."

She said it like it was no big deal; a huge man wanted revenge for the supposed murder of his brother, and targets *me*? "That's insane," I said. "Why would he think that? I never did anything to Burt."

"Well... Come to think of it, a couple of the pictures you took of him weren't very flattering, especially that close-up of him bending over. You know, the dartboard one. I'll bet that stung."

"C'mon! The darts didn't hit his real butt. How does that make me a murderer?"

"I only know what I've heard, but there's a rumor going 'round that Burt was angry at you because of those photos, and when he came after you, somehow you got the best of him."

"It's good to know you stood up for me."

She looked up, as if checking for rain clouds.

"You *did* stand up for me, didn't you? I mean, what he's thinking is ridiculous!"

"To be honest," she said, "being the girlfriend of a wanted man felt kinda exciting."

"I'm *not* a wanted man!" I didn't exactly yell it, but I felt like it.

She pursed her lips and stared directly at me. "I'm not the one you need to convince. Go talk to Buck. But...."

"But what?"

"Don't go alone. From what I hear, Buck is crazy."

"Big *and* crazy?"

"And not real bright," she added.

Chapter Three

*"Scientists have found the gene for shyness. They would have found it years ago, but it was hiding behind a couple other genes." –*Jonathon Katz

Spring, 1981

I managed to avoid Burt's brother for quite a few weeks, but doing it meant adopting strategies I'd seen on TV and in movies. I constantly changed the route I used to go home, along with the timing, but Granville isn't a big town, and there are only so many ways to travel between points A and B. The woods offered the best options since it backed up to our house. It's part of a huge chunk of land the state designated as a park and nature preserve.

That period of my life proved to be more

stressful than anything I'd ever lived through. Constantly being on the lookout for Buck while accommodating all of Malindi's demands left me weary. How I managed to avoid failing out of school is a mystery. I've already mentioned the break up with Malindi, which shouldn't have come as a shock. The fact that it did only solidifies my status as 1981's Naive Loser of the Year.

Then came the breakup after which the daily trek gave me time to ponder my life without Malindi. It's funny how some people treat you after a breakup. I don't mean Malindi; after the dumping, she treated me like I had leprosy. Most of the guys I know never said a word. The girls on the *Gangway* staff, however, seemed sympathetic. Some more than others, of course, but they all treated me nicely. A couple of them even smiled at me, and more than one suggested I was better off without Malindi in my life.

One particular girl on the staff rarely said anything to me, and yet I felt like she could feel my pain. I was pretty sure her name was Jinks, or Jinksie, something like that. A junior, she was probably younger than everyone else, and she was clearly the shyest.

Though of average height, the way she dressed and slouched at school made her appear smaller. She had jet black hair that she wore in a ponytail and dark, Asian eyes which seemed constantly on the move as if scanning for danger.

One day, early that spring, I saw her eating alone in the lunchroom, and I decided to join her. I figured we might be able to cheer each other up.

She seemed surprised when I plunked my books and lunch tray on the table and sat down beside her. After checking to see if I'd dragged anyone else along with me, she relaxed a little bit, but I could see she remained tense. Awkward is the best way to describe our first conversation.

"I'm Denver," I said. "Denver Stow."

She gave me the briefest of glances. "I know."

"I thought you might like some company."

"Why?"

"'Cause you're sitting here all alone."

"Oh."

"And you look like you could use a friend. God knows, I could."

She finally kept her eyes on me for more than a nanosecond. "I thought you *had* a friend, a *girl*-friend. The one you took so many pictures of."

"Yeah, well, not anymore; that's over," I said.

"You're better off without her."

"So I hear."

She responded with a shrug.

"Do you go by Jinks or Jinksie?"

"Jinks," she said. "It's what Dad calls me. He never learned to speak Mom's dialect."

"Well, I think it's a cool name." I hoped for a smile; I didn't get one.

"Most people think it's because I'm unlucky. You know, jinxed."

I shook my head. "That's just dumb."

She shrugged again.

I was getting desperate to find common ground. "At least no one thinks you're a cold-blooded killer."

When not even that got a response, I figured it was time to bail, take my lunch tray, and scurry off somewhere. "Nice talking to you," I said as I got up and juggled my stuff.

"Wait!" she said. "What's that?"

"What's what?"

She pointed at a photo I'd taken of Zeke which had fallen out of my notebook. I'd planned to ask one of the science teachers if they could figure out what kind of critter he is. "Oh, that. It's... uhm... nothing." I reached for it, but she beat me to it.

"I've seen this thing," she said, her voice hushed. "Where did you take this picture?"

"Well... Uh, shoot. I forget. Why?" I didn't want to admit anything about Zeke. At least, not to someone I hardly knew.

Jinks chewed her lower lip before she responded. "I saw it in the forest preserve near the pond. We were... It was right by the parking lot."

"When was that?"

She hesitated again. "I dunno. Back in the fall, I guess."

"And who were you with?"

"I... I'd rather not say."

"Oh, c'mon," I said. "I'd really like to know. I'm interested in learning as much as I can about that thing, whatever it is. Maybe whoever you were with saw something important."

She shook her head. "I doubt that. He— Never mind."

"You can't know that. Just tell me who it was, and I'll go talk to him."

"That's impossible."

"Oh, puh-leeze. *Impossible?*"

"Yeah."

"Why?"

"'Cause he's... uhm... You know. Missing."

"You were with *the Bovine?*" I couldn't believe it.

"He asked me out," she said, a note of hysteria creeping into her voice. "He's a big deal around here, and—"

"Big, yes, I'll give you that much." I tried hard not to giggle. "You had a date with Burt?"

"Well, yeah. Just one. But it didn't go very well.

We went to a movie and afterwards he said he wanted to show me something romantic."

"*Burt* said that? I can't believe he could even spell romantic."

She looked more than a little flustered, so I added, "Sorry. I shouldn't have said that."

"No, it's okay. I'm kinda new at the whole dating thing. Anyway, he drove into the empty parking lot, turned off the motor, and then grabbed at me."

"Aw, geez." I got a vivid, and profoundly disturbing mental image of great big Burt with his hands all over this girl who was barely a quarter of his size. My hands instinctively knotted up in fists as she went on.

"I was trying to push him away, when out of the corner of my eye I saw that weird animal in your picture, and I must've screamed or something because he let go of me and started looking around. I guess he thought maybe someone else might see what he was doing."

"What a sleaze," I muttered.

"No kidding. Anyway, I pointed to the strange animal. Burt said, 'Oh, it's just a dog or a cat. Ignore it.' Only, that's the last thing I wanted to do. I wanted to get the hell away from him, and that animal gave me an excuse. At that point, it looked pretty miserable."

"I'm confused," I said, resisting the urge to scratch my head. "Burt's about to rip your clothes off, and suddenly you're worried about a stray animal?"

"Oh, I was scared, believe me! But I didn't want to panic. I told him if he'd go and get the poor little thing for me, I'd... you know... kiss him and stuff."

"You're not serious!"

"I had to tell him *something*. All I really wanted was to get out of the car and run. I needed a distraction."

"And he agreed to that?"

She nodded. "As soon as he got far enough away, I took off and ran home."

"You didn't think he'd catch you?"

"I run cross-country for H3. Do *you* think he could catch me?"

She had me there. "Maybe. In a car."

"Cars don't go very fast in the woods. The park is loaded with trails, narrow ones. Way too narrow for cars. I know; the cross-country team spends a lot of time running out there. Football players don't."

I couldn't help but smile at her. "You're something else! I'm impressed."

"Don't be," she said, reverting closer to her original, stand-offish persona.

"I'm serious."

"I am, too."

"I don't get it."

She pressed her lips together and exhaled through her nose, then whispered, "Burt was reported missing the next day."

~*~

I suppose I should have expected another call from Detective Weiner right after the news broke in the *Granville Gazetteer* that the Boeheim family car had been located. According to the front-page article—there's not much news to choose from around here when it comes to front pages—the car had been abandoned in a parking lot in the nature preserve. That's not all; Granville's finest were hot on the trail of an unnamed suspect. No one seemed surprised at how long it had taken them to locate the car.

I couldn't help but think about Jinks, and what she went through on her date with Burt. Poor kid. She sure didn't deserve any notoriety after that. I figured Granville PD's ace detective could get along just fine without another highly unlikely suspect. If Jinks decided to tell him about her misadventure with the missing bovine, that was her business.

The following week, however, yet another newsflash appeared on page one: a thigh bone, presumably human, had been located in the park. Speculation was rife about whose body it likely came from, but the size of the thing left little doubt, in my mind anyway.

"Isn't it about time you came clean with me?" asked never-say-die Detective Weiner. He'd caught up with me at home after school but before dinner. I was still a bit unsettled after my afternoon trip through the preserve. The constant lookout for a mugger in the form of Burt's big brother always left me in a non-charitable mood.

"You want me to come clean about what?" I asked.

"You know exactly what I'm talking about," Weiner said. His attitude didn't help the situation. "Did you hear we found one of the missing kid's leg bones?"

"Ah," said I. "You're referring to my dear friend, Burt Boeheim."

"You got it."

"How can I help?"

"You could start by telling us where the rest of his body is."

"Believe me, Officer Weiner—"

"That's *Detective* Weiner."

"Oops. Sorry." *What a jerk.* "I'm going to make a really wild leap here, but if you found a leg bone in the park, there's a pretty good chance the hip bone, the knee bones, and all the rest are probably in the park, too. But that's just a guess; yours is as good as mine."

"Your teacher told me you were a wiseass," Weiner said. "I don't need any of your lip."

"Miss *Lovingood* said I was a wiseass?"

"I never said which of your teachers told me that." He seemed a bit defensive all of a sudden.

"That's not a very nice thing to say about a student."

Weiner humped his shoulders up around his ears. "Hey, if the shoe fits...."

"And it doesn't sound like something any of *my* teachers would say. At least, not about me."

"Knock it off, kid. It's been months. Don't you feel any remorse?"

"About Burt?" I hesitated for a split second, maybe two. "Nah."

The erstwhile cop glared at me. "You'll be singin' a different tune when we finally have enough evidence to arrest you."

"I don't get it," I said. "What makes you think I did anything to Burt? I didn't particularly like the guy, but then, nobody else did either."

"Sorry," he said. "I can't divulge any information during an investigation."

Swell.

~*~

Lots of folks have pets, and I guess that's what I had in mind when Zeke first came into my life. If my parents had been more like normal, everyday people, getting them to accept the fact I had adopted something wouldn't have been a big deal. Unfortunately, Mom claims to be allergic to pretty much any non-human animal, except when it comes to eating them. Then, it doesn't matter. Dad leaves all "domestic" issues to Mom; he's too busy running his business, whatever it is. He doesn't talk about it, and he doesn't have time for things like pets. Or kids, apparently.

That's why I never told them Zeke was now living with us. Okay, with *me*. Luckily, there's a small building at the back of the yard which Mom always intended to make into a place where she could do crafts. It was probably built as an in-law suite, though it doesn't have a kitchen. It does, however, have heat and air-conditioning. It also has all the crap furniture they didn't want in the main house. So, the craft room became the crap room. I moved into it so I wouldn't have to hear them arguing. Once I was safely inside, I barely heard them yell at each other. Best of all, I managed to convert the closet into a darkroom.

Finding a spot inside for a critter Zeke's size could not have been easier; he fit right in. Best of all, he could stand on his back-most pair of legs and reach the door handle—free to come and go at will. He even mastered the lock button!

Since I had no idea what Zeke ate, I experimented with various things, starting with table scraps. After doing the dishes, I would gather the leftovers, plus what I'd squirreled away, and sneak them out to him.

He always seemed happy to see me, but I got the impression he didn't like having me watch him eat. I tried, but he'd just pretend he wasn't hungry. At some point, anything I put out for him would disappear. I assumed he ate it, though I never saw him actually dig in.

What I *can* tell you is that Zeke had the worst farts of any creature that ever lived. I suspect it had something to do with his diet, but I did the best I could for him. I couldn't help but think his farts were some sort of defense mechanism. Lord knows he didn't appear to have anything else to fight with.

Chapter Four

"Nothing defines humans better than their willingness to do irrational things in the pursuit of phenomenally unlikely payoffs. This is the principle behind lotteries, dating, and religion." –Scott Adams

I never planned to follow up with Jinks; she called me. That turned out to be another huge turn of events in my life. Her call came totally out of the blue.

"Denver? It's Jinks."

"Uh, hey!" She took me by surprise, and I mentally reviewed our one previous conversation for something I'd screwed up. Okay, so yeah, I was a teensy bit insecure, especially after what I went through with Malindi.

"Got a sec?" she asked.

"Sure. What's up?"

She paused briefly before going on. "You remember the snapshot that fell out of your notebook in the lunchroom the other day?"

"Yeah. I never did get around to taking it to my bio teacher."

"Good trick, unless you have more than one, 'cause I still have the one you dropped."

"You do?" *Seriously? How'd that happen?*

"And I guess I owe you an apology. Keeping it was a pretty crappy thing to do."

I had no idea where she was headed with all this, so I tried to be... cool. "It's no big deal. Everybody makes mistakes."

She actually laughed. "It was no mistake; believe me. I just needed to be able to look at that sweet little face again."

"Even after what you went through with Burt?"

She exhaled into the receiver, and I thought she might cry, but she didn't. "It's just... I dunno. His little face was so... Happy. It makes me smile, y'know?"

"And *now* you want to return the print? I'm a little confused."

"Well," she said, "I've been feeling uhm... guilty, I suppose. But I kept looking at that picture, and the more I looked, the more I realized it wasn't taken in the forest preserve."

"How could you know—"

"He was sitting on someone's lawn! And since *you* took the picture, I'm guessing *you* know exactly whose lawn he was sitting on."

"Listen, Jinks, I—"

"No. *You* listen. That little guy showed up just when I needed him. He saved me! If he hadn't been there... Well, you know what would have happened."

"And, so—"

"So, I want to see him again." She paused and took a deep breath before going on. "I think you can make that happen. I want you to help me... Geez, I don't know. Reconnect. Find him. Thank him. Give him a home. Whatever."

I didn't respond immediately; I was busy wondering if, by going on, I'd do something I wouldn't be able to fix later. Ultimately, I gave in. "He already has a home."

"Oh, yeah, right. In the park, where anyone could just—"

"With me," I said. "He lives with me."

She made a little gasping sound. "Are you serious? I mean... *Really?* He lives with you? Like a... a pet?"

"Well, yeah. His name's Zeke, and he's not a pet. He's... independent. We're more like roommates."

"Oh-my-God! Will you let me see him? Can I come over now? What does he eat? Can I bring him treats or something? This is incredible! He really lives with you? Seriously?"

Was this the same girl I spoke to in the lunchroom? "Okay, okay. Relax. I guess it'd be okay. I don't— Y'see, Zeke is different. And I mean really different. Like... *profoundly* different."

"Does he bite?"

"To be honest, I've never even seen his teeth. But he's never tried to bite me."

"I'd be very gentle," she said, "so he'd have no reason to bite me. And even if he did, it probably wouldn't hurt. I mean, my God—he looks sorta like a puppy. And that smile!"

"I promise he's not a dog; I'm certain of that. I've spent a lot of time trying to figure out just what he is."

"And?"

"And I still don't know. He—I'm assuming Zeke's a 'he'—has characteristics of a couple different animals."

She giggled. "Like maybe he's a cross between one of those cute little pygmy goats and a baby tree sloth?"

"With a coat like a mink or a bunny," I said. "Unbelievably soft and smooth."

Jinks went into bubbly mode. "I can't wait to

see him! I can be there in no time at all."

"You've got a car?"

"I run cross-country, remember?"

"Do you even know where I live?"

"No, but if you give me your address...."

I felt myself growing flustered. Was I really ready for this? *What if—*

"I'm not kidding, Denny, I'd—"

"It's *Denver*, okay? I'm not a Denny. That's a restaurant."

"Right! Denver. I'm sorry. I didn't... Look, I'd do anything to meet Zeke. Well, *almost* anything."

"Would you go to the prom with me?" I have no idea where that came from. It just sort of erupted, like a surprise burp. And just like that, I'd fallen into a bottomless pit of stupid, uncontrolled madness.

"Do you mean it?" she asked. "I mean, it's only like... what? A week away."

"I'm sorry. I don't know where that came from. If there's not enough time, forget it. I just—"

"No," she said. "It's fine. I'm just surprised is all. I never thought... you know." She paused for a breath. "Do you mean it? For real?"

"Yes!" I would've said more but figured I'd just screw it up. "Does that give you enough time to get ready? I would have asked you sooner except...."

"Except you'd never said two words to me before last week."

"C'mon, I didn't *know* you before last week! Now I feel like I do. At least, a little."

"You're a nutcase. Ya know that?"

The way she said it actually made me feel pretty good. "So, you're in? You'll go?"

"Yeah," she said. "I'd like that. As long as you introduce me to Zeke first. Otherwise, the deal's off."

I gave her my address and told her to meet me in back of the house.

"There's just one more thing," she said.

"What's that?"

"Don't you dare try anything like what Burt did."

I laughed, though I suspect it may not have sounded genuine enough. "I'd never do *anything* like that. In fact—" I paused for dramatic effect "—I bet you'll try to kiss me first."

There followed an all too lengthy silence which she eventually broke with the words, "I'll see you this afternoon."

~*~

Though I didn't know how long it would take Jinks to jog over, I knew I needed to straighten up a little before she arrived. I also needed to alert my mother. She rarely ventured out to see what I was up to because she claimed the smell of the chemicals in

38

my darkroom gave her hives. After all the time I've spent in that tiny space, I must be used to it. It didn't seem to bother Zeke, either.

I tried to imagine what would happen if Mom found a girl in my room. The shock would likely have put her in the hospital. She probably thought I was gay. Dating Malindi didn't prove anything to her, but then, Mom didn't like Malindi. By then, I understood why. Jinks, on the other hand, seemed completely different. I needed time to figure out just how different and how things might work out between us.

I told Mom a friend was coming over who needed help to develop some prints for school. I'm honestly not sure which possibility worried me the most—Mom finding out about Zeke or discovering I had invited a girl to visit me in my room. Either way, the consequences would have been unpleasant, hence my desire to avoid them. It's why I told Jinks to meet me out back.

She arrived sooner than I expected and knocked gently on my door. I'd had just enough time to cram my dirty clothes in the hamper, although the lid wouldn't close all the way. It's not a very big hamper, but it would have to do. For the first time in my life, I wished I had a can of air freshener.

When she stepped through the door, Jinks' first words only heightened my anxiety.

"What's that smell?" she asked, then made a frowny face. "Please tell me it's not Zeke."

I opted not to mention the aroma he generated

when he broke wind and prayed he wouldn't let loose anytime soon. "He doesn't have a strong scent... usually." I pointed to the converted closet that served as my darkroom. "You're probably catching a whiff of the stuff I use to develop film."

"Bleah," she said. "Maybe you need a different hobby."

While she gazed around my room, I gazed at her. She didn't look anything like the shy, introverted girl I'd met in the lunchroom. Dressed in skimpy, hot-weather running gear, she looked amazing and athletic, if a little thin.

She finished her brief scan of what I laughingly thought of as my pad, and said, "This looks a lot like a motel room."

"The Ritz, right?"

Her chuckle lightened the mood. "So, where's your mysterious creature?"

I turned away from her and said, "It's okay, Zeke. You can come out now. It's safe. Jinks is a friend."

"He can understand all that?"

I shrugged. "He seems to, sometimes."

Zeke chose that moment to appear. He stuck his head out from behind the clothes hamper and stared directly at Jinks. Her face immediately softened into a warm smile. "My God, Denver, he's even cuter than I remembered. Can I touch him?"

"That's up to him," I said. "You might want to get down on his level and hold out your hand."

Zeke took baby steps out from his hiding place. When he'd emerged completely, the smile on Jinks' face transformed into a look of sheer wonder. "He's got..." She took a deep breath. "He's got *six* legs!"

"The front two," I said, "are kinda like arms. He uses them to carry his food dish outside."

"But he walks on all of 'em?"

"He can, but arms come in handy."

"And his tail? Please, tell me there's only one of them."

"There is, and it's pretty big. His back legs are larger than the others, kinda like a short, chubby kangaroo."

"He's smiling," she said. "And his eyes. They're beautiful, so... expressive!"

Like yours, I thought, then immediately tried to clear my mind. And failed.

Zeke approached her slowly as if appraising her the same way she examined him. He stopped a few inches from her outstretched hand.

"Zeke, meet Jinks," I said. "She's cool."

He inched closer to her and sniffed her hand. Immediately, his brows dipped in apparent consternation. "Warm," he said.

The word came out in a prolonged fashion

with extra emphasis on the "ar" sound. I was almost as surprised as Jinks.

"He... he *talks?*"

I nodded, trying to look like I wasn't totally stunned. "It sounded like he said 'Warm.'" I glanced at Jinks. "Is that what you heard?"

"Clear as day."

Gradually, the look of wonder on her face faded, and she shook her head as if to clear it. Looking directly at Zeke, she pointed to her hand and nodded up and down. "Yes," she said. "Warm."

Zeke's expression returned to normal, too.

"Cool means nice," I added. "Safe. Jinks is safe."

He repeated the word "safe," stretching the vowel sound as before. Then he closed the gap between himself and Jinks' hand, allowing her to touch him.

"Did you know he could talk?" she asked, a hint of wonder lingering in her voice.

"I— Well, sort of. I heard him once before when I found him in the woods. He made a noise, and it sounded like 'Zeke,' which is why I call him that. I never dreamed he was trying to... you know... chat with me."

She sat back on her heels as Zeke parked in front of her, and tilted his head to the side.

"What do you suppose he's thinking?" she asked.

"I imagine he's still chewing over the whole 'cool' versus 'safe' thing."

"My mom says she was often confused by English idioms," Jinks said. "She didn't grow up here like you and me. She had to learn the hard way."

"Idioms?" I let the word roll around in my head for a moment. I'm pretty sure I'd heard it in class somewhere along the way, but I just assumed it meant people like Burt Boeheim.

Jinks stayed quiet for a long time. She seemed content just to look at Zeke and occasionally shake her head. "I'm glad you didn't tell any of the science teachers about him. That's a terrible idea."

"Why?"

"'Cause once the secret's out—once people know he exists—there's no way you'll be allowed to keep him."

"You really believe that?"

"Yes," she said. "Are you willing to bet his life on it?"

Chapter Five

*"Bureaucracy defends the status quo long past the time
when the quo has lost its status."* –Laurence J. Peter

AARPA (Advanced Alternative Research Projects Agency) Southeast Field Office, Nashville, Tennessee — Spring, 1981

"Fitzgerald!"

"Yes, ma'am," said the agent as he walked into the office of AARPA's Chief of Southeast Operations, Augusta Burnside. The woman occupied a desk chair covertly known to agency staff members as the "GT," short for gilded throne, and she filled it completely. Burnside's office, modeled with Buckingham Palace in mind, had been furnished at the agency's expense, and most of the regional section's budget for renovation had gone into her lair.

Jonathon Fitzgerald stood in front of his superior's desk and tried not to fidget while she perused pages from a file folder labeled "Top Secret" and made noises he would have expected to hear coming from some sort of burrowing animal. In his mind, she not only sounded like one, she looked the part, like a gigantic mole-rat, with hair, and jewelry. He knew better than to smile at the thought.

"Your new assignment," Burnside said. She closed the folder and tossed it in his direction. It landed roughly halfway across her massive, ornate desk, and Jon had to stretch in order to reach it.

"Don't let that out of your sight," she said, squinting at him. "And don't screw up again. I shouldn't have to tell you that after your last assignment—"

"I understand," he said. "I admit, the outcome was unfortunate, but—"

"Save it," she snapped. "This case is more important. And, just so you know, I would never have given it to you if there had been a *reliable* agent available."

"I won't let you down," he said.

She eyed him with suspicion. "You'd better not, or you'll be out on your ass. And good luck finding another job in government service."

He gave her a slight nod. "Seriously, Ma'am, I won't—"

"Be quiet and listen." Burnside checked her watch then continued. "This one's important, so pay attention."

Looking down, Jon opened the folder without thinking.

"I said, 'Listen,' damn it." Burnside's contorted face conveyed anger and impatience.

Jon slapped the folder shut and gave her his full attention.

Burnside shook her head and exhaled as if weary. "Look, we're in a tight situation here. We've got people missing and no idea what's happened to them."

Jon nodded, unwilling to say anything that might rile her further.

"I issued orders recently to shut down a project that had been championed by someone way above our paygrades. When that individual finally retired, I evaluated the work being done. It didn't take long to see that we'd been wasting resources."

She paused to take a sip of what he assumed was tea from a dainty, porcelain cup sporting a golden *fleur-de-lis* pattern.

"William Bledsoe, the PhD who ran the operation, strongly objected to my directive, at least according to his wife. A total loser, that one. The wife, not the scientist. Well, she was, too. Anyway, I contracted a team to secure the research notes and records, dispose of any laboratory animals, and make sure nothing useful could fall into enemy hands."

She glared at him. "You do understand we have enemies, don't you?"

"Yes, ma'am. Of course. But, uhm, what went missing?"

"I'm getting to that," she said. "It's not a what; it's a who. The cleaning crew succeeded in shutting the facility down, packing up the research, and shipping it here. Something happened shortly after that. We're just not sure what, exactly, but the cleaners disappeared."

Jon couldn't help but ask, "What did Bledsoe say?"

"Nothing. Apparently, he had a coronary and died shortly after learning his program had been cancelled. We doubt he had anything to do with the disappearance of our team. He was dead before they arrived."

"Then, how—"

She silenced him with another glare. "Your job is to figure out what happened. I will be reviewing the research materials that were recovered to see if something went on down there that we didn't know about. Bledsoe shared very little information. He didn't have to; his protector saw to that. But once he lost his champion, the rules changed in my..." she paused, then corrected herself, "...in *our* favor. That's it. Now go; get busy."

"Yes, ma'am. I couldn't help but wonder—"

"Are you still here?" she asked without looking up. She had a different folder in her hand.

"Right. Sorry."

Jon scurried out of Burnside's domain and headed for his cubicle. Field agents weren't assigned actual office space; they supposedly spent their time elsewhere, providing for the security of AARPA's many experts and their various ultra-secret projects. Unlike the other field agents in the regional office, Jonathon Fitzgerald didn't have a Navy Seal, Marine Recon, or Army Special Operations background. His appointment had been purely political; his father knew someone who knew someone. Burnside was well aware of that and seemed to have made it the basis for her negative appraisals of him.

Jon knew he had to prove himself in a big way, or he'd remain miserable. A career requiring that he suck up to his overbearing boss in her version of 17th century splendor was simply unthinkable.

His engineering degree and family connections got him into and through field training. But neither of those things aided him in his first assignment, one that ended badly. The scientist whose safety had been entrusted to him refused to cooperate and ignored Jonathon's appeals to exercise caution while vacationing, so Jon accompanied him, much to the scientist's dismay. During a whitewater rafting trip, the researcher fell into the river and smashed his skull on a boulder.

Jon didn't hesitate and dove into the frigid, turbulent river. He grabbed the man and dragged him onto a craggy shore, but resuscitation efforts failed. Burnside held Johnathan responsible despite his heroic rescue efforts.

Things would be different this time, he told himself. With that conviction firmly in mind, he dug into the file he'd been given.

The project in question, codenamed "Live Canary," had been initiated several decades earlier, preceding AARPA's founding in the mid-1950s. Unlike most of the agency's projects, Live Canary operated far from the labs and testing grounds in militarily secured sites like those in Virginia and New Mexico. Instead, Live Canary's research and development occurred in rural Georgia. Run by a single scientist, William Bledsoe, PhD., and his one assistant, Dawn Popkin, the program existed with only one on-site security guard. That fact, more than any other, convinced Jon that Bledsoe's benefactor had to have been a complete idiot.

Based on the limited technical data in the folder Burnside gave him, Jon initially doubted the project had accomplished much. However, the file did contain unredacted copies of correspondence between Burnside and Bledsoe; the latter's responses to Burnside's demands trumpeted amazing results without providing specifics. Having read it all, Jon had no idea what to believe.

In any event, he didn't need Augusta Burnside to remind him of his primary focus, finding out what happened to the three-person crew sent to dismantle

Bledsoe's research lab. That would require a trip to rural southwest Georgia. And while he looked forward to getting away from the AARPA offices, a destination in the boondocks of the deep South held little appeal.

One thing for sure, he'd go well-armed. Whatever befell the cleaners would not happen to him.

~*~

With his initial review of the Live Canary file completed, Jon went straight home. His two-bedroom, furnished apartment near downtown Nashville was pricey but convenient. Since he would be sent out on assignments of varying lengths, he wanted nothing to do with pets, plants, or people needing his care.

Like most government field agents, he maintained a "go bag," a backpack pre-loaded with essentials he might need in the field. For this assignment, however, he opted to bring more clothing since he had no idea how long he'd be away. He'd leave the backpack behind.

As he crammed extra socks and underwear in his suitcase, the phone rang. He assumed it was someone from the office and answered as normally as he did when at headquarters. "This is Agent Fitzgerald."

"Well, of course it is, Jonathon," said a voice he recognized instantly. "This is your mother."

He glanced at his watch, knowing a typically

lengthy call with his mother would plunge him into rush hour traffic. "What's up?"

"You know I don't like that phrase. It makes me think I'm interrupting something important."

"Right. Sorry. I was just packing."

"Packing? That's good news."

"It is?"

"Of course, because I need you to come here and help me with your father."

"Is he okay?" Jon asked, suddenly concerned.

"I wouldn't characterize his condition as spectacular, but he's alive."

"Geez, Ma. What happened?"

"Must you call me Ma? It sounds so... coarse. Rural."

"Please tell me what's wrong with Dad. Did he have another heart attack?" With both of his adoptive parents in their 70s, heart problems were always a concern.

"No, no. Nothing like that. He had a little operation, and his doctor told him not to play golf for twelve weeks or lift anything heavier than five pounds."

"Okay," said Jon, "but what do you need me for? I've just been handed an important assignment. I have to be on the road as soon as possible."

"They can just give it to someone else," she

said. "Family comes first. Always."

"It doesn't work that way, Ma."

"There you go again with that Ma business."

"Please listen," he said through clenched teeth. "This investigation is important; it's important to me, to my career. They only gave it to me because there's no one else available. This is my big chance to prove myself."

"And what am I supposed to do?" she asked. "Do you expect me to travel *with* your father to make sure he's not connecting with his golf pals? You know they carry liquor with them, *in their carts!* Imagine: drinks in the middle of the day, before lunch even! And then, when they're through chasing those stupid, little white balls around, they race back to the clubhouse for more drinks, and cards. Oh, and *cigars!* I'm telling you, the smoke in that bar is so thick and nasty—"

"Mom, please. It's out of my hands. I have to do this." He glanced again at his watch. "I'm leaving in a few minutes."

She paused before responding. "Do me a favor. Let me make one quick phone call."

"What? No. Please. I've gotta—"

"One call. That's it. Give me... thirty minutes. Surely you can spare your mother that much, can't you?"

"I know what you're going to do," he said. "And it's a terrible idea. It could really mess up my—"

"Now you listen to me, Jonathon Andrew Fitzgerald. A thirty-minute delay isn't going to cripple your investigation or your career. You owe me that much, considering all we've done for you over the years. If we hadn't rescued you from that orphanage... well, let's just say, you certainly wouldn't be where you are today."

Try as he might, Jon couldn't recall winning an argument with his mother, ever. "Okay then. I can hold off that long. I just wish you'd let—"

"Good. If all goes well, I'll see you soon. Bye!"

He gazed down at the suddenly dead phone in his hand and then turned toward the suitcase he'd left open on his bed. If he moved quickly, he could shut it, throw it in the car, and be out of town long before the thirty minutes was up.

But he knew he wouldn't do it. As always, he'd live up to his end of any bargains he made with her, though she'd proven notoriously bad at living up to hers. With nothing on TV worth watching in the middle of the afternoon, he turned on a radio and listened to music while he suffered through the countdown.

Precisely twenty-five minutes after the call with his mother ended, his phone rang again.

Chapter Six

"It wasn't that no one asked me to the prom, it was that no one would tell me where it was." –Rita Rudner

Granville, Georgia

By the time I reached the tender age of eighteen, I figured I'd had all the weird chats I'd ever have with my mother. I could not have been more wrong. Females, I discovered, are universally obsessed with the need to prove they understand fashion. If given a position of power, like that of a suddenly caring mother over her socially inept son, the weirdness multiplies.

"You'll need a tuxedo," Mom announced after learning I had a date for the prom, something that had never happened before. Thrilled by the news, she immediately set out to make me into her version of a red-carpet strolling, Hollywood Oscar nominee.

"But I have a suit I hardly ever wear."

"Nonsense. You owe it to your date— Did you tell me her name?"

"Jinks."

She seemed not to hear me, her focus clearly being elsewhere. "You owe it to her to look your absolute best. There will be photos, and they'll be on display forever. You don't want to look like a nobody."

"But I *am* a nobody." Sometimes the truth hurts, especially when it's obvious.

"Not to me you aren't! Prom photos, and the bragging rights that go with 'em, belong to the parents. In this case, me. So, you're going to look great, Denver, whether you like it or not. Now, what color is your date's dress?"

When I admitted I had no earthly idea, nor that I was *supposed* to have gathered this critical bit of intel, Mom remained adamant about the tux. "You'll just have to go with the classic look. If you can find out what color or colors she's wearing, we might be able to get a matching cummerbund."

The word "cummerbund" felt distinctly weird, and I wished I'd had a dictionary handy. The look on my face must have given Mom a clue that I was befuddled. She said, "It wraps around your waist."

"So, it's a belt."

"No, it's much bigger than that." She set her palms about a foot apart.

I envisioned the sort of belt worn by professional wrestlers or rodeo circuit bull riders. I couldn't quite square the image with something dressy like a tuxedo, but I gave in anyway. "Okay, sure. That sounds great."

"Good! Now we're making progress. Why don't you call... What's her name again? Jingle?"

"Jinks."

It was Mom's turn to wear a confused look. "What kind of name is that? She's not a gypsy, is she?"

"I doubt they have many gypsies in China."

While she looked confused before, her expression quickly shifted to alarm. "She's Oriental?"

"Her mother is from China. Her dad's from... I dunno, Montana maybe. It doesn't matter. Jinks grew up here in Georgia, so she's no more oriental than I am. Besides, I'm pretty sure oriental is a kind of floor covering."

"But she's pretty?"

I couldn't help but wonder who this person was, and what she had done with the woman who gave me life. I shifted into wise-ass mode and instantly felt safer. "No, she's repulsively ugly, unless you're into sumo wrestlers, in which case she's drop-dead gorgeous."

"Sometimes you act just like your father," she said.

I presumed she meant that as an insult.

"By the way," she added, flicking a bit of lint from her blouse, "he and I are getting a divorce."

The lint missed me by a good inch.

~*~

After a hurried phone call with Jinks, I embarked on what I knew would be a thoroughly humiliating trip with Mom to a place that rented formalwear. Mom told me it was my fault they ran out of black tuxedos in my size. Apparently, I should have arranged my date earlier, before they sold out. In any event, I started looking at alternatives, mostly in shades of maroon and gold—school colors.

Mom quashed my efforts and dragged me away from the rack featuring "non-traditional" options. "A white dinner jacket and dark slacks will look great on you. And you said Jinks is wearing something in coral, right?"

I shrugged. "That's like... pink?"

"Right, with a hint of red. So, all you need is a pinkish cummerbund. You'll match! It'll be so cute, so... exciting! I can't wait to see you together."

Dressing like a waiter for the prom didn't thrill me, but it got my mother off my back. The white jacket looked okay, but once the photos were taken, the pink "guy girdle" would remain in the car, in a bag, under the seat, and well out of sight.

I was ready for the big dance. Not that I had a clue *how* to dance, or do much of anything else on a date with a girl more interested in me than my camera. But, if nothing else, the awkwardness of prom prep kept me from thinking about Buck Boeheim. The week prior to the "big event" passed without any major trauma. Jinks dropped by twice to see Zeke, and I found myself liking her more and more.

"Zeke can *talk*," Jinks said, as if I hadn't noticed. The three of us lounged around a shaded picnic table in the back yard. Mom was off hunting cummerbunds or something, so we had plenty of privacy.

"He may know a couple words," I said, "but that doesn't mean he can carry on a conversation."

"Yet!" She looked incredibly earnest. "We can teach him."

"Uhm... okay. But just remember, neither of us is Jane Goodall, and Zeke isn't a chimpanzee."

"It wasn't Jane Goodall who tried to teach Koko the gorilla how to use sign language. And I'm well aware that Zeke isn't some kind of monkey. He's way more advanced. Just look at him! I think he knows what we're talking about."

Zeke hadn't said a syllable yet that day, but I got the impression Jinks was right. "So, how do we proceed? Show him stuff and name it?" I pointed to the outdoor table at which we sat. "Tay-bull," I said.

"Let's start with names," she said.

It went on from there, and we covered all sorts of things—trees, buildings, clothing, even my camera. Zeke was a good sport about it, and even tried to mimic the words we fed him in his vowel-heavy way.

Eventually we all grew tired, though Jinks declared the afternoon a success and announced that this would merely be the first of many such lessons for our six-legged friend. I worried a bit when she gave Zeke a hug, but he didn't seem to mind it any more than he had the language lesson.

I wished Jinks had hugged me, too. Watching her jog away through the preserve left me feeling low. Zeke wandered into the woods, but it seemed clear to me he wasn't following her.

Mom returned shortly thereafter and joined me in the backyard "for a chat." Coming from her, "chat" was a trigger word, and I endeavored to proceed with caution. She wanted to talk about her split with Dad.

She seemed oddly unconcerned about their pending divorce. To be honest, I wondered why it had taken so long to reach that point after all the arguments they'd had. Dad spent very little time at home, and Mom never seemed to care. When I asked her about it, she said she had waited to file until I was old enough to live on my own.

On my own? That left me more than a little freaked out.

"With your photography skills, I'm sure you'll be able to find a job somewhere. And when you reach twenty-one, you can use the trust fund your grandmother set up for you."

"I have a trust fund?"

"Yes."

"What's in it?"

"I have no idea," she said. "But she left enough for me to live on, whether your father pays alimony or not."

I was speechless.

"Don't worry," she continued, "it'll take a couple of months, at least, before it's all finalized. He's not contesting it. I think he's relieved."

Evidently, offspring weren't given the option to contest such things. "Will we still live here?"

"For the time being anyway."

~*~

In order to have permission to use Mom's car for the prom, I had to promise to bring Jinks by the house for the photo session. I left my Nikon mounted on a tripod for instant use, hoping for a quick escape once the shutter had been clicked. Knowing Mom, she would likely be armed with a two-dollar, disposable camera she'd found at a discount store.

Jinks met me at her front door. She appeared slightly embarrassed in a pinkish prom dress that hugged her torso in all the right places. For once, she didn't have her hair trussed up in a pony tail. Instead, it draped down over her bare shoulders. My mouth went suddenly dry, and the boxed corsage Mom provided shook in my hand.

"You look... just... wow," I said, struggling for the right word. She smiled at that, and suddenly she wasn't merely pretty; she'd become a goddess, one who'd left Aphrodite behind in cross-country dust. The smile transformed Jinks from the girl I thought I knew into the girl I desperately wanted to know. I breathed a final, "You look absolutely gorgeous," which kept that beautiful and suddenly confidant smile on her face.

Jinks' parents welcomed me in, and we chatted briefly. They helped Jinks with the corsage, took a few snapshots, and told us not to stay out too late. Just as we were about to leave, Jinks' dad asked if I enjoyed being the yearbook photographer.

"Absolutely," I said, trying not to look too proud or overly eager to leave.

"Jinks says you're pretty good, but we haven't seen the yearbook yet."

"It'll be out soon. Some of my stuff is on display in *The Gangway* office."

Jinks gave me a light elbow jab. "There are *dozens* of great pictures there, Dad. He's amazing! You've gotta give him a chance."

I spun my head in her direction. "A chance at what?"

"Dad's the managing editor at the *Gazetteer*. They need a staff photographer, and I told him you'd be perfect for it."

"'Cause I'll take pictures of anything?"

They both chuckled, then her dad grew serious. "If you're interested, drop by my office on Monday and bring some examples of your work. We'll talk it over. But don't leave me hanging. I need to fill that spot as soon as possible."

Jinks and I left shortly thereafter.

I don't often pray outside of church, but I felt like it then. I not only had a date with a goddess, I had a possible job offer—to do something I loved doing! The entire gang on Mount Olympus had to be smiling down on me. I gazed at Jinks and thanked her.

"For what?"

"For... all of it. The prom, the job offer, everything."

"The night's young," she said, still smiling. "Let's not get ahead of ourselves."

~*~

Much to my surprise, Mom didn't embarrass me when Jinks and I made our obligatory appearance. After mooning over my date and her dress, Mom asked me to show her how to use my camera.

"The two of you look so... so *grown up!* I want a great, big, color photo, and I'm going to have it framed. If you'll help me Denver, I'll get just the right shot." She favored Jinks with a broad smile. "I'll make extras for you and your parents, too."

Once the picture-taking ended, Mom asked a question that quickly undid all the good she'd done. "So, where are you taking this lovely girl for dinner?"

"We uh... I thought, maybe...."

Jinks came to the rescue. "This all came together so fast, we didn't really have time to plan anything. So, we'll probably just grab a burger somewhere."

"Nonsense!" Mom said. "This occasion calls for something way nicer than that." She looked directly at me. "Why don't you take Jinks to The Cascades?" She glanced at her watch. "The dance doesn't officially start for over an hour, and besides, it's always better to arrive fashionably late."

She then cast her smile at Jinks. "How does that sound?"

Jinks swallowed. "It actually sounds kind of... uhm... pricey."

Mom waved the objection off. "Hah! It's already taken care of. I play bridge with the owner's wife, and she owed me a favor or two. She set up a reservation for you—best seats in the house, according to her—but you'll need to get a move on."

"Mom, I don't have anywhere near enough—"

"Money?" She laughed. "Don't give it a thought. This is your father's treat, though he doesn't know it yet. Order whatever you want and put it on this." She handed me a credit card. "Have fun, and don't worry about a thing."

I kissed Mom on the cheek, then Jinks and I left, smiling. And hungry.

Over a sumptuous meal at Granville's swankiest restaurant, I confessed that my dancing ability was somewhat limited. Pride kept me from admitting I'd never actually danced at all.

Jinks took the news gracefully. "To be honest, I'm not much of a dancer either." Then she added, "Let's just watch what everyone else is doing and copy them."

That suited me. After a ridiculously expensive dessert, we headed to H3. Nothing says elegant like a high school gym decorated in streamers and balloons by kids who haven't the foggiest notion what they're doing.

Chapter Seven

"No one lies so boldly as the man who is indignant."
–Friedrich Nietzsche

We were met at the gym door by Miss Lovingood and Coach Doobin, both dressed in nice, if not formal, attire. Miss Lovingood flashed me a big smile and a thumbs up. "Nice goin', Denver," she whispered. "That girl's quite a catch. What's her name?"

Are you serious? "It's Jinks! She's on the *Gangway* staff."

"Oh! I— If... Uhm...."

With a shake of my head, I maneuvered Jinks through the entrance, hoping she hadn't noticed our esteemed advisor's colossal memory lapse. I, too, had been most pleasantly surprised by Jinks' appearance, but there was never any doubt about who she was. Miss Lovingood's standing among my most admired instructors took a nosedive.

Once inside the gym, we made a quick tour of the large, streamer-bedecked room. Someone had added colored lights to the decor, and it helped, but the disco ball hanging from a basketball hoop didn't. The aroma in the big room was a mixture of Old Spice and perspiration, tinted with a variety of perfumes depending on who stood nearby. The band had a nonsensical name, and they compensated for their lack of talent by cranking the volume up enough to deafen any potential groupies.

We danced a little, and even held hands for a while as someone from the prom committee made an announcement. That august body decided it would be nice to dedicate the prom to the memory of Burt Boeheim whom the police had declared dead. Had he survived, he would have graduated, alphabetically, near the top of his class.

The pronouncement had a decidedly negative effect on both of us, and we wandered outside to cool off, psychologically rather than physically. As we exited, I noticed that both of the chaperones assigned to the entrance had gone AWOL, but that didn't worry me. In fact, I felt happy to be alone with Jinks.

My joy was short-lived, however. It ended with the arrival of Burt Boeheim's older brother. Buck appeared just as we settled ourselves on a bench outside the building. Buck did not look very steady, and I suspected it had something to do with the half-empty liquor bottle in his hand.

I seriously doubted Buck had shown up to celebrate the honor bestowed on his brother. Despite being wobbly, his great size and the look on his face promised something grim if not ghastly.

"I've been lookin' fer you," Buck said. He stood a few feet away, but I could still smell the alcohol on his breath.

Jinks grabbed my arm. "We should go back inside," she said as she rose. "Now."

"Doan rush off on my account." Buck shuffled sideways, one arm waving dismissively. After stepping between us and the double door entrance to the gym, he put the bottle to his lips, took a swig, made a face, and belched.

"What do you want?" I asked, praying he had a non-lethal objective.

"Jus' wanna talk," he said, pointing at me. "To you."

"I'm going for help," Jinks said, her voice nearly obliterated by the noise coming from the alleged musicians inside the building. She let go of my arm and attempted to sidestep Burt's brother. He stopped her with ease, pushed her back toward the bench, and growled, "Siddown."

"Leave her alone," I said. "She—"

"Shuddup, asshole," Buck said, jerking a hand

toward her. "She's part of this. She's the reason you killed Burt."

"That's insane!" exclaimed Jinks. "Neither of us—"

"You're *with him*, ain't ya?" Buck didn't wait for an answer and turned to me instead. "You wanted his girlfriend."

"You're drunk," I muttered. "C'mon Jinks, this guy's—"

"Shut it!" he yelled. "Everyone knows how easy foreign girls are. They're eager for it. They can't wait to get knocked up by one of us so they can get welfare. Burt got him one, and you couldn't stand it."

"That's bullshit!" I shot back. "She's not—"

"You couldn't wait to git yer hands on that little chink whore, could ya?"

I lurched upright. Buck had been moving forward, and my head collided with his snout. He dropped his bottle of booze as he stumbled away, but the glass didn't break. His nose didn't fare as well; the collision released a torrent of blood.

Buck groaned and probed his face with both hands. I kept my eyes on him while I rubbed the sore spot on the crown of my head. Eventually, he looked down at his hands and saw the gore; that set him off again. "You're dead!" he screamed as he lumbered toward me.

I edged to one side trying to evade him and realized Jinks had somehow disappeared.

Buck's face registered rage and hatred, looks I'd never personally encountered in my life. He lunged at me and grabbed the front of my dinner jacket. The backs of my legs slammed up against the bench Jinks and I had been sitting on.

Blood leaked steadily from Buck's nose as he pulled back a massive fist and paused, a menacing smile curling his fat lips. He wanted me to see it coming. He wanted me to panic, beg for mercy, and crap my pants.

Instead, I punched him square in the center of his squat, ugly face. The blow made an odd, squishy sound. Not what I expected after watching any number of fistfights on TV.

Buck let go of my jacket, his face reflecting both shock and pain. Tears trickled down his cheeks and mixed with the blood already dripping from his lips and chin.

My adrenalin levels had spiked. I couldn't stop shaking, but I was ready to take another shot at him if needed.

"There they are!" shouted Jinks from somewhere behind me, though I wasn't about to take my eyes off Buck. What she said didn't make any sense until she and a uniformed policeman raced into view.

The cop went immediately to Buck; Jinks ran straight to me. "Are you all right?"

"My head hurts a little," I said. "So does my

hand." I couldn't tell if the blood on my knuckles was Buck's or mine. I continued to shake even though the danger had seemingly passed. The cop helped Buck, now strangely cooperative, to his feet. Once steadied, the policeman led Buck away, a gratifying sight.

"How did you find a cop so fast?" I asked.

Jinks still looked worried. "He was directing traffic when we arrived. I guessed he might still be around, and he was. When I yelled, he came running."

She took a long, slow, shuddering breath, then shook her head and tsked at me. "Your jacket's a mess."

I looked down to confirm it. She was right. Buck's blood appeared in vivid contrast to my white dinner outfit; streaks and smears of red were accompanied by a mist of crimson dots.

"Why'd you hit him?" She had her palms on my cheeks, staring at me. "You should've just run."

"He grabbed my jacket, so I couldn't get away, and besides, I… Uhm… I didn't like what he said about you."

And that's when she kissed me.

~*~

I slept late on Sunday morning, the day after the prom. I would have slept even later if it weren't for the noises Zeke made while sniffing the blood on my rented tux. His little nose twitched up and down, and the sounds he uttered definitely weren't words, at least not any found in English.

70

"What's the deal?" I asked him, not really expecting an answer.

He just looked at me for a moment, then went back to sniffing and grunting. From time to time he'd stop, walk to the window, and look out after another round of sounds. Weirdness.

I knew I needed to get the jacket cleaned and hoped I could get it done without Mom knowing about it. The possibility was microscopically thin, but I clung to it anyway. I also needed to get some photos together to bring to my job interview with Jinks' father at the *Gazetteer*. That kind of possibility had a lot more going for it.

Only a couple of the dry cleaners in town were open on Sunday, and neither of them said they could completely get rid of the stains. Settling for less didn't cut it; I would have to tell Mom.

Finding decent photos, however, turned out to be fairly simple. I'd been doing it long enough to recognize good technique from bad, and it certainly wouldn't hurt that I knew how to develop and print my own stuff. I whipped up a selection of nature shots, close-ups, crowd scenes, and even a couple that would soon appear in *The Gangway*.

Feeling good about my pending interview didn't make me enthusiastic about showing Mom my dinner jacket or explaining how it got stained. I decided to wait until I had Jinks by my side for corroboration. Mom had rarely been pleased by my clarifications of past sins.

Jinks agreed to my plan and jogged to the house in the afternoon. We had a brief chat about what we'd been through the night before, without any mention of the kiss. And despite my inability to think about much else, I couldn't summon enough confidence to bring the subject up. Instead, we formed a united front, marched indoors, and presented the wounded wardrobe together.

Mom reacted predictably to the grim, red stains and assumed the blood came from me. Jinks set her straight, although her version of the ambush and my "gallant defense"—her words, I swear—included several details that came as news to me. I couldn't help but wonder if she'd given the same glowing version to the police.

Though unhappy about the condition of the jacket, Mom seemed relieved to know I had not been wounded. I told her I'd taken it to two separate dry cleaners who pronounced it unsalvageable.

"I'm going to the rental shop," she said. "Maybe they'll know what to do." She left without another word.

I felt I owed Jinks a huge thank you for standing by me. "I think that's the first time anyone ever really stood up for me."

"That makes two of us," she said as she, Zeke, and I got comfortable in the backyard at the picnic table in the shade of the nearby woods. "You didn't let that big idiot get away with the things he said about me."

I touched the bump on my head where I'd made the initial contact. "It was kinda accidental. And there's a spot right here that's still a little sore."

"Maybe so, but the jab to his nose was no accident."

I brightened. "Does that mean I get to kiss you now?"

"I— Uh...."

"What is kiss?" asked Zeke.

We both looked at him in surprise. Though he usually repeated the words we tried to teach him, and he appeared to understand them, he never asked any questions. Until now.

"Well, a kiss is—" I began.

"It's something people do when they like each other," Jinks said. "It's a sign of affection."

Zeke squinted at her. "Affection," he said, almost getting the pronunciation correct.

"When two people touch their lips together, it's called a kiss," I said, then turned to Jinks. "We really ought to demonstrate."

Her mouth twisted a bit to one side before she responded. "You're loving this, aren't you?"

"Pretty much. Yeah." I couldn't help but smile.

"Kiss," said Zeke. "Now."

"Don't go getting any crazy ideas, Denver. This is educational, not... you know... romantic."

"Obviously," I said.

I remembered the kiss she'd given me after the run-in with Buck, but this one was different. I expected it to be odd, and more than a little kinky, since we were supposedly doing it for Zeke's benefit. That feeling disappeared the moment her lips met mine.

They were soft.

And warm.

And she didn't pull away.

In fact, she put her hands on either side of my head and gently pulled me closer. I didn't want it to end, even when I realized I'd been holding my breath.

When we finally separated, I inhaled deeply and, I suspect, dramatically. "That was...."

"Educational," she whispered, though she didn't seem as shell-shocked as I was.

"I'll say." I cleared my throat and went on, hoping I wasn't pushing my luck. "I thought you were new to the whole dating scene. But that kiss... Oh, man."

She giggled. "I watch a lot of movies about people in love."

That triggered an idea. "Y'know, maybe we ought to do it again. I mean, in case Zeke missed something."

She promptly looked alarmed, stood up, and backed away. "No! It's... I— I better get going."

"But you just got here!"

"I'm sorry," she said. "I've gotta go."

I watched her race away, back through the woods the way she'd come. I spent the rest of the afternoon trying to figure out what I'd done wrong.

Chapter Eight

"Ask any experienced defense lawyer: the real risks are for an accused person who is innocent. A guilty defendant has many more options available." –Andrew Vachss

All my life I've heard—mostly from other guys—that women are impossible to understand. Jinks proved it. I tried to put the events of Sunday afternoon out of my mind, a good trick in light of my upcoming job interview with her father. My boneheaded attempt to coax her into another kiss had gone train wreck wrong. And I still didn't know why. I actually thought I'd been rather clever, and I hadn't meant to be threatening in any way. Yet, she took off as if some sort of crazed beast was after her.

I didn't feel much like a crazed beast. I felt more like… a loser, maybe the King Kong of losers. If self-confidence was the hallmark of successful job candidates, I hunkered down at the other end of the scale, ground zero, hardly the sort of emotional state to be in when walking into the office of your true love's daddy to beg for a job.

That occurred the following day.

Somehow, I held it together long enough to answer his questions and display my work. He was complimentary and never said a word about Jinks, the prom, or anything that may have occurred the day after. All in all, it went better than I thought possible.

At the end, as I repacked my prints and gear, he told me I was one of two finalists for the staff photographer job and that he would call me in a day or two. He said he needed time to check references. I only had one, Miss Lovingood, and I prayed she'd vouch for me.

"As of now," he said, "you're the leading contender for the position. I'm assuming you don't have a police record; the company has a policy that forbids us from hiring lawbreakers."

I thought I was on pretty safe ground at that point. I thanked him for his time and traveled all the way home without feeling my feet touch the ground.

Much to my surprise, Jinks was sitting on the front steps of the house waiting for me. Dressed in running shorts, t-shirt, and ballcap, she looked really cute. She would have looked even cuter if she'd been smiling.

The garage door was open, so I could see Mom's parked car and assumed she was home. I wondered if she knew Jinks was there.

"How'd the interview go with Dad?" Jinks asked, her tone subdued. Small talk.

"Fine, I think. I'm just... I didn't expect to see you here."

Oh, nice, Denver. Put her on the defensive. Why stop now? Go ahead; prove you're a total loser. What else can you do to turn her away?

She gave me a tentative smile. "I don't know what got into me yesterday. I've been thinking about it all morning, and I realized we need to talk."

Need to talk? Oh, God—code words! Just like with Malindi. No warning, just boom—and breakup.

"Relax," she said. "You look like... I dunno... like you just lost a friend or something. I thought you said the interview went okay."

"It did! Your dad's easy to talk to. But I... Uhm... Does my mom know you're here?"

"Of course. I talked to her when I first got here. She invited me inside, but I told her I wanted to wait out here for you."

I could tell she was eager to dismember whatever budding relationship we had.

"Could we go into the backyard?" She turned to look at the front door then back at me. "I'd rather your mom didn't... y'know... hear us."

"Sure, no problem. I'll see if Zeke's around, too. Okay?"

That prompted a real smile and tempered my misgivings a little. Maybe, thanks to Zeke, we could at least remain friends. A quick fevered memory of our last kiss crept into my head and wouldn't leave. And, to be honest, I didn't want it to. If anything, I wanted to create more memories just like it.

As we rounded the house and headed toward the picnic table, Jinks reached for my hand, held it, and walked beside me. I felt a surge of relief, but my utter lack of self-confidence quickly flooded back. She was just trying to calm me down, *before she let me down*—like a sedative before the fatal dose. *The end is near!*

"I wanted to apologize," she said.

"For what?" *Breaking my heart? Yes, yes, I know we only had one date and it was just... okay... weird. But still....*

"For running away like an idiot, a ninny. I shouldn't have. I should've..." She paused and looked slightly out of breath. A pained expression crossed her face. "Can I be honest?"

Oh, geez. Here it comes. "Of course."

"I really wanted to kiss you yesterday afternoon."

"You did?" *Really?*

"Yes, but I was afraid it might... I thought

maybe it was too soon." She wrapped her arms around her chest and hugged herself. "I worried what you would think."

"What? Think *what?*"

She pressed her lips into a tight line. "That what Burt's brother said might be true. That I'm... you know. Easy."

Are you crazy? I reached out, hoping she'd take my hands. "I never thought that. I never thought anything even remotely like that."

She put her hands in mine and stared at me—a look of distress, or worry, or maybe even fear darkened her features. I felt like all my self-confidence and all my stupid doubts had somehow infected her. I managed a whisper. "I swear to you; I never thought any such thing, and I never, ever, would. I couldn't."

At some point, Zeke put in an appearance; he must have seen us because I didn't take the time to look for him. He climbed up on the table and sat beside us. He seemed intense and examined us as if looking for a hint of something terrible. Just what that might be didn't occur to me. I was too busy being happy I hadn't messed things up with Jinks.

The afternoon passed much as previous ones had until I heard Mom calling me which put a serious damper on the proceedings.

I answered with something lame about being in the backyard, then I aimed Zeke toward the door of the little house where we bunked and gave him a nudge. He took off and was quickly out of sight. Meanwhile, Jinks worked her way around to the far side of the picnic table.

"There's a policeman here to see you," Mom said as she walked around the corner of the main house. She hated using the back door since the latch always stuck. It had taken me quite a while to figure out how to make it do that. The effort was worth it, however, since it gave me a bit more time to prepare for any unplanned visits.

Detective Weiner followed in her footsteps, his expression dour.

"I presume this is about the man who attacked my son the other night," Mom said, addressing the cop. "I'd certainly like to know what you're going to do about it. The dry cleaner said he couldn't get the blood stains out of the tuxedo jacket we rented, so we had to pay for a replacement. Will I need to take that hoodlum to court in order to get reimbursed?"

"I don't know," said Weiner. "I'm a cop, not a lawyer. If you have an attorney, ask him. As for why I'm here, I need to speak with that young man." He pointed at me. "The rest of you don't need to stick around."

"I believe I'll just stay right here," Mom said.

Jinks put her hands on her hips. "I'm not going anywhere either."

"He's the only one I'm here to see," said Weiner, his eyes still on me.

That definitely raised Mom's blood pressure. The rental company had charged her $200 to replace the jacket, and Dad said he wouldn't pay for it. "If it involves my son," she said, "it involves me."

"Suit yourselves. I'm just here to follow up on a police report that came across my desk." He frowned at me. "According to the complaint, you attacked a man the other night and broke his nose."

"*What?*" I suddenly felt a surge of 220-volt anger.

Weiner continued, "It's called assault *and* battery since he says you threatened him first."

"That's insane!" I yelled.

The detective simply shook his head. "I figured you'd be both argumentative and uncooperative. I'm not arresting you. At least, not yet, but you're coming with me. We'll finish this discussion at the station."

~*~

Mom and Jinks followed Detective Weiner all the way to Granville's police headquarters, a small building right next to the county courthouse. I sat in the back of Weiner's car. I tried to be positive and waved to Mom and Jinks through the back window, mostly to assure them I hadn't been handcuffed. Weiner said nothing during the drive, which surprised me, but then, the whole afternoon had been one massive surprise.

When we reached the police station, Weiner led me to an interrogation room and left me sitting alone while he did whatever cops do when they're trying to intimidate lawbreakers. Even though I hadn't broken any laws—at least none I knew of—I remained intimidated. Eventually he entered the room, spread a file of some sort on the table between us, and took a seat.

"Where's my mother?" I asked.

"She's waiting outside. You're almost nineteen, an adult in the eyes of the law. So, your mommy doesn't get to be in here with you. The same goes for your girlfriend."

"You said I wasn't under arrest."

"True. But just so you know, Denver, you're in deep, deep shit."

"Because why?"

"Based on this new complaint—"

"You mean the one from a drunk? The guy who came after me?"

Weiner's attitude didn't change. It was abundantly clear he had no interest in things like evidence, reason, or constitutionality. "We've got you, dead to rights."

"I want a lawyer," I said.

"Hah! That tells me I'm right!"

I glared at him. "It ought to tell you you're full of crap."

Weiner rattled a piece of paper before reading

it. "According to this *sworn* statement, Mr. Boeheim attended a ceremony at Herbert Hoover High School in order to affirm the honor bestowed on his brother." Weiner looked up from his notes. "That'd be the guy you killed."

"I haven't killed anybody. Burt's stupid brother was drunk. He could barely stand. I doubt he even knew about the dedication—"

"Shut up until I finish reading."

I sat through it all. Buck claimed I'd waited for him to exit the building and then attacked him when he tried to exchange pleasantries.

"Buck Boeheim wouldn't know a pleasantry if it bit him on the—"

"Keep it civil, smart guy."

A deep breath did little to calm my nerves. "Do you honestly believe I went to the prom just so I could beat up a guy twice my size? So I could get blood all over my rented tux?" I shook my head at the idiocy of it all. "What possible motive could I have for doing something so... so incredibly stupid."

"Criminals rarely use good logic," Weiner said.

"Evidently, detectives don't either."

He didn't react. "Mr. Boeheim claims he has proof that you hurt his brother, too, that you were jealous of him and wanted to steal his girlfriend."

"Obviously, you haven't spoken to Jinks. She can clear it all up. I can't believe you're after me based on the ravings of a maniac. Aren't you supposed to do sobriety tests on the people you arrest?"

"Why?" He squinted at me. "Have *you* been drinking?"

"No! I'm talking about your star witness, Buck Boeheim, the walking, talking booze bottle!"

Weiner snorted. "Nobody arrested him. He was taken to County General to have his nose patched up after you broke it."

I had never been so angry; nor had I ever been faced with such a towering mass of stupidity. It took a tremendous act of will to keep my thoughts to myself. I took another deep breath and followed it with, "You said I wasn't under arrest, right?"

"Not yet, no."

"Then I'm leaving."

"I'll *tell* you when you can go!" Weiner said with a scowl, his arms crossed as if to confirm he'd have the last word.

"If I haven't been arrested, then technically, you're holding me against my will. That's called kidnapping, isn't it?" I had him, and he knew it.

"Okay. We're done for now," he said. "But this isn't over."

I wondered if Mom's divorce attorney would help me sue the city for hiring someone so astonishingly incompetent.

Chapter Nine

"The only reason for time is so that everything doesn't happen at once." –Albert Einstein

Nashville, Tennessee — Spring, 1981

Jonathon Fitzgerald shook his head. He found it hard to believe the time he'd just spent with his parents—five weeks mostly spent babysitting his father—had finally come to an end. It had begun with the call he'd received over a month earlier which advised he'd been granted a "compassionate leave to care for an aging parent."

He didn't know there was such a thing as compassionate leave. It smelled way more like "political leave," especially since his assignment had been put on an administrative hold pending his return. During the decidedly brief visit to the AARPA offices when he came back, he didn't see or speak to Augusta Burnside. He could only imagine how pissed she was about his mother's interference in agency work.

He wasted no time once he got back. A blitzing re-pack of his bag allowed him to hit the road in record time, and he silently thanked the army of workers who built the Interstate Highway system. It wouldn't take him too long to reach Granville.

After several hours of travel, however, he pulled off the road. He needed food and gas, but more importantly, he needed to call Augusta Burnside's administrative assistant, Cecilia Martin. They weren't exactly "best" friends, but she had made it clear, privately of course, that she disagreed with Burnside about who was at fault in Jon's only other solo assignment.

He had taken pains to get on her good side; having an ally in the boss's office never hurt. It wasn't the only skill he'd learned from his politically well-connected family, but it had come in handy more than once. He found a pay phone just outside a time-worn Stuckey's restaurant and dialed her number.

"I wondered when you'd call," Cecilia said in her low-pitched, Tennessee drawl. Jon pictured the slim, pleasant woman, a dozen years younger than his mother.

He put a smile in his voice. "You know I can't make it through the day without hearing your voice."

"And you know," she purred, "you're more full of shit than all the other guys in this office put together."

"Oh, Cecilia, yer breakin' my heart."

"Your stealin' lines from Simon and Garfunkel now? They did that tune way better."

"What? You don't love me anymore?"

She chuckled. "Nonsense. You're the only fun person around here. Other than me, of course." She paused, and he could sense her turning serious. "Don't take any chances out there, okay?"

"What d'ya mean?"

"There's a reason Miz Burnside sent you down there solo, and why she didn't reassign your case."

"I just assumed she wanted me to fail."

"I wish it were that innocent," Cecelia said. "And we both know; Augusta Burnside is anything but innocent. In the past, when our people were hurt or injured on the job, the department went to great lengths to figure out what happened, why, and who they could prosecute. You, on the other hand, are a team of one."

The call ended on that note, and Jon trudged into the restaurant with pecan pralines and coffee in mind. Neither, however, satisfied him. He simply couldn't get over Cecelia's suggestion that Burnside might have intentionally compromised him and/or his mission. Yes, she was petty and vindictive, a regular prima donna who had risen through the ranks based on her years of... what, exactly? He suddenly realized he had no idea what field skills she had, if any.

Had her rise up the management ladder been just as politically driven as his entry into the department? Did making him look bad mean she looked good? Did she really hate him so much that she hoped he'd disappear like the Live Canary cleaning crew?

The questions in his head reminded him of an operational directive from his training: situational awareness—knowing everything that might come into play during any phase of an operation. He couldn't imagine a scenario where that would include the planning stage. And yet, Cecelia couldn't have made it any clearer: Jon was on his own.

He gleaned a handful of names—contacts and potential contacts—from the file Burnside gave him. Two were directly involved in Live Canary; the others seemed less likely to provide useful intel. Any of them, however, might surprise him. Though he'd studied engineering, his departmental training helped him develop a different mindset, one geared toward collecting evidence and investigating those who didn't share AARPA's goals.

Obviously a newbie, he had no intention of remaining one. Augusta Burnside's goals notwithstanding, Jon saw his mission as a great opportunity.

He made his way through insanely heavy

Atlanta traffic without incident. The long, boring drive to Granville gave him plenty of time to brood about Burnside and wonder what she knew that he didn't.

The drive down I-85 eventually led to the exit for Granville. The town lay several miles to the west, but the area around the exit had been commercialized. In addition to a motel, it featured a gigantic truck stop, a burger joint, and a strip club. Knowing he'd have to wait for reimbursement of his expenses, finding cheap food, lodging, and entertainment was a godsend.

Not wanting to take his chances at having a peaceful night in the truck stop, he checked into the slightly more upscale motel. Too tired to do anything else, Jon turned on the TV and went to sleep just as Johnny Carson finished his "Tonight Show" monologue.

The following morning, he drove to Granville, picked up a county map, and plotted a course to the home of William Bledsoe's associate, Dawn Popkin. A long drive led to a single story, ranch style home on a heavily wooded country lot. Jon rang the bell, and while waiting for someone to respond, he gazed at the woods and fields surrounding the house. There weren't any other buildings.

When no one answered, he walked to the back of the house but found no signs of life there either. Returning to the front door, he scribbled a note on the back of a business card and secured it on the screen door where it would be easily found.

Just then a car pulled up to the mailbox at the end of the driveway. Jon waved to get the driver's attention, then jogged toward the vehicle.

"Howdy," said an older man whose smile would have looked good on a Halloween pumpkin. Jon tried not to stare.

"Ain't nobody home, y'know," said the man as he removed the contents of the mailbox and dumped it on the seat beside him. "Ah'm just collectin' the mail fer Miz Dawn."

Jon worked his way through the man's accent. "Any idea when she'll be home? I really need to speak to her."

"Why's that?" he asked, focusing on Jon's suitcoat and tie. "You a process server or sumpthin'?"

"A what? No. I'm—"

"That poor gal's had enough grief lately. She sure don't need some city type gettin' up in her bidness. Now, why don't you just run along and fergit whatever nonsense you needed to discuss with her."

Jon pulled out his AARPA credentials and held them out for the man's inspection. "I'm a federal agent."

"Well, lookit you," the old man said, totally unimpressed. "Maybe one day you kin git yerself a real job."

"I *have* a real job," Jon said, "and right now you're interfering with it."

"Izzat right?" The man spat a stream of tobacco-tinted saliva out the window which landed a few inches from Jon's shoes. "You work for that Hollywood feller what's in the White House now?"

"You mean *President* Reagan?"

"Yeah, him. He got the peanut farmer's job. Me? I wouldn't touch it, no matter how much it paid. Way too many headaches, like them Iranians. Know whut I mean?"

"I do. So, when is Ms. Popkin due to return?"

"Don't rightly know. She went out west somewhere to visit family. San Francisco maybe, or… I dunno, Idaho. She's been at loose ends since her husband died. Heart attack." He snapped his fingers. "Gone. Just like that. Imagine, workin' all those years for the guv'mint, and all of a sudden, they throw his ass out. No warnin', nuthin'. And then he's dead. Damn feds." He looked Jon in the eye, but he didn't smile. "No offense meant."

"None taken," Jon said. "How long has she been gone?"

"She took off right after the funeral. So, several weeks, I reckon. Asked me to collect her mail and keep an eye on the house. I don't live too far from here."

Jon handed him a business card. "Have her call the number on that card when she returns. I seriously need to talk with her."

"She in some kinda trouble?"

"No. Certainly not. But I need her help with… an investigation."

"My oh my, oh my. Do tell. An investigation, huh? Sounds serious."

"It is," Jon said. "Very serious."

"Okay, if I hear from her, I'll pass it along. But I can't guarantee nothin'."

Jon watched the man drive off and chided himself for not getting his contact information. "Nice, work," he muttered on his way back to his car. "You're such a pro."

He might have continued to berate himself, but his stomach rumbled, reminding him he'd skipped breakfast. He treated himself to an early lunch and consulted his map to locate the shuttered lab where Bledsoe and Popkin had spent the last thirty years. The file provided a rural route address which he eventually located. The complex lay on otherwise undeveloped land separated from Granville proper by a sizeable forest preserve.

It took the better part of an hour to locate the partially concealed drive leading to the gated research facility. Burnside's file provided the combinations to the locks on the eight-foot-high fence and the modest building it surrounded.

He entered the dark space and fumbled for a light switch. When the one he found didn't work, he assumed the power had been cut off, along with the funding for everything else. Opening the blinds covering the windows allowed in enough light for him to operate, though there remained little to see.

One room, obviously used as a lab, dominated the interior. A second, smaller room had likely housed desks and filing cabinets, all of which had since been shipped back to the nearest AARPA warehouse. The files in those cabinets were long gone, either bureaucratically pigeonholed or simply destroyed. He suspected Burnside had not bothered to assign anyone else to study the research materials. He doubted she'd actually do the work herself.

After his brief tour of the interior, Jon ventured through a door in the rear of the building which led to two long rows of cages in various sizes. The smallest could have accommodated a small dog or a raccoon. The larger ones might have housed something much larger, possibly livestock. All were roofed and featured cooling fans at either end.

The concrete floors all contained drains, and water dispensing pipes traced the back walls of each row. A single valve on each side appeared to control the flow. The system must have worked since he smelled nothing but fresh air.

Jon couldn't help but wonder if Burnside had a clue about what might have gone on here. But, without having any of the research material handy nor any way to contact Dawn Popkin for answers, he remained clueless.

Live Canary? The name made absolutely no sense to him at all.

Chapter Ten

*"I've said it before: War brings out the patriotic bullies.
In World War I, they went around kicking dachshunds on
the grounds that dachshunds were 'German dogs.' They
did not, however, go around kicking German shepherds."*
–Molly Ivins

Granville, Georgia

Mom declined my offer to drive home, though she appeared upset, and her hands shook a bit on the steering wheel. She didn't admit it, but I felt pretty sure she was more concerned about not getting a reimbursement from Buck than she was about Weiner's intent to charge me with a crime.

Jinks, on the other hand, appeared seriously concerned about me. As we sat together in the back seat, she threaded her fingers between mine and lightly patted my arm. Suddenly I understood why Zeke liked her so much. She cared.

"I have to run to the store," Mom said. "I'll drop you two off at the house unless Jinks wants to go home."

"Actually," Jinks said, "I think I'll stay with Denver for a while, if that's okay."

Mom looked at me in the rearview mirror. "It's fine with me. Just... Uhm... Don't... You know; do anything... foolish."

Much as I would have liked to think Jinks and I would jump into bed and have hot, crazy sex the instant Mom drove out of sight, I knew the reality would be mundane. After all, I'd had to talk my way into a second kiss. A third might require that I pledge myself to indentured servitude or make a massive donation toward her dowery.

Okay, so hyperbole is my middle name. Sue me.

We returned to the serenity of the shaded picnic table. Zeke wandered out and joined us after taking the time to examine us, visually, before making himself comfy beneath the table.

"What's he doing down there?" Jinks asked.

"Damned if I know," I responded. "Maybe he just likes being close to us." That was a total wag—a wild-ass guess—but he seemed content, so we left him alone down there.

Jinks asked for a recap of my interrogation by

Herr Weiner, the premier defective on the Granville police farce. I gave her the gist of it, including my guess at the likelihood Buck might press charges against me.

"He's an idiot," she said. "Once I testify, they'll laugh him right out of court."

"You'd do that for me?"

"Sure. Why not? We're kinda in this together, aren't we?"

I couldn't help but imagine myself marrying this girl and working wherever I had to in order to support her and the five dozen kids we'd almost certainly have. Zeke's presence completely slipped my mind until Jinks produced a lightweight back pack she'd had with her the whole time.

"What's this?" I asked.

"Snack stuff. You said you'd never actually seen Zeke eat, so I figured I'd try to find something he'd like." She brought out several plastic sandwich bags containing small amounts of cheese, crackers, grapes, cookies, and cut-up frankfurter. The last item was a can of cat food which she delivered with a flourish. "He ought to like one of those, don't you think?"

I had my doubts, but figured the experiment couldn't do any harm. "Let's find out."

After summoning Zeke from beneath the table, Jinks opened the bag of cheese and set it in front of him. "This is food," she said. "Cheese."

"Cheese is food," said Zeke, once again long on vowel sounds.

"This is food, too," I said, setting the open bag of crackers between his front legs. "Crackers." I tried not to say it the way I thought he would.

He sniffed them both then looked from one of us to the other. "Not food," he said.

It went the same way for the grapes and the cookies; one sniff was enough to turn him off. He never tasted any of it. His mouth seemed way too small to eat much of anything anyway, but then, I'd never seen him use it. "Try the hot dog," I said.

Jinks dutifully plunked the neatly sliced, all-beef weenie in front of him. This time he looked pleased. He then picked up each of the pieces and put them back in the bag. Jinks laughed, a sound I loved to hear, and asked him, "Are you saving that for later?"

He didn't answer.

"I doubt he'll like the cat food," I said.

Jinks hefted the small can like a ballplayer readying to make a pitch. "Only one way to find out," she said and popped it open.

Once it sat squarely in front of him, Zeke sniffed it before touching it with a forepaw. A slight shiver shook his koala bear-sized frame, and he pushed the can away. Another rejection.

Holding the bag containing the hot dog in his forepaws, Zeke clambered down from the picnic table. He accomplished the maneuver gracefully, reached the ground, and headed off toward the woods.

"Hey!" Jinks called out. "Where are you going?"

"High-duh," he said, once again stringing out the vowels.

Jinks looked at me, one eyebrow dipped in puzzlement. "He's going to hide?"

"I guess so. He's never eaten a bite in front of me." I was as bemused as she was, and just as curious. We watched him trundle away and silently disappear into the undergrowth.

Alone again, with Jinks close beside me, I wanted to tell her I had feelings for her, but I couldn't think of a way to say it without sounding dumb. One date, especially as bizarre as ours had been, didn't suddenly evolve into love. Or did it? While we'd only had one "official" evening together, we'd spent several afternoons with Zeke. I had looked forward to those more and more.

Jinks leaned forward, put her elbows on the table, and rested her chin on her fisted hands. She seemed content to gaze into the woods in case Zeke returned. Calm and relaxed, a little smile touched the corners of her mouth. I focused on her lips and the memory of kissing them. As corny as it sounds, I knew I'd fallen for her.

"Y'know," I began, intending to give her a hint about my feelings, but not sure quite how to proceed.

She stopped me with an upraised palm and a muted, "Shh!"

"What? I was just gettin' started."

"Didn't you hear that?"

"Hear what?"

"It sounded like a motorcycle. And it's getting louder."

"I heard it," I said. "It might just be a car with a crummy muffler."

When the noise abruptly stopped, Jinks grew apprehensive. "Whatever it is, I think it just stopped in your driveway."

A minute or so later, Buck swaggered into view from around the corner of the house. A white bandage appeared to be holding his nose in place, and both of his eyes were blackened—imagine a gigantic raccoon with a nose job. He'd crammed his bulky body into jeans and a sleeveless t-shirt that hadn't been washed since the fall of Rome. A denim vest covered the worst of the dirt and stains but couldn't disguise Buck's signature paunch. A variety of artless tattoos covered his arms.

"*There* you are!" A quick look at Jinks ignited a scary grin. "And here's sweet cheeks, too. How nice; a two-fer-one deal."

I touched Jinks on the arm and whispered, "There's a phone in my room. Call 911."

"And you...?" She had a tremor in her voice.

"I'll be okay. Just make the call. Tell 'em someone just threatened to kill us."

"Not yet I haven't," grunted Buck, "But gimme time." He swept a huge, grime-encrusted wrench from behind his back and shook it at Jinks. "Don't you go anywhere, sweet thing. Your turn's next. I'm gonna make a little adjustment to your boyfriend first."

Jinks bolted for the cottage. Buck lunged after her, but couldn't catch up. She slammed the door behind her and locked it. While he stood there, fuming, I got a glimpse of the lettering on the back of his ragged vest; it read "Rode Hawgs," in a barely legible script.

Lovely. He's in a biker gang, and they're illiterate. "What d'you want?" I asked, trying to sound calm.

"You know damn well what I want. I want your ass in a sack. And when I finish with you, I'll take care of that little chink; show her what a real man can do."

"I think I showed her that the last time we met," I said, trying a bit of false bravado. "Look in a mirror."

I needed to give Jinks time to call the cops, and besides, as heavy as Buck was, I knew I could outrun him. The path through the woods began right behind me; God knows I'd traversed it often enough. I could do it easily to avoid a run-in with the wrench-wielding gorilla now threatening us. I doubted he'd get lost in the woods, but with a little luck, I could hold him off until the cavalry arrived.

"You'll pay for that."

I shook my head, trying to act as if I wasn't petrified. "It's not likely."

A new voice chimed in, one I recognized from its reliance on vowel sounds: "High-duh!"

Buck squinted, his focus going past my shoulder toward the opening in the forest. "What the hell is that?"

"It's... Uhm... A Siberian spider wolf," I said, knowing he'd spotted Zeke. "Very rare. They love to eat slow, fat morons, so don't piss him off."

"*That* little shit?" Buck's laugh sounded more like a bark. "I'll get ya both!"

I anticipated his attack, but I doubted Zeke had. Buck lumbered toward me, and I yelled at Zeke to run. He took off but didn't bother with the path. Instead, he slipped into the heavy undergrowth and vanished, while I hustled into the woods with Buck right behind me.

He remained too close for me to hide; he could have reached anywhere I might have stopped quickly. I ran as if pursued by night demons, and I was.

C'mon, Jinks! Make the cops move faster! A futile wish. According to my dad, the only thing that might motivate a bureaucrat was a pay raise. As that didn't seem likely, I ran faster. And, because I was worried about what Jinks might do, I circled around through the woods in order to get back to the house.

Fortunately for me, Buck's lifestyle didn't lend itself to long-distance running, not that I had ever competed in track and field events. But since the freight I hauled weighed a couple hundred pounds less than Buck's load, I moved faster.

Eventually, we thundered through the front yard, past Buck's massive Harley, and on into the backyard. As I approached the guest house, Jinks opened the door and motioned for me to join her inside. I gratefully complied, delighted to hear the door locked behind me.

"Get down," she said, "below the window. Buck's coming. You don't want him to see us!"

We dropped to the floor together, but I couldn't resist peeking through the bottom of the window to watch events in the yard. Jinks squeezed in right next to me.

Much to our horror, Zeke popped up again. He stood in the center of the path that led into the woods.

Utterly astounded, Jinks asked, "What on Earth is he *doing?*"

I could only shrug; I still hadn't caught my breath.

We watched in fear as Buck lumbered into view, saw Zeke, and crashed into the woods after him. His breathy epithets did nothing to calm our nerves.

Moments later, we heard a horrible scream, as if some poor slob was being drawn and quartered, a gruesome method of execution practiced after the

Dark Ages, according to Miss Lovingood.

Jinks tugged my sleeve until I looked at her. "You don't think Zeke did something to him, do you?"

"Seriously? Zeke couldn't scare anything. You've seen him. He's like a stuffed animal with cartoon eyes. He couldn't hurt anyone if he wanted to."

"We need to go look for Buck. What if he's injured? He might have fallen and hit his head on a rock or something. What if he's bleeding?"

"What if he's not?" I asked. "That bothers me a lot more."

"Still, maybe I should dial 911 again and ask for an ambulance."

"Suit yourself," I said. "But honestly, I'd be tickled to know he was in serious pain. Coming after me is one thing, but threatening you?" I shook my head. "I hope he's dead."

Chapter Eleven

"Fear is a powerful beast. But we can learn to ride it." –Justine Musk

Mom got home before the two cops who responded to the 911 call Jinks made. While the officers tromped around in the woods looking for Buck, we huddled together on the front stoop.

They couldn't find Buck, which didn't come as a surprise; the search had lasted all of ten minutes.

"He's gone," concluded the first officer. "He had too much of a head start for us to catch up."

"What are we supposed to do with this stupid motorcycle?" Mom asked.

"Just leave it," said the cop. "We've got the tag

number and registration info, so we can find out who the owner is and where he lives. But it might be stolen. That's an expensive bike; it's not likely to be abandoned."

"Well, it *is* likely to get run over," Mom said, never one to miss an opportunity to argue. "I want to put my car in the garage, and that thing's in the way."

I tried to process all this without getting snarky, a serious challenge. "Here's a thought," I said, "what are the chances that Harley belongs to the guy who came here to kill us? I've already given you his name. Does it by any chance match the name on the registration?"

Cop number two rewarded my query with a frown. "We're going to have to pass this whole mess on up the ladder. We called it in when we arrived, and there's a detective on the way to follow up."

Oh, joy! Weiner was mobile. I could only imagine how he would twist this episode in Boeheim's favor.

"I don't understand why Buck parked here in the first place," Jinks said. "If he came here intending to commit a crime, why wouldn't he park out of sight and sneak in like any normal lowlife? Why announce his presence?"

Like any normal *lowlife?* My innate sarcasm had rubbed off on Jinks. It didn't seem fair. Especially not to her.

"Criminals don't always use good logic," replied the second officer. I recognized the source of his deep dive into the criminal psyche. *Thank you, Detective Weiner.*

It wasn't long before the detective arrived, and he opened with his usual candor. "You," he said, pointing at me, "go sit in my car."

"I'm comfortable right here."

"You gonna start that crap again?" Weiner pursed his lips.

Jinks tugged his sleeve to get his attention. "Don't you want to know what happened? Denver wasn't the only one Buck came after."

Weiner looked at her and exhaled in exasperation. "Okay, go ahead."

Jinks gave a quick recap leaving out the scream we heard from the woods and any mention of Zeke.

"You're telling me he came after the two of you, chased Denver through the woods, and when he finally cornered you both in the little house out back, he turned tail and ran off?"

We nodded our heads in unison.

Weiner made no effort to hide his suspicion. "You really expect me to believe that?"

Mom then chimed in. "If you ask me, instead of badgering these two, I think you need to go after this Buck character. He's obviously the one at fault. He came *here*, remember?"

Staring straight at me, Weiner said, "So, he

comes to visit Denver, and now he's disappeared. Sounds kinda familiar to me."

I asked, "What makes you think he's disappeared?"

"Because he left his motorcycle behind, just like his brother left his car behind. That's a pretty huge coincidence in my book."

"And next," I said, "you're going to tell us you don't believe in coincidences." That made sense to me; it's what TV detectives said all the time, and I felt reasonably sure that's where Weiner got his training.

"As a matter of fact, no. I don't believe in 'em." He gave a little sigh as he surveyed the three of us. "You'll be hearing from me, kid."

"I want that motorcycle hauled off my property," Mom said as Weiner stalked back to his car.

He waved in response, climbed in his car, and drove away.

Mom glared at him as he departed, then turned to me. "I want it gone before I put the house on the market."

"What?"

"I'm tired of all this, Denver. I've decided to move to Florida. I'm going to leave all this behind."

I struggled to process her statement. "Do you mean leave Dad behind? Or me? The divorce isn't even final, is it?"

"No, but it won't be long before it is. And the sooner I get out of here, the sooner I can start living the rest of my life."

"Am I supposed to give up everything and move, too?"

"That's for you to decide, honey, but you'd probably be better off staying in Granville. You've got a job now, and I'll pay your tuition if you go to the community college in the fall. At least for the first year. That should be plenty of time for you to get settled."

"I haven't even started my job, assuming I can still get it. For all I know, Weiner will be hanging 'Wanted' posters all over town, just so I can kiss my job goodbye. And even if he doesn't, where am I supposed to live?" *And what on Earth will I do with Zeke?*

"You'll stay here, for now. It's going to take a while to sell this place. The neighborhood is obviously headed into the toilet. You've seen the gangster who moved in next door, haven't you?"

"Just because he owns a pit bull and wears his ballcap backwards doesn't make him a gangster."

"It's not 'just' a pit bull," she said. "It's a *gigantic* pit bull! The idiot who owns him has to use a chain for a leash, and he needs both hands on it to keep that monster from going after people. The last time I went out to the mailbox, I thought he would attack me."

"Is his backyard fenced?" Jinks asked.

"Yes, thank God."

"Does he let the dog run loose?"

"Not usually."

"So, you've seen the dog outside the fence?" I asked.

"Once or twice," she said. "And that was enough to scare me silly."

~*~

I met with Jinks' father the following morning. He said the job was mine if I wanted it, provided I could start that day. Though still recovering from Mom's one-woman declaration of independence, I eagerly accepted the position. "I'll go home, grab my camera gear, and be right back!"

"Hold on, son. You don't need to rush anywhere. And... don't you want to know what the job pays?"

I resisted delivering a well-deserved palm to my forehead. "Oh, right. That's important." *Okay dummy—this is the real world; wake up!*

"You won't actually be on the payroll; we'll pay you by the photo. It's a flat rate, but we usually add a little extra for shots requiring more than an aim and a click. I've got the details in here." He handed me a sheet of paper with several items typed on it.

"As you probably know, *The Gazetteer* is only one of several papers we publish. We also do weekly editions for several other small towns in the area. Your photos will appear in all of them, assuming you can travel to them as needed."

"I've been hoping to find a good used car," I said. "In the meantime, I'm sure I can borrow my mother's."

"Jinks told me your mother plans to move to Florida but didn't think you'd be going with her. She also mentioned something about you attending our community college in the fall. Is that right?"

"I got accepted faster than I thought I would. I wasn't exactly a stellar student," I admitted. "And yes, Mom's decided to move. It's... I'm not exactly sure what all I need to do. I'm still kind of in shock. It all happened so fast."

"Working for the *Gazetteer* might just be a blessing. We'll give you your assignments ahead of time when we can, but you'll need to be on call for unusual things."

I had no idea what he meant by "unusual." My expression must have said so.

"Fires, unexpected things, oh, and local sports. We'll keep you busy, I promise."

He wasn't kidding. I took a moment to glance at the list he'd given me. In addition to a note about the pay-per-print, there was a list of photos they wanted to have.

"Forget the first two," he said. "Those are for today. I'll shoot 'em myself. A ribbon-cutting and the presentation of a garden club award can't be too hard. Why not use the time to find yourself some wheels?"

Having only recently repaid my father for the money I borrowed to buy an enlarger for my darkroom, I had little left in savings. A "good" used car was out of the question; I couldn't even afford a wreck.

I talked Mom into co-signing a loan so I could buy a used Vespa scooter, but only after I swore an oath never to ride in bad weather or without a helmet. Suddenly I began to think of Coach Doobin's ratty little Fiat as a limo. Jinks, thank God, promised she'd never make fun of me or refuse to ride with me, provided the weather was okay and I got her a helmet, too. She swore she hadn't talked to Mom, but as I've learned, guys can't understand females. They have some kind of code.

Little happened in the weeks immediately following my graduation from H3, except that a second Boeheim had gone missing. That led to yet another Q&A with Detective Weiner, but nothing came of it. I eventually mentioned to Jinks' dad that I thought the Granville PD's detective had it in for me. He merely smiled and said journalistic ethics forbade him from rendering an opinion about any of Granville's finest.

Over those few weeks, my relationship with Jinks deepened into something I'd only dreamed of, a real live romance. Zeke figured in as well, and his grasp of English slowly grew. Much of that, I later realized, was just as much the result of him watching

TV as it was with our efforts to tutor him.

Zeke adored soap operas, especially those in Spanish. Go figure.

Jinks and I were discussing this very topic in our usual educational venue, the picnic table in the backyard, when she abruptly changed the subject. "Where will you go when your mom sells the house?"

It was a topic I'd avoided as much as I could, though I knew I'd have to deal with it eventually. "There's some student housing available at the community college," I said. "My classes start in the fall."

"And if you move in there, where will Zeke go?"

"Yeah. That's a problem."

"A big problem."

I tried to mimic Zeke's "Oh, poor me" look and said, "I don't suppose he could live with you, could he?"

She didn't laugh at me, but I could tell she was tempted, and then reality kicked in. "That'd never work. My folks know everything that goes on at our house." She shook her head and sighed. "They'd find him in a skinny minute."

"Well, would that be so bad?"

"C'mon, Denver! Mom works for the National Science Foundation. You think she'd keep quiet about an oddball creature like Zeke? Not in a million years."

"I know; you're right." The admission didn't thrill me. "What I need is something cheap and close to the woods."

Her face lit up. "Shady Grove!"

"The trailer park?"

"The sign says it's a *mobile home* community."

"I dunno. It's a scary place. I had a paper route once, and one of my customers lived there, an old lady with a bunch of cats. Everything around there is either run-down or weird. Or both."

"But it's perfect!" she said, still fired up. "It's gotta be cheap, and it's real close to the woods. It'd do until you found something better."

"Well, maybe. But I'm not sure I'd want you going near there," I said. "It may not be safe. And your dad would kill me if something happened to you."

She straightened her ballcap, a determined look on her face. "At the very least, we need to find out if they have anything available and what it would cost."

"I s'pose. Maybe we should run it by Zeke?"

"You need Zeke's seal of approval?" Jinks giggled. "Where is he, by the way?"

The words had barely left her mouth when Zeke appeared. I'd never seen him move so fast, and the reason soon became apparent; the new neighbor's vicious pit bull was in hot pursuit. How he got loose was anyone's guess.

Chapter Twelve

"The voyage of discovery is not in seeking new landscapes but in having new eyes." –Marcel Proust

There are moments in life that imbed themselves in one's memory forever. Seeing the terror on poor Zeke's face as he raced to evade the massive jaws of the mindless pit bull was just such an event.

What surprised me nearly as much as Zeke's mad dash was the warning he shouted. His high-pitched "High-duh" seemed like a waste of breath. In one short instant, all three of us were in plain view of the beast; none of us would be able to hide, much less run for cover.

I made a tentative move toward the dog, but

Jinks grabbed the collar of my shirt and yanked me back. We then scrambled up on top of the picnic table. "Zeke!" I cried, "Up here! Come up here!"

In retrospect, that was an idiotic thing to suggest. If Zeke could've made his way to the tabletop, so could the damned dog. All three of us would have been primed for a mauling.

Still, I had the thought in mind that maybe all three of us, or at least Jinks and I, could kick the animal in the head before he finished his climb. Who knows if that might have discouraged him.

Zeke had something else in mind. Instead of joining us on the table, he dodged around it, continually screaming, "Hide-duh" as if we didn't hear him the first few times. Fortunately for him, the pit bull didn't corner very well, and our little friend was able to stay out of range for what seemed like a long while. In reality, it couldn't have been long at all, and eventually Zeke got tired. The dog quickly closed most of the gap.

I reached down and snatched Zeke off the ground, surprised by the weight he'd gained over the past few weeks. The pit bull lunged at me but only grazed my leg. Jinks landed a toe in the vicinity of his ear which elicited a short squeal followed by a fierce and frightening growl. It only seemed to make him more determined than before to eat us.

Why *we* weren't screaming for help remains a mystery to me. We certainly should've been. But then, if someone had responded, they would not only have put themselves in jeopardy, they'd have seen what happened next. It was another of those part and parcel memories one can never forget.

Something bizarre burst from the woods.

Imagine a madman's nightmare as it hurtled directly toward the pit bull. A scorpion-like creature the size of a chaise lounge, it briefly left the ground and shifted slightly to compensate for the dog's attempt to turn and face it. The pit bull stood no chance; its fearsome, snarling rage went ignored as the spider-thing struck. A barbed tail stabbed the dog while dual pinchers lanced out and held it by the ears. The animal's eyes went wide with fear.

It let loose an agonized howl that lasted two heart-rending seconds before the canine dropped to the ground. I assumed it was dead since it didn't even twitch.

"Hide-duh," said Zeke proudly as he pointed to the newly arrived menace, which completely ignored us and concentrated on hauling its prey back into the woods. The dog must have weighed nearly as much as Jinks, and yet the creature Zeke summoned had no difficulty dragging its burden into the shelter of the forest.

Jinks and I stood and stared, too stunned to do anything else. "Hide-duh," when translated from Zeke-speak to English became "Hide," or more aptly, "Hyde," like the monster from Robert Lewis Stevenson's bizarre novel about Dr. Jekyll.

~*~

I got no arguments from Jinks when I suggested we take a ride somewhere. Pretty much anywhere would have been fine. Neither of us felt like sticking around after what we'd seen. The fact that Zeke's response was the complete opposite of ours only made us want to leave sooner and stay away longer.

It's difficult to have a good conversation when both parties are wearing motorcycle helmets and riding a Vespa in desperate need of a tune-up. Nevertheless, we tooled out into the countryside and tried to get the image of the hound and Hyde out of our heads.

Eventually we stopped for a rest on the far side of Granville and only a short hop away from Shady Grove. It felt good to get off the scooter.

"We should go talk to them," Jinks said. "And see what it might cost to stay there."

The idea had zero appeal, and for good reason, which I pointed out. "Shady Grove is the closest thing Granville has to a slum."

Even without smiling, she looked cute with her helmet tucked under her arm. But that didn't alter the truth of her words. "It may also be the only place you can afford to live without abandoning Zeke."

We got back on the scooter and made a slow pass by the entrance to the "park." Aside from having an abundance of big trees growing near all of the trailers, it didn't look very park-like. The condition of the units seemed to deteriorate the farther we moved from the center. The trailer in the middle, a double-wide, bore a sign proclaiming it the domain of the resident manager. A mangy-looking cat lay in the shade of a nearby tree.

An astonishingly skinny woman in shorts and a sleeveless t-shirt stood outside the boxy abode and stared at us. She kept her hands on her hips and held a cigarette in her mouth. Her dry, stringy hair hung limp as if she'd just come out of the shower.

"Let's go talk to her," Jinks said.

"Why? She looks kinda mean."

"Geez, Denver. Don't be such a wuss. If she's not in charge, she can point us to whoever is."

Though still harboring doubts about the wisdom of entering the Shady Grove grounds, I couldn't prove Jinks right and admit to being a complete chicken. I drove up the gravel track that led to the manager's office.

The bony woman didn't move as we parked next to the trailer and dismounted. She looked us over without changing her expression, a heavily wrinkled frown. "What d'ya want?"

"We wondered if you have any rental units," I said.

The woman fixed her eyes on Jinks. "Neither of you look old enough to sign a lease."

That didn't sound promising, but Jinks gave me a gentle rib shot with her elbow, and I continued,

"I can get a co-signer, at least to start. But the thing is, I need to find housing while I'm in school, and this may be the only place I can afford."

"The school don't have rooms?"

"None for freshmen who don't want roommates."

The woman nodded at Jinks. "So, she's not gonna be yer roomie?"

"No," said Jinks. "I've got another year of high school to go."

The gaunt woman took a long drag of her cigarette. "You in public school? I fergit the name. No, wait. I 'member now. Pervert Hoover High."

Ouch. "That's the place," I said. "Now, about renting a trailer—"

"They ain't trailers. They're mobile homes."

"Right. Sorry. So, are there any uhm... *units* available?"

"Maybe," she said. "You got a job? References?"

I nodded yes.

She squinted and exhaled smoke in my face. "You ever been arrested? Served time?"

"Does he look like a criminal?" Jinks asked, putting her hand in mine. I'd never seen her lose her temper, but it felt like she was getting close.

"Honey, I've seen all kinds," the woman said.

"It don't matter how pretty a thief or a killer is. They'll rob ya, or murder ya, just the same." She leaned closer to me; her breath reeked of unfiltered cigarettes. "So, answer the question. You got a record or not?"

"No," I said, trying to sound convincing. I had no idea what sorts of records Detective Weiner may have created about me. "None that I know of."

"Aw right then, maybe we can do some bidness. But I'm still gonna have to check you out."

After quoting the going rate, which was well outside my meager budget, I asked if all the mobile homes were the same size.

"No," she said. "'Course not."

"Do you have a small one? Like a one-bedroom model?"

"Or maybe a studio?" Jinks asked.

The woman looked at Jinks as if she'd just stolen her wallet. "The hell's a studio? We don't have no artists 'round here."

"A studio," Jinks explained, "is even smaller than a one-bedroom. It's more of a one-room deal with everything all together, except the bathroom, of course."

"Of course," said the woman, mimicking Jinks' voice. "We don't got nothin' like that. There are standards, after all." She paused as if mulling over some deep, dark option. "Listen. There is one really small one, but it's not in very good shape. It needs some work, but if you're willin' to split the cost of repairs, we might work something out."

It sounded reasonable to me. "Is it close to the woods?"

"Hon, they're *all* close to the woods, in case you hadn't noticed."

I filled out a tenant questionnaire while the woman, who finally introduced herself as Wanda Vickers, filled me in on the rules for residents.

"We don't allow no pets, 'cept maybe goldfish. Dogs, cats, rabbits, and what-not ain't allowed."

"But—" Jinks went quiet when I gave her the stink eye, something I'd never used on her before. I anticipated a repercussion at some point since we'd both seen a cat on our way in.

"If yer gonna smoke, do it outside," she went on. "These damn things catch fire if you rub yer legs together."

I resisted the temptation to look at her spindly stems.

"Rent's gotta be paid weekly. No exceptions. Don't miss a payment, or I'll have yer stuff tossed in the road. Garbage gets picked up on Wednesdays, and trust me, they'll take anything if it's stacked right." She paused briefly to cough.

"Don't bring no cops around, ever. I don't care what you might be up to, or what somebody else might be doing to you. No cops. Period. Got that? If you have a problem, bring it to me. I'll take care of it."

"So much for public safety," I muttered as I finished filling out the form.

"You say sumpthin', boy?"

"Nothing worth repeating," Jinks said, a worried look in her eye.

Wanda took the form from my outstretched hand. "Okay then. I'll need some time to check this stuff out. I'll call if everything's okay. After that, you can move in whenever."

"I'd kinda like to take a look at the uhm... mobile home before I agree to anything," I said.

She looked as if I'd asked her for a kidney. "Aw right." She fiddled with a massive keyring and finally removed one marked with a three-digit number that she handed to Jinks. "It's down there near the end," she said, pointing.

"Thanks. We'll bring the key back when we're done."

Wanda eyed Jinks with undisguised suspicion. "Don't you two do nuthin' stupid in there, y'hear? I done seen enough knocked up teenagers in my life. I don't care to see another."

"That's not going to happen," I shot back.

"Hey," she said. "Yer not the one pays the price!" She aimed a thumb at Jinks. "*She* is."

Jinks ignored her, which I was having a hard time doing. "Why are some of the tra—uh, mobile homes—on blocks while others are still on wheels?"

"Yer kiddin' me, right?"

"No. But I guess it's not important, so never mind."

"The ones on blocks are paid for. The others can still be hauled off if the owner can't make the payments."

I felt confused. "I thought they were all rentals."

"Nah," said Wanda. "Only some of 'em."

Jinks had my sleeve at that point and pulled me toward the scooter, but I dug in my heels. "I used to deliver newspapers here a few years back."

"So?"

"Well, there was an old lady on my route who used to have a bunch of cats. Is she still here?"

Wanda shook her head. "I've only been here a couple years, and that's when the 'no pet' rule went into effect. If she had cats, they're gone now. She prob'ly is, too."

We hopped on the scooter and started down the gravel lane, reviewing the house numbers as we went. When we reached #103, we stopped.

"I don't think I wanna go in there," Jinks said.

From the looks of it, I couldn't have agreed more.

Chapter Thirteen

"Fantasy, abandoned by reason, produces impossible monsters; united with it, she is the mother of the arts and the origin of marvels." –Francisco Goya

"Y'know," I said as we sat on the scooter contemplating Shady Grove's unit 103, "if nothing else, it's really close to the woods. In fact, it's pretty much in the woods."

"Uh huh." Jinks squinted at the deep shade of the nearby trees. "I think I saw something moving in there."

"Like what? A squirrel?" *Please let it be a squirrel!*

"Bigger. More like a— Look!" She pointed to a space between unit 103 and the matching dump labeled 105 sitting beside it. "There it is. See it? A cat."

Not Hyde? Thank God. Time to be cool. "Yep. Definitely a cat. So what?"

"The manager said no one could have pets."

"Maybe it's a feral cat," I said. "I didn't see a collar, and it looked skinny."

"And dirty," Jinks said. "Just like the other one we saw on the way in."

I got off the scooter and stretched. "I don't think it's something we have to worry about. First things first; we've got to decide if we're going to look inside this trailer."

We approached the boxy housing unit tentatively, as if it were a sleeping dragon, or more likely, a pile of dragon poop that would give rise to another Hyde-like monster. Rather than go in, we stood at the door. I suspected we were both debating whether to actually go in.

"It's just a trailer," Jinks finally said. "It's no big deal." She stepped forward, key in hand, unlocked the door, and gestured for me to proceed. "After you."

I swallowed my pride, and a significant chunk of my apprehension, and pushed the door open, fully expecting to be run over by fleeing scorpions the size of cruise missiles. Instead, I was met with darkness.

After fumbling around, I found a light switch and flipped it on. A single, small ceiling fixture cast a feeble light on a living room/kitchen combination which featured a tiny table with two straight-back, metal chairs, a worn-out sofa, and a TV stand with no TV.

"Wow," breathed Jinks, "it's the Taj Mahal. No. Wait! It's more like the Palace of Versailles."

"It has a stove and a fridge," I said. "That's good."

"Assuming they work."

I opened the refrigerator and immediately regretted it. The odor went well beyond pungent, and I quickly slammed the door shut.

"That's gotta go," Jinks said. "There's no saving it."

"Maybe we could haul it outside and hose it down."

"That'd work, provided you had a tanker truck full of bleach. And even then, I doubt you'd get rid of the stink. You'd be better off junking that thing and buying an ice chest. At least for the time being."

We discovered the stove didn't work very well either; of the three electric burners, only one got hot. There were enough dishes and silverware for two place settings, provided no one minded having totally mismatched utensils, plates, cups, and glasses. Pots and pans were similarly limited and near the end of their useful lives.

The bedroom featured a single bed with a mattress that sagged halfway to the floor, a three-drawer dresser sans drawer pulls, a cracked mirror, and a ceiling fixture in need of a working bulb.

We expected similarly disastrous conditions for the bathroom, and we weren't disappointed. The sink, tub, and toilet were stained a shade of brown I'd only seen on hiking boots. Surprisingly, the room didn't smell bad. That conclusion may have been clouded by the lingering effects of the aroma from the fridge. I held my breath and flushed the toilet, fairly certain it would overflow.

Oddly enough, it didn't.

"I'll bet we could scrub those stains off," Jinks said.

I smiled at her. "Aren't you the optimist?"

"One of us needs to be."

"Do you think we could make this place livable?"

She shrugged. "Maybe. I didn't see anything on the ceilings to suggest a roof leak. That'd be a deal-breaker."

"It couldn't be that hard to re-roof this thing," I said. "It's not that big."

"What do you know about roofing?"

She had me there. I'd never roofed anything. "Okay. If the roof's bad, the deal's off. The furniture sucks rocks, but that's actually a good thing."

Jinks didn't respond. Instead, she gave me a look that plainly said, "Huh?"

"I doubt my mom wants to move all the

furniture in the house we have now. And she sure won't want anything that's in my little place. I could haul it here."

"On the Vespa?"

"Maybe I could borrow your dad's truck."

"And what about all this lovely stuff?" Jinks spread her arms wide to include all the flotsam in the rental unit.

"We toss it. By the time I'm ready to move out, I'll be able to buy new stuff wherever I end up."

I suspect it was the confidence I tried to put into the declaration that carried the day.

"Yeah," she said. "That'd work." She looked around thoughtfully. "We could paint it, too. Maybe come up with a color scheme that doesn't scream roadkill."

As we prepared to go back and see Wanda Vickers, Jinks paused, turned to me, and whispered, "Don't look now, but there's a kid under the trailer right behind me."

Of course, I looked, but I didn't see anything at first. "There's no...." But there was. A little boy. And he'd been crying, quietly. Almost silently.

"Geez. What do we do?" I asked.

"We go see what's wrong," Jinks said, already moving toward the child. "It's probably nothing. I've done enough babysitting to know kids don't always need a reason to cry."

But this kid had a definite reason. Sitting in the shadow of the single-wide trailer, he cradled his hand and wouldn't let us touch it, or him.

"What happened?" Jinks asked.

The boy just shook his head.

"It's okay," Jinks said. "You can talk to me. What's your name?"

"Tucker," he said.

She gave him her warmest smile. "I'm Jinks. And this is Denver. Do you live here?"

His eyes rolled up toward the trailer overhead while tears dripped down his cheeks.

"What happened to your hand?" I asked, looking down at the nastiest burn I'd ever seen.

"It hurts," he said.

Jinks took a closer look at it. "I'm sure it does. Where are your parents?"

"Mommy's at work."

"And your daddy?" I asked.

"No daddy. Just... him, up there," he said, once again looking at the underside of the trailer.

"Why don't we go see him," Jinks said. "I'm sure he'll want to—"

Tucker voiced a shrill, "No!" then drew back further under the trailer, a look of fear clouding his pale face. "I want Mommy," he blubbered.

"That burn looks terrible," I whispered to Jinks. "We've gotta do something."

"C'mon," she said. "Let's go talk to whoever's inside. This little guy needs a doctor."

Jinks tried to reassure the child that everything would be okay, but he didn't believe her. We told him we'd be right back, and then made our way to the front door of the trailer. Jinks knocked.

A man yanked the door open and stared at us. "What d'you want?"

"There's a little boy under your trailer," I said. "He's hurt. It looks like a burn. We thought—"

"You thought what? That I gave a damn? He got what he deserved, sassin' me like he did."

Oh, my God! He did it. He burned the boy. "It's just—"

"I don't know you, and I don't have to talk to you. It's none of your damn business. Now go on, git outta here."

"But the boy—"

The man cut Jinks off before she could continue. "His momma's comin' home any time now. She'll take care of him. Now leave me alone!"

It's the first time I could recall being happy that someone slammed a door in my face.

"C'mon," Jinks said. "We need to stay with him 'til his mother gets here."

Fortunately, that didn't take long. Tucker's mom drove up in a Toyota Corolla that hadn't seen a bath or a body shop in decades. She must have seen the three of us crouching under the trailer, because she bolted from the car and raced toward us.

As soon as she got close, she dropped to her knees and gathered the boy in her arms. "Tucker? What's the matter, honey? Are you okay?"

When the boy didn't answer right away, she looked at us. "Who are you, and what did you do to my son?"

We both backed away instantly.

Jinks responded first. "We just tried to comfort him until you got here."

"His hand looks pretty badly burned," I added.

She unwrapped herself from the child and examined his wounds, shaking her head and muttering all the while.

Jinks continued, "We tried to talk to the boy's father—"

"*Who?*"

"The man in the trailer," I said. "He didn't seem very concerned. Said you'd take care of Tucker when you got home."

"Right. Right," she said. "I will. I'll... I'll take care of him. Thank you for staying with him. I'm sure he appreciated it. But you can go now. You don't need to hang around. I'll deal with his uhm... daddy."

"He needs to go to the ER," Jinks said. "That's a bad burn."

At that point, the man we'd tried to talk to earlier walked out of the trailer and confronted us. "You still here? Damn busybodies. Go on; git!" He looked down at the woman and child. "It's dinner time. You gonna sit on the ground with that whiny kid all day? I'm hungry."

I wanted to drop a piano on the jerk. Sadly, since we weren't part of a Roadrunner cartoon; nothing like that was available.

"We'll be going now," Jinks said to the boy's mother.

Mr. Sunshine managed a surly growl, "Good riddance."

We waved goodbye to Tucker, climbed on the Vespa, dropped the key off with wonderful Wanda and put Shady Grove behind us. By the time we got to Jinks' house, where I intended to drop her off, I'd made up my mind. "I'm moving into that little trailer, and I could use your help."

"To move, or to do something about that creep who lives next door?"

"Both," I said. "And the sooner the better."

"You think Zeke will be safe there?" she asked.

"I hope so." But his welfare, at that point, was not the most important. "We need to have a chat with Zeke."

"Then, let's get to it," she said.

By the time we got to my house, I had worked myself into a righteous dither. I couldn't get the image of the boy or his injury out of my head. It took me a while to figure out that the burn pattern on his fingers and palm were probably made by the cooking element of an electric range. Either the child had inadvertently placed his hand on a red-hot burner, or the man in the trailer had forced him to do it. Having met them both, I suspected the second theory was more likely.

That led me to wonder why the woman put up with him. Even if he didn't actually abuse the kid, his indifference seemed criminal. I'd never met such a complete butthead, and that included the Boeheim brothers. If my own parents could get a divorce so easily, I figured the kid's parents could, too. If not, I'd love to hear the explanation.

We sat down with Zeke, who also had some explaining to do.

"Care to tell us about Hyde?" I asked. "Who is he? *What* is he? Where did he come from?"

Zeke appeared confused by the avalanche of questions. "Take 'em one at a time," I said.

Imagine trying to interpret the expression on the face of a tree sloth or one of those endearing creatures from Australia, the names of which practically nobody outside of Oz knows. That was our challenge as we looked at Zeke. He projected an image of pure, undiluted innocence.

And yet, we'd seen him summon a monster.

Chapter Fourteen

"A day without sunshine is like, you know, night." –Steve Martin

Jonathon Fitzgerald decided he didn't like Granville, and if pressed on the issue, he would have admitted he didn't care much for the rest of the state, though he'd seen very little of it. What he wouldn't have admitted to was a fear of impending failure.

Following his tour of Bledsoe's shuttered research site, he got in touch with the Granville police detective whose name had been mentioned in the file from Burnside. A hand-written note suggested that the initial investigators had little faith in the man and opted not to share details of the cleaning crew's disappearance. Nevertheless, Jon decided the man ought to be aware of major crimes which occurred in his jurisdiction. Maybe he'd learned something of value without knowing with whom to share it.

The meeting with Detective Weiner produced nothing of interest with the exception of validating the suspicions of incompetence noted in the file. Weiner claimed he only knew of two mysterious disappearances, neither of which involved any feds. He claimed to have a suspect in mind but doubted the individual even knew there was a research facility in the county. After all, it had come as news to Weiner.

Disappointed by his lack of progress, Jon called it a day and returned to his motel room. He had seen a very nice restaurant in town when he drove to the Granville PD headquarters, but decided he could get by on less expensive fare. Besides, sitting right next door to the Sweet Dreams motel was a restaurant called Babe's Burgers. The parking lot appeared nearly full which he took to mean the food wouldn't be too bad.

The restaurant had slightly more atmosphere than a franchise fast food joint, but its real selling point was a bar that served beer and wine. Jon ordered a brew and parked at a two-person table where the bar met a wall so he could keep an eye on everyone. He complimented himself on his situational awareness.

A pretty young blonde sat at the bar a few feet away. Jon couldn't help but notice she was heavily made up, as if ready to go on stage. He guessed her age as somewhere between late teens and early twenties. She'd been eating alone when a man approached and sat down beside her. His neck and arms were covered in tattoos, and it was all too obvious that he wanted the world to see them. A heavily stained, wife beater t-shirt made that possible.

Jon watched as he tried to chat the girl up, but she wasn't interested. That didn't deter her suitor at all. He kept pestering her despite the fact she told him she merely wanted to eat her dinner in peace. When he pulled on her arm as if to drag her out of the restaurant, Jon stepped in.

"Why don't you let this young lady finish her meal in peace?"

The man responded with a smirk. "Why don't you mind yer own damn business?"

Jon smiled at the girl and nodded at the man. "Is he bothering you?"

"Yes, he is."

Jon turned toward the man. "That's it then. Leave her be."

"Who the hell d'you think you are? John Law?"

"Actually, yes. I'm a federal agent. Would you like to see my badge?"

"You don't have no damn badge. You look more like a preacher than a cop."

Jon dug out his badge and held it in front of the man's eyes. "That look official enough for you?"

The man backed two steps away. "I ain't done nothin'."

"That's a good thing. 'Cause now you can go on about your business and not have to worry about being arrested."

"For what?"

Jon shrugged. "I'm sure I can think of something, and if you'd like to find out what, just keep pestering her. Otherwise, move along."

"Go on, Tats," said the girl. "I'm sure I'll have to look at your ugly face later."

"Damn right you will," he said, then turned and walked away.

Jon settled into the bar seat beside her. "What was that all about, if you don't mind me asking."

"He's one of my regulars. Thinks he's entitled to somethin' extra." She poked her salad with a fork. The shredded lettuce didn't look fresh.

"Can I buy you something a little more... Uhm... Interesting?"

"Like one of Babe's Specials?" She pointed to a poster featuring a mound of meat and cheese bursting from a bun.

He grinned. "Why not? I'll bet it tastes pretty good."

"It does," she said, her face turning wistful. "I used to eat one nearly every day until I noticed my G-string was getting kinda tight."

Jon choked on his beer.

She patted him on the back. "You okay?"

"Yeah," he wheezed. "Just... y'know, startled."

"It's all about the tips," she said. "I work across the street, at Sweet Dreamz. That's dreams but with a 'Z' at the end."

"So, the motel and the place where you work have the same name?"

"Almost. Like I said, the club's name is spelled with a Z. The motel uses an S. The same guys owns 'em both."

"Interesting."

"Anyway, what we wear is pretty simple. When the guys in the audience tip the dancers, they've gotta put the money somewhere. And I'm not a fan of garters. I think they make the girls look cheap." She smiled and changed the subject. "So, you're with the FBI?"

He shook his head. "Nope. Different agency. Not nearly as well known, but we do have impressive looking badges."

"I really appreciate you trying to look out for me." She offered her hand. "My name's Malindi. Well, it is in here, anyway. At work I use a stage name."

"Lemme guess. Stormy?"

"No." She giggled. "I started out as 'Amazing Gracie,' but nobody liked it. Said it was too biblical. So, I decided to do something really different. You know, like wear a bright pink wig and think up a clever name." She tapped her chest. "Now I'm 'Natasha, the blushin' Russian.'"

"The blushin' Russian, eh? That's cute."

She dropped her voice to a whisper. "I'm not really Russian. I was born right here in Granville."

"Oddly enough," Jon said, "I *was* born in Russia."

She stared at him. "Really? I mean, you don't have an accent or anything." Her eyebrows suddenly dipped. "What's your name?"

"Jon Fitzgerald."

"That doesn't sound—"

"I was adopted. Long story short: my folks couldn't have kids of their own, and they were deemed too old to be parents by the adoption agencies in the US. So, they went to the USSR and found me." He smiled. "I consider myself pretty lucky."

"And now you're like a secret agent. That's very cool."

"But not very secret," he said, "although I am working on some stuff that's... you know, classified." He didn't bother to add that he didn't have the clearance to see any of the actual research data.

Malindi checked her watch. "My shift starts in about a half hour, and I need to get ready." She smiled and batted her artificial eyelashes at him. "Maybe you could... uhm... sorta drop by the club later on?"

Jon smiled back. "I'd like that, Natasha."

She put her hand on his shoulder as she slipped off the stool and got to her feet. She gave him a wink and a squeeze. "A real, live secret agent. That really is way cool."

He watched her prance to and through the exit, and noticed she'd caught the attention of several male customers. He couldn't blame them. The more he thought about it, the more he wanted to see her perform.

After taking his time to consume one of Babe's Specials and another beer, Jon returned to his motel room to change. He assumed a suitcoat and tie would stand out too much at Sweet Dreamz, so he changed into jeans and a golf shirt. The weather was nice; it would be a short walk. He told himself he wouldn't stay long.

The parking lot seemed crowded, and he was glad he'd left his car at the motel. Very little sound leaked from the inside of the club to the outside. For obvious reasons, the place had no windows.

He paused at the entrance and surveyed photos of dancers posted on a wall. Each image bore a name, and he quickly found Natasha, in bright pink hair and lipstick, long lashes, and very little else.

Standing just inside was a man easily twice Jon's size. After checking out the new arrival, he collected a ten-dollar "un-cover" charge and waved Jon into the loud, brightly lit interior.

Percussive rock music drowned out conversations, and those ordering drinks had to shout. Two small stages flanked a larger one, all three of which sported gyrating females surrounded by admiring male patrons.

Amused, Jon found a corner spot and merely watched until the voice of an unseen host announced the arrival of a new performer. "Feast your eyes on the center stage and welcome Natasha, the blushin' Russian, who escaped to America just to entertain you!"

Laughing at the absurdity of the claim, Jon worked his way closer to the stage, hoping to catch Malindi's attention. He got no closer than a wall of leering males standing three-deep in front of her. When he waved, she responded by blowing him a kiss.

Though he liked rock music, the tunes played and the volume used soon turned him away. After watching her and listening for about fifteen minutes, he pointed toward the exit in case Malindi still had him in view, and then made his way outside.

With a moonless night sky above, he paused to clear his head. A mental image of the blushin' Russian persisted in his brain as he prepared to go back to his motel room.

A slight noise caused him to glance back toward the lounge. An instant later, something hard slammed into his back and drove him to the ground. Groaning and trying not to inhale the dirt and cigarette butts in which he'd buried his nose, Jon struggled to figure out what happened.

Those efforts ended when he was hit again, this time in the head.

Chapter Fifteen

"When I say that human beings are just gene machines, one shouldn't put too much emphasis on the word 'just.' There is a very great deal of complication, and indeed beauty, in being a gene machine." –Richard Dawkins

Though it hardly came as a surprise, Zeke didn't respond well to interrogation. He backed away from our questions about Hyde and appeared flustered and wary. At that point, I feared I'd somehow adopted Detective Wiener's complete lack of empathy, so I backed off.

"We still need answers," Jinks said. "I mean, there's a lot to consider."

"I know. And not the least of it involves my new neighbors, assuming I move into Shady Grove."

I tried to be as non-threatening as I could toward Zeke. I smiled a lot and only used gestures I thought would be reassuring. "It's just... Ya see, we don't understand Hyde."

"He scares us," Jinks said.

Our little friend blinked, thought for a moment, then said, "High-duh good. Feed Zeke."

Jinks and I looked at each other in surprise.

"You don't feed yourself?" she asked.

"High-duh feed."

"Like a mother bird feeds her chicks?" I asked.

Zeke's silence made it clear he knew nothing about other animals.

"He doesn't understand," Jinks said, "but I think you may be on the right track."

What? Nonsense. "They're two totally different species."

"Really? How do you know? Do I call you Doctor Stow now?" Jinks had her arms crossed and her lips pursed. "Did you even take biology?"

"Yeah, but... Okay. Only 'cause I had to."

She closed her eyes and shook her head like a tutor annoyed by a pupil who failed to grasp the concept of addition, or maybe quantum physics. "It's called symbiosis."

"Sym—"

"It's when two animals from different species

cooperate for survival. There's a much fancier definition, but I never memorized it."

I finally got it. "Like those nasty sucker fish that hang onto sharks and eat the leftovers?"

"I think so, yeah. But I was thinking more along the lines of clown fish and—"

"Clown fish? Like with colorful make-up and big floppy shoes?" *I can be so clever.*

"Just stop." Jinks gave me an academic's lofty frown. "Clown fish are cute little orange and white striped fish that hang around sea anemones. The plants have stingers that don't hurt the clown fish, but the fish feeds on tiny critters that could hurt the anemone. The fish is safe, and the plant is, too."

"That's it?"

"I think anemones like clown fish poop, but I could be wrong."

"Wow! You're beautiful and smart," I said.

"Kinda makes ya wonder why I hang around with you, doesn't it?"

I tried to sound superior. "It's the excitement factor. Who wants a dull, boring existence?"

She slugged my shoulder and pointed at Zeke, who had been patiently listening to us. As I think I mentioned, he's big on soap operas, and we presented the nearest thing to the real deal, except for love triangles, mistaken identities, and unknown paternity issues.

"So," she continued, "Hyde feeds Zeke. What does Zeke contribute?"

We both looked at him, but he remained silent.

"What do you do for Hyde?" I asked him.

Zeke shrugged, which looks weird when it involves two sets of shoulders.

Jinks reached out and gently held Zeke's face in her hands to keep him focused. "Do you help Hyde?"

"Food come to Zeke. High-duh kill."

"Oh my God," I whispered. "He's bait!"

"Zeke bring. High-duh kill. Eat. Feed Zeke."

"Symbiotes," Jinks said, her voice low. She slowly raised her eyes and looked straight at me. "Hyde could be preparing to eat... *us*!"

Zeke stopped her with an upraised paw. "Jinks safe. Denver safe. Zeke find mean food."

"Mean? Like... bullies?" I asked.

"Bull-leez," he said.

"I have another question," Jinks said. She gave me a look I'd seen before which suggested she knew what she was up to even if I didn't. "Where did you come from? You and Hyde, both."

He appeared not to understand, so I chimed in. "Where are your parents?"

"Pear-entz?" he asked, clearly not acquainted with the idea.

"Your Mom and Dad," Jink said. "Who raised you?"

"Bee-lee?"

It sounded like he was speaking with an Italian accent.

"Dawn," he added, stringing out the "aw."

"Billy and Dawn... who?" Jinks asked, ever so gently.

"Bee-lee and Dawn. Bee-lee and Dawn!" His voice rose with a tremor.

"It's all right," Jinks said. She made her voice sound soothing, and it seemed to help; Zeke relaxed a bit,

"Bullies come. Bee-lee gone. No Dawn. High-duh stop bullies. Go trees."

It dawned on me that our little friend had somehow managed to cram several, more-or-less complete sentences together. We didn't know what it meant, of course, but that seemed irrelevant at the time. The greater mystery, if we chose to look into it, was identification of Bee-lee... Sorry, Billy... and Dawn. We presumed they were human, mostly because we couldn't bear to think of any critter that might have generated the likes of Zeke and Hyde. One or the other, maybe, but not both.

Not in a bazillion years.

~*~

Wanda Vickers, Shady Grove's wraith-like

resident manager, gave me a key and the okay to move in. We briefly discussed my plans for renovations, and she agreed as long as it didn't cost her anything, and any furniture I removed was replaced with something at least as good. It would have been harder to find things in worse shape.

Jinks' dad gave me the use of his truck, provided I didn't miss any photo assignments, and Jinks offered to help, provided I let her make any decorating decisions. It's a girl-thing I suppose, kinda like selecting prom gear. I told her I would be good with anything short of zebra stripes on the walls and pink flooring. That earned me another shoulder punch. I should mention that those blows were landing with a little more frequency than before and with a good deal more zest. Fortunately, I don't bruise too easily.

We painted the inside of #103, hauled the old furniture out, and replaced it with stuff I'd had in the little house behind Mom's. That property sold, to Mom's delight, shortly after I moved out.

Removing the nasty refrigerator proved to be a bigger challenge, but Jinks and I managed it without injury. We parked an ice chest in its place. I learned how to replace heating elements from a guy at an appliance store and got the stovetop working. I didn't intend to use the oven. Mom donated a toaster, some cookware, and a pristine *Better Homes and Gardens* cookbook I'm pretty sure her grandmother received as a wedding gift.

Jinks wanted to replace the ratty Venetian

blinds with curtains, but by that point, I was already over budget. And tired. Very, very tired.

Our biggest concern was Zeke. He simply had to live with me. That way, if nothing else, we might have some control over Hyde's menu. And trust me when I say we agonized over *that* subject day after day. But there were other subjects. Zeke mentioned other bullies, but we couldn't understand who or where they were. We doubted he meant either of the Boeheim brothers, or the pit bull, and those three tallied our slate. Our immediate problem, however, was the relocation of Zeke and his hideous cohort. That became Job One.

"I could always put Zeke in the truck and drive him over here," I said.

Jinks immediately vetoed the idea. "You gonna haul Hyde here that way, too?"

Try to imagine the logistics of loading and unloading a deadly insect weighing as much as Jinks and I combined, probably more. I tried, and failed. "There's gotta be another way."

She gave the problem two full seconds of consideration before announcing the solution. "He can walk."

"Beg pardon?"

"The preserve is chock full of hiking trails. The cross-country team uses 'em all the time. I'm sure there's one that comes fairly close to the trailer park. We wouldn't have to trek through too much forest to get there. And best of all, nobody'll see him, especially if we do it in the rain."

"I'm not much of a hiker, and it's gotta be several miles at least. Are you sure you want to lead a flesh-eating monster through the woods, in the rain, all by yourself?"

"Heck no," she said. "That's why you're coming with me. Zeke is, too."

"I'm not sure he could go that far." *I didn't want to admit doubts about my own ability to go that far without a tent and supplies for a week.*

She closed her eyes and gave her head an unsubtle shake. "It's not 'Westward Ho' across the great plains, Denver. Geez. And it's way, way shorter than the Trail of Tears. If you can hack it, so can Zeke. If we have to, one of us can carry him."

"He's gotten bigger since I first found him," I said. "He's probably doubled in size."

"I noticed."

"Evidently, recycled Bovine suits him."

"That's gross!" she said as she whacked me in the shoulder again.

"What?"

She quickly sobered. "Actually, Burt deserved it. They both did."

We settled for discussing the idea with Zeke as best we could. He gave assurances that he could command Hyde to follow us without eating us. At least, that's what we hoped he meant. He seemed sincere.

Jinks brought up another point, one I hadn't thought much about. "If Zeke lives in the trailer with you, where does Hyde live?"

Lacking even the slightest clue, we asked the little guy.

"High-duh sleep in ground," Zeke advised. "With food. He dig. Hard to find."

It felt like I was communicating with Tarzan, or his chimpanzee, Cheeta.

After considerable back and forth with Zeke, we determined that Hyde would eventually need to move in order to find more food. That delayed our expedition a bit. It wasn't just a matter of Hyde getting hungry; we needed lousy weather to ensure no one else would be using the hiking trails.

We got it mostly right.

At the start of the march, Jinks took the lead since she claimed to know the way. Zeke trundled along beside her, his nose even with her knees, and I took up the rear behind Hyde. The view was... less than inspiring, but the creature's built-in tool set for killing and dismantling its prey provided all the stimulus I needed to keep moving.

The rain didn't help despite providing the cover we needed to herd Hyde toward the trailer park. Unlike his mad dashes toward food, his efforts along the trail were boring. He moseyed along, stopping here and there to sniff, or fart, or whatever it is creatures of his ilk do. None of it was endearing.

Roughly halfway to our destination, the thunder and lightning kicked in. Hyde all but dissolved in a puddle of quivering bugness. If it weren't for his great size, his wicked pinchers, and his deadly appendage, he'd have been thoroughly pathetic.

Zeke raced to his side to comfort him while I stood there watching as raindrops dripped off my ears and chin. Jinks squished through the accumulating muck to stand beside me as the sky lit up, and the thunder rolled like a bowling tournament for the gods on Mount Olympus.

"What's he doing now?" Jinks asked. "I thought he just had the shakes."

"He dig," Zeke said. "Go in ground."

"No!" I yelped. "Not here. We've gotta keep moving."

"Oh, crap," Jinks groaned. "Someone's coming." She nodded at the trail behind us. "And whoever it is, they're moving pretty fast."

I turned to look and spotted a woman with a very large and very wet dog. The canine strained at the leash attached to its harness as if it were pulling a sled. The human at the other end of the leash struggled to keep the animal under control.

"They'll be here any moment," I said.

Ditching her poncho, Jinks ran toward Hyde.

"What are you doing?" I tried not to sound frantic.

"C'mon, hurry! We'll cover up Hyde before they get here. Take off your poncho."

I yanked off the garment without argument and added it to Jinks' efforts to conceal Hyde. He had already kicked up chunks of muddy earth in his hysterical attempt to dig a fox hole. Scorpion hole? Whatever. More wet dirt followed as he crammed himself into an ever-deepening pit.

The dog "walker," a bedraggled and weary-looking female about my mother's age, skidded by. She tried to slow the impulsive dog pulling the leash, but her feet merely slid on, leaving shallow tracks in the gravel and mud.

"Are you all right?" she yelled as she went by. "I'd stop and help if I could. Do you want me to call someone?"

"That's okay, there's no problem. We're fine," Jinks replied, her voice partially drowned out by another burst of thunder.

From a distance, we heard the woman respond with, "Good luck!" She and the dog then quickly faded from view.

We wasted no time retrieving our raingear and putting it back on, even though we were both thoroughly soaked. Only about a third of Hyde's insectoid body remained above ground, and my patience had worn down to nothing.

As the rain began to slack off, I yelled at Zeke to make Hyde stop digging. When Zeke's efforts failed, I repositioned myself behind the tunneling monster and kicked him as hard as I could.

"Stop!" Jinks screamed, "are you insane?"

Hyde didn't react until I got the third kick in. Evidently, the first two didn't hit anything sensitive. The third one, however, did.

He scrambled backwards out of the ground, and I jumped aside to avoid being run over. In the process, I slipped and landed on my backside amidst wet, thorny undergrowth. Hyde spun around and faced me with his talons clacking and his great ghastly stinger poised to run me through.

Chapter Sixteen

"There is a group of people who would like to silence everybody and have everybody go along to get along, but that's not going to be very helpful for us in the long run, in terms of solving our problems. And somebody has to be courageous enough to actually stand up to, you know, the bullies." –Dr. Ben Carson

I prayed for another crack of thunder and a few zillion amps of undiluted lightning, and I wanted it all directed at Hyde. I got squat from that. The monster staring down at me from above wasn't actually drooling. He didn't have to. His mandibles looked like a bench vice equipped with sawtooth edges. I supplied my own drool.

A furious blast of clicks and clacks, nearly as sharp as the thunder, erupted close by, momentarily distracting Hyde. Zeke leaped toward me, clambered up on my chest and stared straight up into Hyde's nightmarish mug.

They chittered away at one another, Zeke's sing-song speech rising continually until Hyde lowered his head, his pincers, and his stinger, and backed away.

"What'd you say to him?" Jinks asked my little savior, her voice hushed in awe.

"High-duh bully," he said. "Zeke stop."

"How?" I squeaked. "*How* did you stop him?"

"I say, 'Denver not food. Go now; eat later.'"

Jinks leaned close and whispered, "Got any idea what he intends to feed that thing... you know... later?"

I didn't have a clue and admitted it.

When the rain finally let up, Zeke cajoled Hyde into moving once again. Eventually, we settled down in or near Shady Grove's charming unit #103.

Despite having left us drenched and weary, to say nothing of the years Hyde scared off my life, the hike wasn't as bad as I'd first feared. I not only didn't have to carry Zeke, I got to watch Jinks navigate through the woods, make quick and rational decisions, then act on them. If I hadn't fallen in love with her before, that little woodland jaunt would have done it for sure. Jinks was the girl of my dreams. Sorry, Ms. Lovingood.

Hyde and Zeke

~*~

Life in the trailer park had both good and bad elements. The good consisted of having a place where Jinks and I could be together during the day when I wasn't working. We often watched TV with Zeke, although his program selections, mostly soap operas, left a lot to be desired, and the only person with cable seemed to be Wanda Vickers.

The bad consisted of the neighborhood. There just weren't many "normal" people living there, not that I'd actually met many of them. Far from it. The people I saw didn't appear interested in friendly conversation. In fact, most seemed to scurry about as if they didn't want to be seen at all, rather like roaches when a light flicks on.

My next-door neighbors provided the biggest exception: Tucker, Ivo Petrova, and Tucker's mother, Ruth. I really felt sorry for Ruth and the little boy. It seemed like angry voices were all I ever heard coming from that trailer, and that anger was always aimed at the mother and child.

The terrible burns on Tucker's hand appeared to be healing, though he'd worn bandages for quite a while. Once they came off, he seemed in better spirits, right up until the day Ivo broke the boy's arm.

"We've gotta do something," Jinks declared.

"Like what? Sic Hyde on old Ivo?"

"Sure," she said. "Why not?"

"Because it's not exactly our job to dispense

justice. We need to notify the child welfare people."

Jinks wasn't buying it. "We need to get the cops after him."

She was well aware of my history with local law enforcement, so it didn't come as a surprise when I told her I needed to touch base with Wanda Vickers first.

"Fine," she said, sounding way too much like my mother. "Go talk to her, but just understand, there's no chance she'll do anything."

I suspected Jinks had sized up Wanda accurately. But the woman had made it abundantly clear she would handle any issues occurring in the park. I couldn't wait to see her take on Ivo.

I found her lying face up on a folding aluminum lawn chair in heavy shade. An electric fan whirred away from the top step of the stairs leading to her trailer.

"Miz Vickers?"

"Go 'way. I'm busy."

"We've got a problem," I said.

"Not that I'm aware of."

"This is about the guy who lives in the trailer next to me, Ivo. I don't know his last name."

"Doesn't matter," she said.

"I think he's abusing the woman and child living with him."

She slipped her sunglasses off and raised her head ever so slightly to look at me. "So? What business is it of yours?"

"I think he broke little Tucker's arm."

"You didn't answer my question. What business is it of yours?"

In the space of ten seconds, she'd gotten under my skin. I could feel myself shifting into smart ass mode. "You said nobody around here should call the cops. They should come to you instead."

"You got it."

"Well," I said. "Here I am. If you won't do anything, then I'll have to find someone who will."

She rolled to a sitting position, and though her weight couldn't have been that much, the webbing on the ancient lawn chair strained as if responding to a critical mass.

"There ain't a damned thing I can do about Ivo. He's connected."

"Connected to what?"

Apparently, my appearance had taken on some bizarre form since she stared at me as if I had morphed into a T-rex or quite possibly the archangel Gabriel.

"You really are a dumbass," she said after a long pause.

I may not have been the class valedictorian, but I can out-think the average mouth breather every time. "I'm usually on the other end of that accusation."

"You ever heard of the Cossack?"

"*The* Cossack? Like there's only one?"

"Gee-zus, kid! You gotta be shittin' me. I'm talkin' about *THE* Cossack. The only one. The guy that pretty much runs this whole stinkin' town!"

And suddenly, I had the feeling she'd gotten it right; I was a dumbass. That didn't stop me from proving it, however. "Never heard of him. He's what—a pro wrestler or something? I'm not really into that stuff."

"Ivo works for the Cossack. Got it? He's what's called... muscle. If somethin' bad needs to be done, Ivo's the guy who'll do it. Understand?"

"So, that means he can break a kid's arm, and nobody will say anything about it?"

"Pretty much, yeah."

"That's the stupidest thing I've ever heard in my life. Does this Cossack guy know Ivo's a total whack job?"

"Why d'ya think the Cossack hired him? 'Cause he's a sweetheart? Geez. You just keep gettin' dumber by the minute."

~*~

While I stewed over what to do about Ivo, Jinks brought up a topic I hadn't thought of. Nothing odd about that; she did it a lot, but this time she mentioned something that really got me thinking. Namely, if Hyde spent his time tunneling, when he wasn't eating whatever Zeke had designated as food, where did he put the dirt he removed from the ground?

I asked Zeke about it, but he either didn't understand the question or chose not to answer. So, rather than badger him about it, I did some investigation on my own. After all, Hyde had to be living pretty close to my trailer.

It took me longer than I thought it would to find the entrance to his burrow. He'd hidden it behind a huge tree with extremely large, exposed roots. I'd looked at it a number of times before I recognized what it was. I'd expected to find piles of freshly dug dirt nearby. If ants didn't bother to disguise their diggings, why would Hyde?

Looking back on it now, I'm sure he just didn't want to be found.

So, what did he do with all the extra dirt? Even compressed, his body would still have been a good three feet in diameter and three times that in length. And then there were all those legs of his—too many to count. They'd have to fit in the tunnels, too. Moving just enough soil to create a hidey-hole big enough for him would result in dozens of wheelbarrows full of dirt, if not more.

Further complicating the mystery, we'd seen him dig frantically when we made our trek through the preserve to reach Shady Grove. He didn't make any effort to hide the debris then. The dirt flew behind him as he dug.

And yet, in the woods behind the trailer park, there were no dirt piles, no obvious signs of excavation. Once again, I put the question to Zeke, but he continued to be coy.

The puzzle remained unsolved until I noticed Tucker experiencing some difficulty working his way out from under Ivo's trailer, and not just because of the cast on his arm. The first time we'd seen him, there was a reasonable amount of clearance, enough to require three steps to reach the front entrance.

I took that as a clue and inspected the space underneath #103. The ground there featured a great deal of loose soil. It wasn't as compact as I thought it should be. The same proved true of several more trailers leading back toward Wanda Vicker's spot.

How he'd managed to transport the dirt without leaving some sort of trail remained a mystery. I managed to push the problem aside, however, in order to figure out how to deal with Ivo.

"We've got to do something," Jinks said. "Tucker's life is in danger whenever he's around Ivo."

I had a minor brain tickle. "What kind of name is 'Ivo' anyway?"

Jinks smirked. "Bulgarian. I looked it up. You won't believe what it means."

"Butt breath?"

"Jehovah's gift."

I groaned. "Must've been from a white elephant exchange."

"A what?"

"Never mind. Dumb joke. Kinda like Ivo. So, what are we supposed to do? We aren't cops; we don't have anything at risk. And besides all that, Ivo's connected."

"What's that mean?"

I couldn't believe Jinks hadn't watched enough movies about mobsters to know what "being connected" meant. She looked so innocent; I just couldn't tease her about it.

"It means he works for people with a lot of power. In his case, it's someone called The Cossack."

Jinks' shoulders slumped. "Yuck. I've heard of him."

"That puts you way ahead of me. I only recently learned he exists."

"I've heard Dad mention him several times. The guy's a crook—a regular gangster—but he's smart. He's never been caught. Dad thinks he's got the cops in his pocket."

"All of 'em?"

She shrugged. "The ones that count, I guess."

I immediately thought of my old pal, Detective Weiner.

Jinks looked out the window at Ivo's trailer. "Oh, crap."

"What is it? Is he beating up Tucker again?" Suddenly, I craved a baseball bat.

"Nope. He just wheeled your scooter up next to his front steps."

Acting on pure outrage, I stomped outside to confront the thief. Ivo occupied the top step. He leaned back against his front door, a cigarette dangling from his dark jowls.

"What do you think you're doing?" I asked.

"Smokin'. What're you doing?"

"I came to get my bike back."

"You mean that thing?" He glanced at my sole form of transportation and laughed.

"Yeah."

"I'm not through with it yet," he said.

"I never said you could use it!"

Looking utterly bored, he took a deep drag on his cigarette and exhaled smoke in my direction. "Yeah, 'bout that. I don't need no permission."

"I'm calling the cops."

"Don't bother. I already called. Told 'em you parked your crappy little scooter on my property, so I'm holding on to it until you pay me a storage fee."

"I didn't— You can't—"

"Yeah, I can. You want it back?"

"Damn right I do!"

"That'll be... Oh, I dunno." He drummed the fingers of his free hand on the top step as if in deep thought. "Make it five hun'erd bucks. Double that tomorrow."

"That's crazy!"

"Yeah, ain't it just." He didn't mean it as a question.

After a final puff of his cigarette, he flicked it over my head. I didn't bother to look at where it landed.

"Tell ya what," he said. "My old lady and her kid ain't here right now, so why don't you bring your little gal pal over here? She can entertain me while you roll that piece of junk back home."

"You're insane."

He snickered. "Y'know? I git that a lot."

Chapter Seventeen

"A person should not be too honest. Straight trees are cut first, and honest people are screwed first." –Chanakya

I wandered back to #103, not knowing quite what to do. Trade Jinks for the return of my scooter? Right. That was never going to happen. But could I tell her what Ivo said? That amounted to yet another terrible idea. Jinks would likely go after him with the baseball bat I didn't have. Okay, so I'm not terribly logical under stress.

Jinks stood in the doorway, a look of dread on her face. That look changed only slightly as I came into view. The girl has dimples the gods envy, but they only appear when she smiles. At that point, she wasn't.

"You know that was an incredibly stupid thing to do," she said.

I agreed, but it didn't satisfy her.

"Now what? How am I supposed to get home—jog?" She shoved her hands in the pockets of her shorts, a signature indication of how irritated she'd become. "You know it's about to rain again, right?"

Up until then, I had ignored the weather. Threats to my girlfriend's well-being were way more important.

Standing side-by-side while wedged in the door to the trailer, we peeked up at the sky, a starkly dark, grim view. Summer storms in Georgia can be ferocious. We don't often get the tornados that plague the Midwest, but our frequent run-ins with Mother Nature's secondary efforts can be heart-stopping, literally. The only thing that makes them worse is living in a trailer park. It's common knowledge that such places attract the worst the weather has to offer.

"I can call Mom," Jinks said. "Either she or Dad could pick me up. I really don't want to run when it's storming out."

"Besides which, I wouldn't let you," I said, then quickly changed the subject before she could object to my being so possessive. "We've still got to deal with Ivo the Asshole."

"What did he say when you asked him to give back your scooter?"

The background theatrics of thunder and lightning only dramatized my impotence. "I dunno," I said, knowing it was lame.

"You don't *know* what he said? *Come on, Denver!*"

"He said he'd trade the Vespa for you," I mumbled.

That left her totally stunned. "What did you tell him?"

"I told him to go pound sand." Which is what I would have said if I'd actually thought of it at the time. That didn't change my resolve. I wouldn't trade my girlfriend for a motorbike—to anyone, let alone a psychotic earthworm like Ivo.

"Maybe we could get Zeke to call on—"

"Hyde?" My laugh came out sans humor. "With thunder and lightning on the menu? He's curled up in a hole somewhere busy peeing on himself."

That elicited a giggle. "A real killer, that one," she said. "So, what are we—"

An astounding clap of thunder cut her off in mid-sentence. That was followed by the onset of ferociously high winds.

"I don't think either of us is going anywhere for the time being," I said. "We need to wait until—"

An enormous whooshing sound cut me off. It was immediately followed by a thunderous crunch. We both raced to the window overlooking #105, the trailer belonging to the man who stole my Vespa: Ivo the child-abuser.

~*~

Georgia's official state tree is the Southern live oak, which I understand is plentiful near the coast and on the many islands in the state's portion of the Atlantic Ocean. Around here, however, tall, long-leaf, yellow pines abound. These are the kind of trees that produce enough pollen every spring to cover everything like yellow snow. And who needs yellow snow, right? Achoo. And bless you.

These big pine trees, however, concentrate more on growing tall than on growing roots or limbs. Wind storms regularly knock them down, even when giant scorpions like Hyde *haven't* dug tunnels under them. So, I can't say it came as a huge surprise to see one of those massive trees lying squarely on top of Ivo's trailer—not across it mind you, but end-to-end.

The exterior wall which faced my trailer appeared fairly intact. The shallow roof, however, had disappeared. The tree trunk, too, could not be seen from the side. It protruded, however, from the front and rear, as if the trailer had been run through. Very little clearance remained between the tree and the floor of the formerly mobile home. I imagined a layer of seriously compressed furnishings. I tried to be discreet while guiding my scooter back where it belonged.

"Call 911," Jinks said. "Ivo might still be alive. Thank God Tucker and his mother weren't in there."

Based on what we could see of the flattened trailer, Ivo's chances of survival appeared minimal at best. "I suppose it's possible he's alive in there," I said. "But, honestly, do we even want that scumbag to crawl out and rejoin the living?"

She conceded that I had a valid point but immediately countered it. "Just because Ivo's a rotten, low-life, conniving, despicable piece of crap doesn't mean we are, too. We have morals, don't we?"

"Well..." I began, "as I recall, it wasn't too long ago we were discussing the possibility of arranging for Hyde to pay him a visit. That wouldn't have ended well for him, would it?"

"True," she said. "Okay then, I think our best bet is to call it in and just pray he's already deader than a bag of hammers."

Someone else, however, beat us to it. As the rain slacked off, the wail of a siren grew louder and louder. Huddled under a single umbrella, we bustled outside to await the arrival of whatever emergency vehicle was headed our way.

"Let's go 'round to the other side of the trailer. We might be able to see a little more."

A police car arrived just as we rounded the top of the now prone pine and began working our way toward the back of the trailer. The cops yelled for us to stop and get out of their way.

We complied and wandered back toward #103 while keeping our eyes on the uniformed officers. They attacked the mangled door to Ivo's home, presumably to get a better look inside. While trying not to be too obviously nosey, we shifted our position to see if we could get a glimpse inside, too.

"I see a hand," said one of the officers as he crouched in the doorway.

"Can you reach his wrist? Check for a pulse?" asked his partner.

"I'm trying," said the first cop as he wiggled his way into the squished interior. "Hang on, I'm— Oh, Lord... There's so much...."

"What? Blood?" asked the second cop.

"Yeah. And other... stuff." He backed out and away from the carnage, his face pale and shaken. "There's no way we can pull the body out until the tree is removed. And even then... I dunno, man. As far as I can tell, the guy inside has been... flattened."

His partner handed him a camera. "Get some pictures of the exterior while I mark off the site." He glanced down at the roll of yellow, plastic crime scene tape. "Hope I've got enough."

"There's plenty more in the trunk," said the cop in the doorway. They quickly went about their tasks while people from other parts of the trailer park gathered to watch.

Once they'd secured the tape and taken their photos, they turned to face the growing crowd of gawkers. The officers appeared ready to shoo us away when a blast of static accompanied a voice coming from their squad car. The larger of the two lumbered over to the vehicle, opened the door, and reached inside for a microphone. After a few moments of dialog with the voice on the radio, he gestured for his partner to join him.

I strained to hear them. "We've gotta roll," the larger of the two said. "Can't do anything more here, and we've got other calls coming in. Trees down all over. Roads are blocked. EMTs are hung up; can't get through. C'mon, we've gotta go."

They both stood up and looked at us, ready to issue a warning or commands.

"Go on back home," said the cop who had crawled into Ivo's trailer. "There's nothin' here to see. I promise y'all that, for sure." He still looked pale. "We'll get somebody out here to cut up and remove the tree; then—"

"You gonna pay for that?" Wanda Vickers asked. "'Cause I sure as hell ain't." She made her way to the front of the gathering and assumed a stance directly in front of the cop. "That tree didn't grow on Shady Grove property. It fell outta the park. Besides, I'm pretty sure the city has more money than we do. Come to think of it, the gov'mint shoulda hauled a bunch of them trees outta here before they started crashin' down on our homes."

The cop just shook his head, climbed into the car with his partner, and drove away.

~*~

Two days after the weather gods voiced their displeasure with my neighbor, I got a visit from my favorite Granville police detective. He knocked on the door and let himself in when I opened it.

"I've gotta tell ya, Denver, I wasn't too surprised when I looked up the registration info on that girlie bike you left parked beside Ivo Petrova's mobile home. I didn't know you had moved, but when I heard there were questions about the whole falling tree thing and that portions of the body had gone missing... Well, frankly, your name was the first one that popped into my head."

He'd just begun his investigation, and I'd already grown weary of it. *Parts of Ivo's body were missing? Damn it all, Hyde!* "I can't imagine why you'd think of me."

"Seriously? Missing bodies... Missing body parts... Sounds kinda familiar, don't ya think?"

"I don't know anything about missing body parts. Which parts, exactly?"

Weiner chuffed. "Don't play dumb."

"I have no idea what you're talking about! I was out taking pictures for the *Gazetteer* when somebody cut up the tree, and I was working in another town when they recovered Ivo's body."

"Don't you mean what was left of it?"

Yuck! "Listen, I—"

"And don't pretend that just 'cause you weren't here when the remains were found, that you didn't have anything to do with mutilating the body.

That was done way earlier, when you *were* here."

Weiner faced me straight-on, looking smug. I could feel the smart-ass remarks beginning to boil up from somewhere inside and struggled to keep them under control. "You're so—"

"My guess is you also had something to do with that tree coming down." He crossed his arms like an angry parent. "How do you explain the fact that someone dug up the ground under the roots? Hm? Answer me that."

"I didn't dig up a damn thing," I said. "I don't even own a shovel."

He switched tactics without missing a beat. "Why did you park your motor scooter next to Mr. Petrova's trailer?"

"I didn't!"

"Then explain this." Weiner produced a photo taken the night of the storm, which clearly showed my Vespa parked a few feet from Ivo's door.

"Ivo parked it there."

"Oh, so you loaned it to him?"

"Of course not," I said. "He stole it."

"And parked it outside his trailer where the whole world could see it?" Weiner scrunched up his face as if struggling to think through an equation. "Nah. I don't buy it. He wasn't that stupid."

"That's debatable."

"Besides, he'd already called in a nuisance

complaint about you parking it there."

I wanted to scream but managed not to. "Can't you see what he was trying to do? He set me up in case I refused to do what he wanted me to do."

"Yeah?" Weiner feigned interest. "And what was that?"

"He wanted to trade my bike for my girlfriend."

Suddenly, Weiner *did* look interested. "Is this the same girl you took to the fancy high school dance?" He pointed to one of the two framed photos of Jinks on my wall. "Her?"

"Yeah."

"The same one that led you to kill the Boeheim brothers and hide *their* bodies?"

Chapter Eighteen

*"Terre Haute. They used to call it 'Terrible Hut'
because it was so wide open. Gambling, red-light
district, speak-easies. I entertained for all the
gangsters. Can't name a gangster that didn't come into
the place where I worked." –Scatman Crothers*

"Listen, Zeke, this may come as a surprise, but you and Hyde can't just chomp down on any old body or handy body part you run into."

We were sitting in my dinky trailer shortly after detective Weiner's visit. I'd invited him to inspect my quarters, and he immediately took me up on the offer. He didn't try to disguise his disappointment when he couldn't find anything that actually tied me to Ivo's death or dismemberment. Weiner hadn't supplied any details about that, so I had no idea which parts of Ivo were in the wind, that being a handy way of avoiding thoughts about Hyde's digestive tract.

"High-duh hungry," Zeke said. "Zeke hungry, too."

I still hadn't mastered reading his expressions, limited though they were. "You need to stick with wildlife," I said. "Squirrels, rabbits—"

"Cats?"

That scored a massive ick, and I made no effort to disguise my reaction.

He ignored me. "Cats gone," he said.

I allowed myself to think they'd all moved away or found adoptive homes. "There are deer and wild pigs in the forest preserve. Why not eat a few of them?" If I'd had snapshots of them handy, I'd have shared them with Zeke. Alas, my photo files weren't very well organized. Though I knew I had pictures of deer somewhere in my pile of prints, finding them would have taken a while, and he wouldn't have hung around.

"Listen," I said, thinking of my conversation with Jinks about serving Ivo to Hyde, "there may come a time when I'll need you and Hyde to go after a human."

"Hew-mahn?"

"A person, people." I pointed to myself. "Like me and Jinks."

I wish I could say we reached some sort of agreement.

~*~

"Maybe you need a lawyer," Jinks said.

We sat in the living room of her parents' home, awaiting their arrival at any moment. Jinks had invited me to come for dinner, and since my cooking skills were limited to can opening, water boiling, and egg scrambling, I promptly accepted the offer.

"I dunno about getting a lawyer," I said. "I haven't been charged with anything. And lawyers aren't cheap."

"You just haven't been charged yet." She frowned at me. "By the way, have you had a chat with Zeke about Ivo and Hyde?"

"I think so."

"You *think* so?"

"Zeke still hasn't quite grasped all the nuances of the English language."

"He's not the only one," she said. "And what about little Tucker and his mom?"

"They showed up the day the tree fell, but it was late and dark out. That's probably a good thing, 'cause they couldn't see the destruction clearly. I heard them pull up in that beat-up old car of hers. I didn't know how Ruth would react."

Clearly concerned, Jinks put her hand on my arm. "And?"

"She looked frantic at first, as if Ivo might pop up and blame her for knocking the tree down. She asked me if I'd seen him. The best I could do was point at the wreckage and shake my head." I patted Jinks' hand. "Ruth put her arm around Tucker, held him close, and then asked if I was sure about Ivo."

Such an odd memory. "'They haven't pulled him out yet', I told her. 'He's... gone.' And then she smiled."

"That's it?" Jinks asked. "She just smiled?"

"I can still see her in my mind. She took a deep breath, exhaled, then said, 'Thank God.'"

Jinks had grown pretty tense as I related the encounter, but when she heard Ruth's response, she relaxed. "And Tucker? How did he react?"

"Once Ruth let him loose, he headed straight for the crushed trailer. I think he might've been looking for some of his toys. He didn't seem upset. I asked Ruth if they had a place to stay for the night. I was about to offer my trailer, but she said they'd go to a motel and that she'd be back the next day."

"So, did she come back?"

"Yes. By then, the roof of the trailer had been removed, along with whatever remained of Ivo. The police tape was still up, but she ignored it and climbed right into the wreckage. It didn't take her long to find what she was after, but once she had it in hand, she gathered up her son and loaded him in her car. I asked her what I should say if someone came looking for her. Her eyes went wide for a split second, then she shook her head. 'Tell 'em I'm dead,' she said. And then she drove away."

Jinks' parents arrived a few minutes apart, and she helped her mother fix dinner while I chatted with her dad. For some reason, I felt comfortable around them even though her dad was my boss.

"I saw the photos of the smashed trailer you turned in," he said. "Based on the address, it sounds like it was pretty close to you."

I chuckled. "It was, literally, right next door."

"Criminy, Denver! You've gotta get outta there. It's not safe."

"It's not like it's raining trees everywhere," I said. "And it's not like Shady Grove will be my permanent residence. With college classes starting in a matter of days, I'll barely spend any time there."

I'd never seen him look so serious. "That's not what I meant."

Crap, I thought. *Had he somehow found out about Hyde and Zeke?* "Okay. So, what am I missing?"

"It's not just the trees; it's the people who run the place."

"Wanda Vickers? She's kind of a jerk, but she's not—"

"I don't know who Wanda Vickers is," he said. "My concern is the Cossack. He's the guy behind much of the crime around here, and not just in Granville.

He's active in several nearby towns, too. So far, the law hasn't touched him. I have a theory about that, but I can't prove it. Anyway, I first heard of him quite a while back, but I discounted much of it as gossip—unproven comments by disgruntled people. Lately, I've gotten better information."

So, he didn't know about Zeke and company. Hallelujah! "Cossack seems like an odd title for a criminal."

"Nah. Just think 'kingpin' or 'mob boss.' I think the title is meant to frighten people. It makes him seem a little mysterious, not just some run of the mill racketeer, and it makes his gang seem more powerful."

"But why here?" I asked. "Why focus on small towns?"

"I don't really know, but I suspect he may be afraid to compete with other gangs. Then again, if you add up the populations of all the towns in this part of the state, there are plenty of people to extort and plenty of idiots willing to pay for the illegal things the Cossack's gang sells."

I struggled to get it all sorted in my head. "But, how is Shady Grove involved? Surely, he doesn't live there. I thought mob bosses had luxury homes." I wanted to add something like 'with hot and cold running babes everywhere,' but thought better of it. Jinks might have been listening. Besides, I didn't want to give her dad the wrong idea about what kind of person I was.

He didn't hesitate to explain. "There's a woman at the *Gazetteer* who handles most of the crime reporting, and she's been digging into this issue for over a year. She's kept me advised on an expose' she's writing. And, who knows, it could lead to something big for her."

"Like a Pulitzer Prize?"

He grinned. "That'd probably be a leap, but it could lead to a job offer from a bigger paper. The *Atlanta Clarion* perhaps. I don't know. I'd hate to lose her, but to be honest, she's too good to stick around here much longer."

"Okay, so back to Shady Grove, which you think the Cossack controls. Why is that a bad thing?"

Jinks' dad tapped his fingertips together the way evil bankers do in the movies. "He could be selling drugs from there. Or storing them. Or worse, he could have someone making them. You've heard of methamphetamine, right?"

"Sure."

"Well, it's the drug of choice outside the big cities 'cause it's easier to find than cocaine. Just ask someone in a biker gang. From what I hear, they control the trade."

Buck Boeheim and his tattoos instantly came to mind. *So, maybe he wasn't drunk; maybe he was high on something else.* Either way, I didn't know anyone who missed him.

"Anyway," he went on, "that's why I don't want

Jinks anywhere near that place, and it's why I think you need to get out of there as quick as you can."

Jinks gave the "Dinner's on" announcement and ended our conversation, but it did nothing to quell the thoughts racing around in my head.

~*~

The next few weeks proved to be as busy as they were boring. Jinks' classes started before mine, but between buying a real vehicle, getting registered for classes, and making deadlines for the various papers carrying my photos, we saw little of each other. It certainly didn't help that her father told her she was forbidden to go anywhere near Shady Grove. Evidently, no one mentioned that edict to her cross-country coach who regularly had his team jogging through the woods behind the trailer park.

I'd gone through those woods more than once just to watch Jinks go by, a heart-warming sight to be sure. On those rare occasions when she wasn't accompanied by other runners, she'd join me for a little rest. The more we were apart, the more those brief encounters grew in importance.

I had grown tired of driving the Vespa when it rained, and with fall coming on, cold, wet weather wasn't far off. So, it was time to find something else to get around. That turned out to be a bit of an ordeal since, according to the credit bureau, I didn't exist. Or rather, my credit history didn't. It seems one can't get credit unless one already has it. The only alternative was to seek credit when you didn't really need it.

How, I wondered, did lenders stay in business? Very reluctantly, I approached the Bank of Mom and Dad. My father told me to call Mom. Mom told me to stick with the Vespa and invest in a good, heavily lined raincoat. "You're young; you can tough it out," she said. "Put whatever money you can set aside in a savings account."

Finding a fur-lined hazmat suit seemed highly unlikely, but it seemed to be the only thing that would realistically meet Mom's requirements. So much for a savings account. It made more sense to survive until I could get my hands on the trust fund she'd once mentioned, ever so vaguely. I convinced myself, without a great deal of effort, that riding the Vespa in the dead of winter, even in Georgia, was an open invitation to pneumonia or worse.

I thought about it, but couldn't bring myself to beg Jinks' dad to co-sign a loan. But eventually, I found a used car dealer who seemed eager to help me.

Okay, so "help" in this instance requires a bit of explanation. Keep in mind that at this time, the country was experiencing some serious inflation. The local savings and loan offered a two-year, used car deal at twelve percent, provided I had a co-signer to make the payments if I defaulted. Not helpful.

The used car dealer said he could get me a loan—*in my name only*—for a "slightly" higher rate. "Slightly" turned out to be twenty-five percent over twelve months.

"So, I have to pay the loan off in a year? I thought most car loans ran for twenty-four months"

"Sure, but those loans are harder to get." The dealer seemed very sure of himself. "You don't want to carry around a lot of debt, do you? That'd be stupid, and I can tell, you ain't no dummy. Besides, this way, you'll get to establish some real credit."

I knew it would be a stretch, but if I could live on pot pies—three for a dollar at the Piggly Wiggly— and didn't spend too much on dates with Jinks, I could probably pay off the nifty little Ford sedan I'd had my eye on.

Chapter Nineteen

*"A street thug and a paid killer are professionals—
beasts of prey, if you will, who have dissociated
themselves from the rest of humanity and can now see
human beings in the same way that trout fisherman
see trout."* –Willard Gaylin

It took a few days, but the ever-resourceful detective Weiner eventually realized that yet another pair of people had gone missing whose last known contact had been me. Once more he arrived at my door, notepad in hand, and with a smarmy expression decorating his complacent mug. I didn't let him in.

"What'd you do with Ms. Darby and her kid?"

"Who?" I asked, honestly not connecting anyone with his question. *Darby?*

"Ruth and Tucker Darby. They were living with Mr. Petrova. Witnesses claim you were talking to them the afternoon they disappeared."

"They didn't disappear; they just left town. I asked her about it before she left. She said if anyone asked—and I'm quoting her—'Tell 'em I'm dead.'"

"Dead?"

"Yep."

"So, you're saying she's dead."

"I'm not saying that at all!" *What the hell is the matter with you?* "As far as I know, she's off enjoying life, probably for the first time in years. I have no idea why she chose to stay with Ivo the Irritable for more than five minutes. That's a lot longer than it took him to get under my skin. He didn't need to break any of *my* bones to prove he was a jerk."

Weiner's expression didn't change a bit. "You've got it all figured out, haven't you?"

I shrugged. "You seem to think *you* have, but you haven't produced anything that even vaguely resembles evidence of the horrible things you keep accusing me of doing."

"I've got my eye on you, kid."

"Whoa. No kidding? Seriously?" Much as I hated to admit it, he'd hit the jumpstart button on my smart-ass engine. "Who'd have ever guessed that?"

"That mouth of yours is gonna git you in big trouble one day."

"It wouldn't be the first time," I said, having had more than my fill of the idiot. "Please let me know when you're ready to start investigating instead of just making shit up." I emphasized the point by slamming my door shut.

I doubt Weiner was terribly impressed, but it made me feel better.

~*~

My first encounter with Regina Hornsby came unexpectedly. I knew she'd been writing for the *Gazetteer* for a long time, but since I didn't work behind a desk, I'd met only a few other employees. I usually just turned my photos in at the front office and went on my way. One day, not long after the tree and trailer incident, Regina was waiting for me when I came in.

"Denver? Denver Stow?"

Someday, maybe, I'll respond to a greeting like that without suspicion. At the time, however, it felt sort of like an ambush.

"Uhm, yeah?"

She introduced herself, and complimented me on my photos, several of which had included a byline. I got paid a little extra for those.

"I'd like to talk to you about a project I'm working on," she said.

I felt sure Regina was the writer Jinks' father told me about, the one who'd filled him in on the Cossack and his gang.

A potential Pulitzer Prize winner wanted to talk to me? I tried to present my best imitation of someone knowledgeable and said, "How can I help you?"

"I understand you live in that mobile home park near the edge of town."

"It's called Shady Grove, and yes, I do live there. But, hopefully, not too much longer." I lowered my voice and added, "I'm told it's not terribly safe."

She nodded. "I don't know if you're aware of what's going on over there."

"I've heard some rumors," I said, trying not to sound too innocent.

"You and one or two others who live there may be the only ones who aren't involved to one extent or another with gang activity."

I swallowed. "You're talking about the Cossack, right?"

"And his little band of cretins."

Cretins, I assumed, were bad, but the only other time I'd heard the word, my mother used it to describe little chunks of toast sprinkled on salad.

"Anyway," she continued, "I'd love to have some photos from there. You know, images that capture illicit activities."

My imagination kicked in, and I envisioned taking pictures of the kinds of people I'd only heard about in movies, truly unsavory types: drug dealers, pimps, and morons like Ivo who beat people up for the hell of it when they weren't doing it for some crime boss. "And you want me to take 'em?"

"Why not? You already live nearby. It shouldn't be that hard to grab a snapshot or two."

"Of what, exactly?"

Regina thought for a moment. "I imagine drug deals would be the easiest to get. Somebody drives up to one of the trailers; a dealer appears, and an exchange is made."

She made it sound all too easy. "Isn't this something the cops should be doing?"

"Of course it is, but according to them, no one's filed any complaints, so they have no reason to suspect anything illegal is going on." That was followed by a shallow laugh. "And then there's the whole issue of the department being understaffed. By that I mean there's only one investigator."

"My dear friend Detective Weiner."

Regina suddenly looked apprehensive. "You're *friends* with him?"

I instantly shook my head. "I was being sarcastic. It's... It's a problem I have."

"Weiner or sarcasm?"

"Both, actually. But that's not important right now." The last thing I wanted to do was drag out the saga of the Boeheim brothers and Ivo. "I'm just...."

"Apprehensive?" She waved her hands

dismissively. "That's okay. It was a crazy idea. I apologize. There's no reason I can't go over there and get my own pictures. How hard could it be?"

"That depends on a lot of things," I said. "Not the least of which is the kind of camera you're using; how far you are from the subjects; whether or not there's decent lighting, and that doesn't even begin to touch on things like—"

"Okay, okay. I get it. You're a photographer, and I'm not. So how do you suggest I get the pictures I need?"

"I might be able to get them for you," I said. "But I don't want to promise anything until I know more about what I'm shooting. Do you know which trailers are being used by the drug dealers?"

We talked for another twenty minutes or so during which time she shared her thoughts on how to identify the proper location, then I had to leave or be late for class. I wasn't ready to start cutting classes even though they were all entry level, freshman courses taught by graduate assistants. Meanwhile, the idea of being a crime buster had put down roots. Tentative roots, to be sure, but they were there, and the more I thought about the prospect, the deeper they went.

~*~

Growing up, I discovered, requires more than just ticking off the years until you're old enough to vote. You have to learn certain things about survival in the modern world, things they don't teach in high school. I'm talking about things like auto insurance, utility bills, unscrupulous car dealers, and car repairs. All of which conspired to make it impossible for me to meet my financial obligations in the timely manner I'd promised.

"The dealer said the car's odometer only showed 37,000 miles. How could the transmission be worn out?"

The mechanic Jinks' dad recommended gave me a sympathetic look. "Son, there's no way on Earth that car's logged fewer than a hundred thousand miles more than what's showing. probably double that. Somebody rolled the odometer back."

"Isn't that illegal?"

"Yep. Sure is."

Having dealt with Detective Weiner, I wasn't entirely new to outrage, but this represented a whole new flavor of it. "Then, I should be able to get my money back. They cheated me!"

The man shrugged, and he looked doubtful. "The thing is, it's hard to prove who did it. Outfits like the one you did business with know all the angles. They're pros at cheating the system. That doesn't mean you can't work something out with 'em, but if I was you, I wouldn't get my hopes up."

He was kind enough to arrange a ride home for me while he figured out what it would cost to bring my car back to life. All during that ride I pondered what I would say when I confronted the con artist who sold me that useless piece of junk. All such thoughts evaporated however, when I saw a lean, dark-complected man sitting on the steps of my trailer, the door of which stood wide open behind him.

Dressed in a sleeveless T-shirt, worn jeans, and sweat, with an array of intricate tattoos on his hands, arms, and neck, he stood when I arrived. His sneer suggested a disposition as charming as Ivo's. While I'd have dearly loved to turn around and go back to the garage where my useless car sat, I had photos to take and classes to attend. I needed the Vespa, or I wouldn't be able to do either of those things.

"'Bout time," he growled as my ride navigated away, down the gravel track leading to the main road.

"Didn't know I had a visitor." I hoped I didn't sound as shaky as I felt.

He took a few steps closer. "I'm takin' over for Ivo since he got himself killed, otherwise you'd be payin' him."

I couldn't make out exactly what he'd had for lunch, but his cigarette breath only partially clouded the smell of garlic. "I hate to admit it," I said, "but I uhm... I can't make my payment today. I've gotta hold back some money to cover car repairs."

"Life sucks, don't it?" He shuffled even closer. "But yer gonna pay what you owe right now." He held up an eight-by-ten print of a prom photo Mom took. "I found this hangin' on the wall inside yer place. Who's the babe?"

"My girlfriend."

"She any good in bed?"

Anger quickly began to supplement my anxiety. "I don't... She's not that kind of girl."

"Oh yeah, right, right." He laughed as he tore the photo in half from top to bottom and discarded the portion with me in it. "Listen, dumbass, when it comes down to it, they're all that kinda girl. So, if you can't pay me, today, then just bring this little honey around. Give her an hour or so with me to work it off."

I took a step closer, unsure of exactly what I might do. Crazy thoughts raced through my head. The idea of lashing out and punching him in the throat definitely appealed to me, provided I could get a little closer.

"Fergit it kid, I ain't waitin'."

"Listen, I—"

Suddenly, I had no breath; my stomach hurt like hell, and I found myself sitting on the gravel strewn ground looking up at the guy who'd just punched me in the stomach.

"Git up," he said, the words erupting in a sort of grunt.

I still hadn't regained my wind. "Gimme a sec," I croaked.

"You got the money on ya?"

"No. I told you before— Stop!"

He'd drawn his leg back to deliver a kick. I had

both arms extended, palms out, hoping he'd at least pause. Desperate to get away from him, I briefly considered crawling under the trailer, not that it had done much good for little Tucker Darby.

"Nobody gits a free ride, kid. Now stand up, go inside, and grab some cash. Yer payment's already late. You owed a hun'erd yesterday. The late fee is fifty bucks. It'll be another fifty tomorrow. Don't screw around; pay me now."

"I— I can't. I need more time."

"That ain't my problem."

"Please. Come back tomorrow. Same time. I'll be here, and I'll get the money somewhere."

"All two hun'erd?"

I said, "Yeah," but I had no idea where I'd find it. I needed the Vespa, and I needed my camera. I didn't own anything else of any real value that I could sell or pawn.

He shook his head. "If you wanna pay more'n ya have to, well, that's yer business. If ya ask me, I think it's stupid. And bring the girl." He dropped the other half of the photo. "Otherwise, it's just you and me."

I couldn't resist asking, "And just who are you?"

"They call me Tats."

It figured. I watched him saunter away, climb into a late model Chevy, and drive off. Slowly, a plan emerged, a possible way out of my dilemma. I needed to find Zeke.

Chapter Twenty

"There cannot be a crisis next week. My schedule is already full." –Henry Kissinger

"You're damned lucky to be alive, Mr. Fitzgerald."

Jonathon struggled to identify the voice, then realized he didn't care. His head hurt; his vision was blurry, and he knew he wasn't thinking straight. "What... happened?" He croaked.

The voice continued, "You've been unconscious for quite a while."

His voice reduced to a harsh whisper, Jon asked, "How long? Where am I? Who are you?" He tried to sit up. "What's—"

A hand on his chest gently pressed him back down. "Easy, champ."

Jon squinted at the speaker. "I don't... understand. Geez. My head...."

"It's still attached."

The voice sounded female, but it was pitched low. He still couldn't see well. "Seems kinda bright in here, doesn't it?"

"You'll get used to it," said the voice. "Your reaction is quite normal. Now, if you'll just lie there and relax, I'm going to contact some folks who really want to see you."

"Wait!" he called to the rapidly retreating figure, but he had no volume. "Who...."

The woman was already gone. Moving slowly so as not to cause himself additional pain, Jon worked his way to a sitting position. It helped that the back of his bed had been angled upward.

Had he done that? No. Not possible. Had he fallen? Had he tripped? And why did his back hurt, too?

He remembered going to the Sweet Dreamz lounge. A pretty girl. Bright pink hair. Loud music. He recalled the heavy bass, a rhythmic thumping he could actually feel. What the hell was he doing there? He couldn't remember leaving.

As slowly as he'd eased himself up, he eased himself back down. He couldn't decide if the pain in his head was worse than the pain in his back. It hurt to move. Hell, it hurt to *think*.

A large person, presumably female and wearing light blue clothing—*scrubs?*—came into the room. "Good, you're still awake."

It sounded like the same person who'd spoken to him earlier.

"Your parents are on their way. Should be here in twenty or thirty minutes."

He shook his head, and instantly regretted it. "Where... Where is here? I mean where—"

"You're in a rehab facility. About halfway between Granville and Columbus."

"Okay. And how'd I get here?"

"Ambulance."

"I mean... What happened? Why—"

"You were transferred here from County General. I don't know why you were there to begin with, but I feel sure your parents can fill you in. Now, why don't you just relax and get some rest? There's water there beside the bed. Someone will be in later to discuss your physical therapy plan."

~*~

It seemed like no time at all had passed when Jon next opened his eyes. His vision had improved considerably, enough to see his mother and father sitting in his room, looking at him.

"It's about time," his mother said. "They called and said you were awake, so we rushed right over. But when we got here you were sleeping. As if you haven't had enough sleep in the past few weeks."

Few weeks? How could that be? "I don't understand."

"We don't, either," she said. "We've been waiting for an explanation, but no one has given us anything useful. Now that you're awake, we'd like you to tell us what happened."

"I... Uhm...."

"That's a dreadful way to start, Jonathon."

"Things are sorta hazy."

"I'm sure."

He looked to his father for support, but he was reading a newspaper, and didn't offer any encouragement.

"They said you were found outside some sort of sex club." She looked at her husband. "Henry? What was the name of that awful place?"

"Sweet Dreams," he said looking up briefly from his paper. "Or something like that. It's a redneck strip joint. No telling how many laws get broken in there."

"Okay, yeah," Jon said. "That sounds right."

"*Sounds right?*" His mother's voice had shifted into indignation mode. "What in the world were you doing there?"

"There was a girl—"

"Oh, dear God!"

He squinted at her. "What?"

"You were consorting with a prostitute? A... harlot?"

"No." He would've shaken his head, but he'd already learned that lesson. "I spoke to her, earlier. In a restaurant."

"Never mind that. Tell me why you got hurt. Who attacked you?" She looked toward Henry and cleared her throat to get his attention. "I told you we should never have let him get involved with that stupid government agency. I was right, admit it."

"I got hit from behind," Jon said. "I didn't see who did it."

She stared down at him over crossed arms. "The doctor told us you were struck with a pipe or a bat. Something hard and round. Fortunately, it was a glancing blow, or you might've been killed. Whoever did it also took your wallet, your ID, and your car."

"They got your sidearm, too," added his father.

"Men and their guns," his mother muttered. "Anyway, the police didn't know who you were, where you came from, or who to contact."

Henry chimed in with, "You were a John Doe for quite a while."

"Then how—"

His mother made no effort to disguise her displeasure. "Some girl showed up and said she knew you. Melanie, I think she said her name was."

"No," said Henry. "That's not right. It was Molly, I think. Or maybe Melody. Something like that."

"Malindi?"

"Yes!" said his mother. "I'm told she came to visit twice. Of course, you were never awake. She told the staff she didn't know your name, but she felt sure you were some sort of secret agent. Can you imagine anything more absurd?"

Jon finally mustered a rational thought. "How did you find out I was here?"

Henry put his paper aside and approached the bed. "There's a woman in your department who got concerned when she didn't hear from you. She contacted the local police who eventually connected you with her missing AARPA field agent."

"Must've been Cecilia," Jon said, smiling for the first time since he woke up. "I owe her, big time."

His mother looked suspicious. "What's the story with her?"

"She's a friend," he said. "A good one."

Thoughts of Burnside's assistant triggered another thought. "My investigation! Did—"

"Don't worry about it," Henry said. "It's on hold."

"Which strikes me as thoroughly ridiculous." Jon's mother had her arms crossed once again. "They should have given it to a real agent."

"I *am* a real agent!" Despite his protest, Jon

couldn't believe Burnside hadn't turned the whole thing over to someone else.

"You are definitely a real, live agent," Henry said, ignoring his wife and the look of disapproval she beamed at him like a searchlight. "I made a few inquiries and put in a word or two here and there with some people I know in DC. It's done. Once the doctor says you're up to it, you should be able to go back to work on whatever case you were involved in."

"Just like that?"

Henry nodded.

"Do you ever *not* get your way?" Jon asked.

"All the time." He looked up at his wife, then back down at his son, and smiled.

~*~

Jon's physician wouldn't commit to a specific date when he'd pronounce his patient well enough to return to work. That didn't sit well, and Jon grew determined to hide whatever symptoms he might have. Other than a headache which wouldn't go away, he felt reasonably well.

A few days after he woke up, Malindi appeared. "Well, look who's up and around," she said. "You had me worried."

"I heard you dropped by to check on me." He paused and scratched his chin. "Please don't take this the wrong way, but what prompted that? I'm mean, we only just met, and—"

"It was me."

"What was you? I don't understand."

"I'm the reason you got whacked. And I'm pretty sure I know who did it." She looked apprehensive. "I know I should have said something to the police, but since I didn't actually see him do anything, I can't be sure he was the one."

Jon blinked, still unaware of what she meant.

"I think it was Tats."

"Who?"

"Tats. He's the guy who was bugging me in Babe's Burgers. You flashed your badge and got him to leave me alone."

It wasn't a terribly distinct memory, but he did recall being put off by all the tattoos, which probably explained why he couldn't remember the man's face. "He hit me just because of that?" It didn't seem likely.

"I saw you at the club. We waved, remember? I was on stage, and I saw you walking toward the exit. Tats was right behind you, and he had a mean look on his face. But then, he always has a mean look on his face. Anyway, when I finished my set, I threw on a robe and ran out into the parking lot. I looked around for a little bit, and then I saw you. I had Eddie, our bouncer, call nine-one-one." She twisted her lips to one side. "He's had to do that a lot."

Jon stared at the young woman standing beside his bed. She looked prettier without all the stage makeup she'd been wearing the first time he saw her. She looked younger, too. "I'm just glad you dropped by. My mother comes by every day, but she can be... tiring."

"If *my* son was a spy, I'd want to check on him regularly, too."

Jon chuckled. "I'm not a spy. I'm an investigator."

She smiled knowingly. "Right. I get it." She took a quick look around the room, then whispered, "Your secret's safe with me."

"Seriously," Jon said. "It's my job to find out what happened to some people who went missing." He chewed his lower lip. "But there's not much more I can say about it."

"Missing, huh?" She cleared her throat. "Funny you should say that. I used to date a guy, kind of a weirdo. Nerdy, y'know? And really into photography. Anyway, the cops were interested in him because of some people who went missing."

"Did they arrest him?"

"I don't think so. But I haven't seen him in a long time."

Jon thought back to his brief discussion with the sole detective on the Granville police force. The cop claimed he'd heard no mention of any missing persons other than the two he sought.

"Who went missing?" Jon asked.

"The Boeheim brothers. I had a couple classes

with one of them. They were both big guys."

"How big?"

"Giant economy? I know one of them played on the football team. He was probably the biggest guy on the squad. Funny thing though, his older brother was even bigger. That's why I don't think Denver did anything to 'em. He's closer to my size than theirs."

"A bullet doesn't much care how big the target is," Jon said. "I don't see what harm it would do to have a chat with him. You say his name's Denver?"

She nodded yes. "Denver Stow. Last I heard, he worked for the newspaper."

Jon made a note of the name. If he ever got the opportunity to go back to work, Denver Stow would be at or near the top of his list of people to contact.

Chapter Twenty-one

"There's only one basic principle of self-defense. You must apply the most effective weapon, as soon as possible, to the most vulnerable target." –Bruce Lee

While sneaking around in the woods isn't very hard, avoiding things like poison ivy, snakes, bees, and bugs can be tricky. So, I took my time when preparing to reconnoiter the trailers at the other side of Shady Grove, the ones Regina suspected of being used by drug dealers.

Getting into a position where I could take photos of drug buyers and sellers meant finding a hiding place in front of the trailers where a strip of trees and underbrush separated the buildings from the road. Getting to that area without being seen by any of the folks I intended to photograph, meant going through the woods behind and beside the targets.

My hope was that I could get some decent shots and sell them to Regina. If the price wasn't right, I hoped she would be willing to advance me some cash for photos I'd take later on. I just wasn't keen on using Hyde and Zeke to handle Tats. They might eat him, sure, but I'd still owe money on the stupid car. Though no one had confirmed it, I assumed the Cossack was my lender, and I guessed he had plenty of people willing to beat the money out of me. So, even if I got rid of Tats, there'd just be another goon to take his place.

Thus, getting the photos seemed like my best bet. Thankfully, there's still enough light in the early autumn evenings to allow shooting without a flash. I needed to be stealthy, so I moved slowly and carefully, but I worried constantly about Hyde's tunnels. He'd had enough time to do extensive burrowing. I just didn't know exactly where, and thoughts of a cave-in which would land me close to him left me extra shaky.

I did my best and put in a couple of hours of effort, but by the time the sun finally set, I'd seen only one potential customer greeted by someone from the suspect trailer. Even though I used a long-range lens, I couldn't get a clear enough shot.

So, it was back to Plan A.

Zeke listened patiently while I attempted to explain my predicament. I hoped his fascination with watching soap operas on my little TV set had given him a better grasp of human communication. After talking with him about my problem, I felt reasonably sure it had. At the very least, he'd begun speaking in sentences of more than two words, and he occasionally responded to questions with answers that made sense, from his point of view anyway. He had finally become more conversant than the average cigar store Indian, if not using quite as many facial expressions.

He did perk up, however, when I mentioned food and asked if either of them had eaten anything lately.

"No. Zeke very hungry. Hide-duh hungry, too," he said.

It was the answer I'd been counting on.

I caught up with Jinks on the cross-country trail behind Shady Grove. She'd been running in the middle of the pack, but there was considerable distance between her and those ahead and behind. I got her attention as she rounded a curve, and we slipped quietly through the woods to a spot we'd used for a rendezvous before. Once we were hidden from the view of other runners, I told her about my encounter with the bill collector.

"Why can't you just go to the police?" she asked.

"Who am I gonna call, Detective Weiner? Not

exactly a sympathetic ear. He'd probably be happy to know Tats mugged me."

"Tats?"

"The guy they sent to collect my payment." I absently rubbed the bruise on my belly which still hurt.

"I've got a little money in savings," she said. "And I'm sure my parents would be willing to lend you some."

"You're amazing, and generous, and if that's all it took, I'd happily borrow the money from you and pay it back as fast as I could. But I can't ask your parents to help me. What kind of message would it send if I told them I owed money to a loan shark? I don't want to admit I'm really that stupid. Besides, unless I pay off the whole thing, whoever Tats works for—"

"The Cossack, right?"

"That's what I think, yeah. And if I can't pay the whole thing off, they'll just keep coming after me."

"So, what're you going to do?"

I exhaled. "I've got a plan."

"Does it involve... You know... Zeke?"

"It's better that you don't know anything about it," I said. "That way, if the Weiner-Meister comes calling, you won't be able to say a word."

"If you're gonna do what I think you're gonna do...."

I shook my head. "Don't go there, okay?"

"Right. It's just... It's not... ethical. You know what I mean?"

"You think I should treat the Cossack and his thugs *ethically?*" I wanted to laugh, but held it to a smile. "No. I think they've got a surprise coming. They've earned it. If not from me, then from all the other people they've done this to. I don't believe for a second that I'm the only one."

"And Weiner isn't the only cop in town," she said. "There are plenty of others."

"That's true. The problem is, I don't know which ones also work for you-know-who. Your dad has some suspicions, and so does Regina. She's—"

"A reporter. I know who she is." Jinks reached for my hand. "I just don't want to see you get hurt." With that, she leaned into me for a quick kiss. "I've gotta go before somebody reports me missing."

"Someone's bound to notice you aren't in the middle of the pack anymore."

"That's no problem. When nature calls, you can't exactly stop in the middle of the trail." She pointed to the woods all around. "I'm not the only one who's ever had to...."

"Gotcha," I said.

After another quick kiss, she was gone.

~*~

Tats was late. I'd had to pass on a Halloween

photo assignment because I expected him to arrive at the same time as he had the day before. Jinks' dad wasn't happy about the cancellation, but I had no choice, and I wasn't about to tell him the real reason I couldn't make it.

The longer Tats stayed away, the more nervous I became.

I sat in the shade in what amounted to my backyard on one of the two folding chairs that normally flank the card table in my trailer. Jinks called it my dining room set. I remember chuckling about that the first few times she said it. Thinking about it didn't ease my mind.

Though I hadn't seen Hyde, Zeke assured me his symbiotic pal was nearby then ducked into the darkness under my trailer. At that point, neither one remained in sight.

In an effort to look nonchalant, I cradled the textbook from my English 101 class in my lap. If I'd had a conventional weapon of some sort, I could have hidden it there. If I needed to slow the proceedings down, I figured I could just pretend I was armed. Tats hadn't displayed a knife or a gun during his first visit, so I assumed he'd be unarmed for this one.

I was wrong. He showed up with a black, Louisville Slugger baseball bat.

He wore the same T-shirt and jeans as the day before, although the shirt bore a ketchup stain that made him look as if he'd been shot. "Got the money?" he asked.

"Yes," I said and waved an envelope I'd stuffed with dollar-bill-sized pieces of newspaper.

"It's funny," he said as he leaned against my trailer. "I've been doin' this for a while now, and it seems like whenever I come 'round a second time, people think they can do somethin' tricky, y'know? Like... Try to get the drop on me."

"Sounds like a bad idea to me," I said.

He bobbed his head, yes. "So, g'wan. Go ahead and do whatever it is you think you're gonna do to me. I'm ready." He stared directly at the textbook in my lap. "What'cha got under there?"

"Nothing."

"Prove it."

I tossed the envelope containing the faux cash over my shoulder in what I presumed was Hyde's direction. Then I made a show of slowly lifting the textbook to reveal the vacant spaces over and between my legs.

"Glad to see you ain't done nothin' stupid," Tats said. "Now, git up, go back there where you threw the money, and pick it up. Bring it to me."

"You're going to have to get it yourself," I said as I stood up and folded my chair. "As far as I'm concerned, my payment's been delivered. Now, if you'll excuse me, I've got some studying to do."

I started toward the trailer when he poked me with the Louisville Slugger. "That ain't how it works."

I dropped the textbook and raised the folded metal chair in both hands. They trembled, but I didn't care if Tats noticed. "You might get in a whack or two," I said, "but so will I. Is it worth it?"

He responded with a snort and a shrug. "Damned kids these days," he said as he headed toward the envelope.

When he did, I called out to Zeke, "Time to eat!"

He answered with, "High-duh!"

Tats turned first to look at me, and then in the direction of Zeke's voice. He never saw the massive scorpion-like creature which rose up from the undergrowth in the woods and sped toward him.

Hyde's lance-like stinger made quick work of the thug who had time to squeal briefly before dropping the baseball bat and the bogus cash and succumbing to whatever venom had been squirted into him. Hyde's stinger was the size of a turkey baster, and the dose he injected must have been both fast-acting and fatal. Tats was dead before his corpse came to rest on the ground.

Hyde wasted no time. He clamped an arm and a leg in his over-sized pincers and dragged his meal into the woods. Zeke clambered out from under the trailer and hurried after Hyde.

I yelled for him to stop. He didn't appear happy about it, but he complied. "Food!" he exclaimed, a note of anxiety in his voice.

"Yes, I know. And it's all yours. But there's one more thing," I said. "I need his car keys."

"Kahr keez?"

"Yeah."

Zeke responded with an utterly blank look. He was a master at that. I dug the keys for the Vespa out of my pocket and dangled them in front of him. "Keys," I said. "I need Tats' keys."

"Keez," he said, still baffled. "Denver have keys."

"No," I said. "I need *Tats'* keys."

"Tat-skeez?"

"Yes!" I pointed in the direction Hyde had dragged the now permanently retired leg breaker. "Keys with food." I hated using Zeke-speak, but he usually responded to it more quickly than he did to conventional English.

"Get his wallet, too," I added, flashing my own for good measure.

After a moment or two, Zeke made the connection. At least, I hoped that's what had happened. He took off as quickly as he could move on his six, funky little legs and charged into the woods after Hyde.

I did a bit of scouting to see if anyone else from Shady Grove might have witnessed Tats' demise. Satisfied that no one had, I returned to the shade and unfolded my chair. While waiting for Zeke's return, I searched the area for anything incriminating. I collected my English textbook, the discarded baseball bat, and the envelope full of cash-size newsprint.

Ordinarily, I'm a pretty patient guy, but my motor was idling way too fast for that. Zeke was taking entirely too much time. Tats had, at most, four pockets, and Zeke had demonstrated a good deal of dexterity with his front paws. He could open doors and drawers, and had mastered the device which allowed him to surf the TV networks for soap operas. In short, picking a dead man's pockets should have been quick and easy.

And yet, he didn't show.

I began to imagine what that might mean for me. I absolutely had to do something with Tats' car. I couldn't leave it anywhere near my trailer. That would have amounted to erecting a billboard for Detective Weiner, one with a gigantic arrow pointing at me. But if Zeke didn't return soon with Tats' wallet and keys, I'd have no choice but to go looking for them myself.

An image of what it might be like to crawl through one of Hyde's tunnels flooded my overly anxious brain. Gore and body parts would surely be strewn in my path. Mental images of faces crowded in, too: the Boeheim brothers, Ivo, and now Tats.

None of them looked happy.

Chapter Twenty-two

"When you are in young love, your pulse pounds, your palms sweat, and there are butterflies in your stomach. It's like diarrhea for your heart." –Daniel Tosh

I'd been sitting in my folding chair for what seemed like hours. The only sounds I heard coming from the woods were the natural kind—birds and squirrels. On that note, it occurred to me I'd never heard any sounds coming from Hyde. But then, he might have been quite noisy underground where such would have been muffled.

Even though I felt sure Hyde wasn't any sort of ordinary scorpion, I'd spent some time studying the nasty things. The two species most likely to live in my home state of Georgia were both small; one averaged an inch in length, the other sometimes growing slightly more than twice as long. And while they both were capable of injecting venom, neither of the wretched little bugs represented a deadly threat to healthy humans.

If Hyde really was a scorpion, his size made him the biggest one to ever roam the Earth. There had been a strictly aquatic version of similar size in the prehistoric past, and it claimed the title of "Biggest Bug of All Time," at least until Hyde showed up. In modern times, the pre-Hyde record-holder for size, called the emperor scorpion, measured a paltry eight or nine inches.

My point here is simple: I did not fancy the thought of crawling through Hyde's underground lair in order to retrieve Tats' car keys. My only other option seemed to be to figure out how to hotwire his vehicle. Sadly, when it came to most things mechanical, my skill set was limited to doorknobs and camera hammers.

Unable to sit still any longer, I went to inspect Tats' vehicle and found the driver side door unlocked. I climbed in, tossed his baseball bat into the backseat, and made myself comfy behind the wheel, despite the overwhelming smell of cigarettes. I rolled both front windows down.

Tats, I quickly discovered, could have been the poster boy for Slobs-R-Us. Crumpled napkins, empty paper cups, and other assorted fast-food flotsam littered the floorboard on the passenger side. The backseat looked much the same. A ledger of some kind and a nearly empty bag of garlic knots occupied the bucket seat beside me.

Curious, I flipped open the heavy paper cover of the ledger and took a look. The pages consisted of several columns of information. The first were obvious: names and addresses. Two more contained numbers, presumably dollar amounts. I guessed these represented total amounts owed and the scheduled monthly payment. The final column held what I assumed to be late fees, penalties, and other extra charges. I confirmed that when I found my own name and debt. Evidently, the Cossack wasn't content to charge outrageous interest rates; he made another killing on penalties and fees.

I thumbed through the pages in hopes of finding something that specifically tied the information to the Cossack. An actual name would have been nice, but I found nothing.

Finally, I opened the glovebox and discovered something even more interesting than the debtor list. I found the money Tats had collected that day, a sum several times greater than what I owed.

And no one on Earth knew I had it.

A brand-new element had entered my formerly not very complicated life.

Before I could even begin to understand the depths of this new element, Zeke appeared. He didn't see me at first, so I exited the car, waved my arms, and called out. In short order he made his way to my side, and in his front paws he held Tats' keys and a plain, leather wallet.

"Did you hang around for the banquet?" I asked.

He blinked. It may have been critter code for "Huh?"

"Did you eat?"

"High-duh eat now," he said. "Zeke eat soon."

I relieved him of the keys and wallet, then motioned for him to return to Hyde, where he could do whatever gruesome things they did. I didn't want to think about it. My immediate need was to move Tats' car as far from Shady Grove as necessary. But before I left, I needed to secure the ledger, wallet, and cash from the glovebox. I sealed them all in a plastic freezer bag.

Then I had to find a place to hide it, but everything I thought of I'd already seen discovered in movies or TV. That included the water closet in the bathroom, under the mattress of my bed, beneath the seat on the Vespa, and/or taped to the underside of any piece of furniture, scarce though they were in my factory-built home.

With Zeke nowhere in sight, I wandered back out into the woods behind the trailer park and cruised as straight as I could to the entrance of Hyde's tunnel system which I'd located earlier.

"Hey, Zeke! You in there?" I expected an echo, but didn't get one. After all, it was merely a hole in the ground roughly the diameter of a cast iron sewer lid.

"Zeke? You hear me?"

I took a seat on a heavy root overlooking the tunnel entrance and waited. Other than the usual forest sounds, I heard nothing. That turned out to be good and bad. On one hand, I hoped to hear Zeke responding to my summons. On the other, I dreaded the appearance of Hyde.

Meanwhile, the sun had worked its way lower on the horizon, not that I could see much of it from where I sat. It was getting late, and I had no desire to sit in the woods, in the dark, waiting for the symbiote of a man-eating scorpion to pop up and say hello. Unfortunately, I didn't have much choice. I used some of the time to count the money I'd liberated from Tats' car.

Zeke showed up shortly before shadows put the woods to bed.

"Have a nice nap?" I asked.

Sarcasm worked on Zeke about as well as it did on the average human toddler. It's just no fun if they don't understand. Zeke didn't.

I handed him the plastic-wrapped package. "Can you put this away somewhere? Hide it?"

He stared at the bundle, his little face working up what for him passed as a frown. "Not food," he said.

"Nope. It's not. But can you hide it?"

"High-duh?"

The hopelessness of the situation loomed

large. "This is important," I said. "No one must find it, but me. Can you put it somewhere and bring it back when I ask for it?"

He seemed to understand, though his track record on that score remained far from perfect. "When I ask, you will bring it. Understood?"

Zeke nodded.

I prayed.

With any luck, he would return it all when I asked for it.

~*~

"Jinks? It's Denver. Have you got a minute?"

"Of course," she said.

I imagined her sitting in her bedroom with a pink, Princess phone pressed to her ear, and wished I was whispering into it instead of the grungy handset that came with my trailer. "Remember telling me about how much trouble you had learning how to drive?"

"You mean when Dad insisted that I learn how to drive a stick shift?"

"Yes. You said you already knew how to drive your mother's car, which was an automatic."

"So?" she asked.

"Do you s'pose you could kinda walk me through it?"

"You want me to retell that particular tale of

woe: learning how to drive Dad's Volkswagen?"

"No. I mean... Hang on. Let me back up. I have to drive a car across town, but it's got a clutch and a stick shift, and I don't know how to operate them. I've only ever driven an automatic."

"Then you've got a problem."

"I *know* I have a problem! That's why I'm calling you." I tried not to let my exasperation leak into my voice, but I knew it had. "Please, you've gotta help me. I'm really getting stressed out."

"It'd make way more sense if I just came over there and drove it myself," she said. "I could try to explain it over the phone, but unless you had a phone in the car, I doubt you'd make much progress."

Tats the leg-breaker had outfoxed me; dead guys really shouldn't be able to do that. "I never thought I'd need to know how to drive anything other than an automatic. Now I'm screwed."

"Maybe not. My parents are out for the evening, so I've got a couple hours. If you can come get me, I can drive it. I'll follow you in your car—"

"It's in the shop. I'll have to use the Vespa."

"Whatever. Once we move the car, you can take me home again. There's just one thing...."

I swallowed and tried not to sound whiny. "What one thing?"

"The Homecoming dance is coming up in a week or so. You haven't said anything about it, and...

well… someone else sorta asked me."

"Wait. *What?*" I suddenly felt dizzy. Malindi had made my head spin this way any number of times, but it was a first for Jinks. "What did you… I mean, how did you answer?"

"How do you *think* I answered?"

I tried to read something in her tone but came up empty. "I hope you said you already had plans to go with someone."

"Well, *maybe*, if that someone had actually *asked* me about it. Or, maybe, who knows? *Mentioned it*? In passing?"

Somewhere in her remarks I heard a familiar echo of my mother's tone. I chalked it up, at least for the present, as a girl-thing. "Sweetheart, you know I'm a dingbat, right? It's not a big secret. And when it comes to stuff like this—"

"Damn it, Denver! Are you going to take me to the Homecoming dance, or not?"

"Yes! Absolutely! Please—and I mean please in gigantic letters—*please* let me take you to the dance. I'll even practice new dance steps if you'd like."

"New *steps?*"

"Yeah, like the Watusi, or whatever."

"No one's done that stupid dance in a thousand years!" she said after a brief moment of silence, but I could hear a giggle in her voice somewhere.

"The Freddy?"

"Just stop, okay?"

"The Twist?"

"That one's absolutely prehistoric!"

"The Lindy?"

"The what?" she asked.

"It's a dance, I think."

She sighed. "What am I gonna do with you?"

"Dance?" I asked, hopefully.

"Of course."

"And drive?"

"To the dance?"

"No," I said, "across town. This evening. Okay? I'll hop on the Vespa and be there as quick as I can."

"Have you had dinner?"

Food was the furthest thing from my mind at that point. "Uhm...."

"I thought not," she said. "After we move the car, you're buying me a burger."

"I'd love to."

There was another brief silence before she continued. "Say that again, please."

"I'd love to?"

"That's not exactly what I heard."

She made me smile in more ways than I could count. "What I said was, 'I love you.'"

"Really? You mean it?"

"With all my heart."

~*~

Nobody will ever break any land-speed records on a Vespa, but I pushed mine as much as I dared. Having a wreck on a little scooter like that never works out well for the person driving the scooter. I made it to Jinks' house quickly enough, and she was waiting for me when I arrived.

I took a wee bit more time driving back to Shady Grove and Tats' car. I'd already given Jinks the keys, and she hurriedly got in and leaned forward and down to adjust the seat. Her head popped back up almost immediately.

"Denver? Did you bother to look under the seat?"

Recalling the volume of wastepaper and garbage in the vehicle, I confessed that I had not.

"Look what I just found," she said as she waved a handgun out the window.

Startled, I hopped off the scooter for a closer look.

"What're we going to do with it?" she asked.

I stared at the weapon in her hand. "For starters, we need to wipe your fingerprints off of it."

As soon as the words left my mouth, Jinks let

228

go of the gun. It hit the ground with a thud. She looked at me with a worried expression. "What do we use to wipe it down? Bleach or something?"

"That's what they always use in the movies," I said. "But I don't have any here. I'm lucky to have a bar of soap."

"So, what do we do with it?"

I bent down and picked up the gun, then asked Jinks to hand me a bag, preferably plastic, from the debris strewn throughout Tats' car. She found one and tossed it to me. I wrapped the weapon in the plastic bag and buried it in the loose soil Hyde had recently deposited under my trailer.

"That's it?" Jinks asked. "You're just gonna bury it?"

"For now," I said. "For now."

Chapter Twenty-three

"Punishment is justice for the unjust." –Saint Augustine

I avoided roads going through town and drove the long way around while Jinks followed in Tats' car. We kept to the back roads, hoping to avoid as many people as possible. We had no idea who might recognize his car, either by sight or smell. Jinks kept all the windows open.

Babe's Burgers, a fast-food joint located near Granville's sole exit from the Interstate highway seemed like an appropriate place to leave the car. I figured it was a favorite of Tats based on the volume of their wrappers and bags that littered the floorboard.

We approached Babe's as quietly as possible,

parked the car near the back of the building, and left on the scooter.

Having a conversation while riding double on a Vespa is tricky, if not pointless, so we kept our thoughts to ourselves during the trip to Jinks' house. Once there, we slumped onto the padded glider on her front porch. I felt exhausted.

"You okay?" Jinks asked.

"Not really. I'm... worried."

"That someone will find out about Tats?"

"It worries me that I'm the kind of person who would do what I did! I'm worse than Tats. Worse than the Boeheim brothers, too."

"Worse than Ivo?" She shook her head. "The tree that fell on him should get a public service award."

"Agreed. It's just... The thing that sticks in my head is the image of Tats ripping up the print I had hanging on the wall of my trailer."

"Our prom picture?"

"Yeah. He ripped it in half and kept the part you were in. He said some things that... Well, let's just say they were way outta line and really pissed me off."

She gave me a puzzled look. "He got the photo out of the trailer? I can't believe you let him in."

"I didn't. The door was open when I got there."

"You've gotta keep it locked! What if he'd seen Zeke? What if—"

"I always lock it." And suddenly, I recoiled from a psychic slap. "How *did* he get in?" Things had instantly gotten squirrely. "The door wasn't damaged, so he didn't break in, and I'm positive I locked it when I left. I always do. Geez. It's Shady Grove. I don't trust anyone who lives there."

"Then he must've had a key," Jinks said. "Where could he have gotten it?"

"It had to be Wanda. Just damn." I put my face in my hands.

"Well? So what?"

"It means she knows Tats was there. Somebody, maybe the Cossack himself, will be looking for the money Tats collected. I found it in the glovebox of his car."

"And you *kept* it?"

I couldn't help but roll my eyes. "Well, yeah. It's not like I can give it to anyone else."

"Why not? Maybe a charity or—"

"I'm going to pay off my car loan and get the junkheap fixed. If there's any money left, I'll be happy to give it to charity."

We sat quietly for a while before I added, "They're going to check every name on the list and find out who paid. Eventually they'll get to me."

She stared at me. "What list?"

"The one Tats had in his car, a ledger. It has names, addresses, loan amounts. Everything."

"If you've still got it, how will they—"

"It can't be the only copy. These people may not be accountants, but they're not stupid."

"So? Tell them you paid, too. Let 'em move on to another name."

"And when the person after me says they never saw Tats? How long do you think it'll take them to figure out I'm the last one to see him alive?"

~*~

Of the many things I loved about Jinks, her willingness to talk about virtually any topic ranked high. Issues of importance to us, of course, came first. But secondary topics also got their fair share of discussion, one of which, much to my consternation, focused on where Hyde and Zeke came from.

Jinks' mother worked for the National Science Foundation, and Jinks often quizzed her about topics introduced at school. Over dinner one evening while I was a guest, and shortly after the Tats incident, Jinks carefully brought up the question of finding a new animal species.

I tried not to squirm during the conversation, but Jinks' mom offered some interesting insights into Earth's critters. The one that surprised me the most was her belief that there is a rough balance between species that go extinct and those that are newly discovered. The whole concept of a recently discovered species was new to me.

"You're mostly talking about little creatures, right?" Jinks asked. "Bugs?"

"For the most part," her mother responded, "but there have been discoveries of some big creatures, too. And recently, there's been some debate about what to make of newly discovered cross breeds. There have been sightings of a hybrid bear for instance: the offspring of a polar bear and a grizzly. Is that a new species?" She shrugged. "I don't know. It's not my area of expertise."

"Bears are big, for sure," Jinks said, "but I meant animals nobody's ever seen before."

"Like Komodo dragons? As I recall, they were discovered shortly before the first world war. The thing is, some remote islanders probably knew about them much earlier."

Jinks pressed the point, ignoring my admittedly subtle efforts to get her to hush. "So, you're saying it's possible that really big animals could exist without anyone actually knowing about them?"

"Sure." Jinks' mother chuckled. "I'm a scientist, dear. Very little surprises me anymore. But what brought this on? Have you seen something new and exciting? You're not thinking of some new costume for Halloween, are you?" She frowned. "You're a little old for that, don't you think?"

I coughed. Jinks stuttered. "Like, for trick or treat? Not a chance. I was just curious. Somebody mentioned it in one of my classes, and it... you know... made me wonder."

"Sounds like a great topic for a term paper," I said, hoping to change the subject.

"Yeah. I guess. Maybe," Jinks said as she kicked me under the table. "What's for dessert?"

~*~

The next evening, I again posted myself in the shelter of the woods which stretched between the highway and Shady Grove. I picked a slightly different spot this time, which gave me a better view of anyone who drove up to the trailers I thought might be the scene of drug deals.

There were a few more visitors than the evening I'd spent watching before. They arrived later, however, and night had fallen. Since I didn't own an infrared camera, my shots ranked somewhere between sad and dismal.

Except for one.

I had packed up my stuff and headed through the woods in the dark when I saw a fancy sports car roll up and park beside Wanda's trailer. It looked as out of place as a buffalo at a baptism. I couldn't resist getting a photo and moved into position, hoping to shoot the license tag. The light over the plate wouldn't cooperate and went out before I was ready. I couldn't get a good look at the driver since he bolted from the car, hurried to Wanda's trailer, and let himself in. I couldn't imagine the owner of such a hot car having anything to do with wicked Wanda.

Unless she worked for him! Could this be the Cossack? In the flesh?

Moving as quickly as I dared, I snuck closer and snapped several shots of the car's license plate using different shutter speeds. One of them would surely generate something legible, and that's all I needed.

I could hear raised voices inside Wanda's trailer, but they weren't shouting loud enough for me to make out exactly what they were saying. By the time the door opened and Wanda's visitor left, I had hidden myself once again in the underbrush, safe and sound.

Once the exotic sportster roared out onto the highway and raced out of sight, I headed back to my humble digs to process the roll of black and white film in my camera. I couldn't wait to share a print or two with Regina. That woman had more contacts than an eye doctor. If she couldn't figure out who owned the sports car, no one could.

I never imagined that a photography job could be boring. How naïve of me! My assignments consisted of store openings, award presentations, group shots of civic club officers, and the occasional car wreck. Some of the car wreck shots proved interesting, but the more gruesome ones never made it into the papers. Fall also meant shooting high school football games, and once those were under way, things got a little better. I managed to get some decent action pix, mostly of H3's opponents. Between work, classes, and studies, my free time shrank, so I spent far less of it in my trailer. And I absolutely cherished whatever time I could spend with Jinks.

That left Zeke on his own for longer and longer periods. I tried explaining my absence to him, detailing what I needed to do and why, but he just couldn't get a handle on things like jobs, bills, and education, to say nothing of Homecoming celebrations.

So, I concentrated on the one thing which could impact him directly, and quite possibly physically. I confessed to being in trouble with Granville's version of the Mafia, or whatever the Cossack chose to call his gang. Unfortunately, Zeke's idea of right and wrong or good and bad, were heavily influenced by what he saw on TV. It would have been much easier to get such ideas across if the soap operas back then focused on situations like mine.

They didn't. But, when it came to the topic of bullies, Zeke got the message.

I returned home late after attending the Homecoming dance with Jinks. Though tired, I'd had a wonderful evening. Several of my former classmates actually talked to me, most likely because they were shocked not only to see me with a date, but with a pretty one.

Just out of curiosity, I looked for Malindi and learned she had gotten a job as a dancer at the "gentleman's club" located near Babe's Burgers, a truck stop, and a motel, all conveniently clustered around the exit from the Interstate highway. Little Malindi no longer danced just for fun. Bada-bing!

That thought twirled in my head as I parked my recently repaired vehicle and walked up to the threshold of my home, shabby though it was. The door stood wide open, and the lights were on. I had no idea how long the interior had been exposed to the outside world, but it wasn't anywhere near long enough to disperse the awful stench coming from within.

Rather than go in, I held my nose, peeked through the door, and got a first-hand look at the destruction. My trailer had been thoroughly ransacked. My belongings lay strewn across the floor. Drawers had been dumped, along with their contents and lay scattered on the ratty linoleum. Anger boiled up from within, along with a profound fear that Zeke had been discovered by the Cossack's goons.

Recoiling from the sight, I stumbled through the dark toward the woods behind the trailer. I called out to Zeke but stopped when I reached the underbrush which marked the start of the forest preserve.

"Den-verr," he said from somewhere in the woods.

"Are you all right?"

"Bull-eeze come," he said from a distance.

I finally caught a glimpse of him as he waddled

toward me. Dropping down to his level, I gathered him up in my arms and gave him a gentle hug, despite knowing he wasn't a huge fan of snuggling. In the process I caught a whiff of the same pungent aroma that nearly overwhelmed me when I first arrived.

"What is that godawful smell?"

"Zeke smell."

"How could you *not* smell it?"

It may have been the first time I'd left him wishing he could smack me. "No. Smell from Zeke. Zeke make."

"But, why? To chase the bullies away? Lord knows, I'd back away if someone threatened to squirt something that stinky on me."

"Bull-lee hold Zeke. Hurt Zeke."

"So, you sprayed him? Like a skunk?"

That earned me a puzzled look.

"No. Zeke smell make bull-eeze sleep."

Chapter Twenty-four

"If you prick us, do we not bleed? If you tickle us do, we not laugh? If you poison us, do we not die? And if you wrong us, shall we not revenge?" –Will Shakespeare
"The Merchant of Venice"

It was too late to call Jinks, and she'd told me at the dance that her mother wanted her to do something at church the following day, so I knew I wouldn't be able to talk to her for a long while. Still, I was dying to tell her what I'd learned—or thought I'd learned—from my conversation with Zeke.

I found a window fan which hadn't been destroyed amidst the wreckage of my trailer. I turned it on and aimed it at the door, hoping to persuade the pervasive stench to leave. I got the windows open, too, but ultimately, the aroma proved more than I could handle. As a result, I knew I'd be spending the night in my car.

Zeke went back into the woods, presumably to cuddle with Hyde. That mental image kept me awake until he returned. He'd obviously learned something from our earlier encounter with Tats, since he brought me two wallets and a set of car keys. The names in the wallets meant nothing to me, but at least I now knew who ransacked my home. I suppose I could have waited until the following morning to make my next request, but I figured the evening had already reached the disaster stage, so a little more delay wouldn't matter.

I had him accompany me to the spot under the trailer where I'd hidden the gun I found in Tats' car. Digging it up required little effort since I'd only buried it a couple of inches deep.

"Did either of the bullies have something like this?" I asked, holding up the handgun.

Rather than answer, Zeke spun around as only something on six legs can, and took off again for the woods. He returned a few minutes later with two more guns, neither of which looked like the sort seen in Hollywood westerns. These were automatics, just like Tats'.

I thanked Zeke for his efforts and told him to rejoin Hyde, since the trailer remained uninhabitable. Even though he'd brought that particular stink into the world, I doubted he liked it any better than I did.

By the following morning, most of the smell

had dissipated, and I began the task of cleaning up. I hadn't gotten very far when Wanda knocked twice then entered without bothering to wait for an invitation.

"It stinks in here," she said, scanning the destruction. "Quite a mess."

"Not really," I responded, "I'm just a lousy housekeeper."

"You ain't funny, ya know."

"I get that a lot," I said as I reached down for another handful of debris and shoved it in a wastebasket. "I don't suppose you know who did this."

"How would I know that?" Her voice dripped innocence.

"When it concerned Shady Grove, I thought you knew everything. And now I'm faced with a decision. Do I call the cops to report this, or will you take care of it?"

She fired up a cigarette, took a deep drag, and exhaled in my direction. "I wouldn't do either. The cops won't do anything 'cept shake their heads and tell you to call your insurance agent. And as for me, there's nothin' I can do. Loan you a broom, maybe. Or some extra garbage bags."

After waving the cigarette smoke from my face, I said, "I guess the only thing that matters is making the Cossack happy."

"What d'you mean?"

"Oh, like you don't work for the Cossack?"

She shook her head. "I have no idea who the hell yer talkin' about."

Rather than argue with her, I told her to make herself at home while I straightened up. She poked around in the wreckage for a while, then left without a word. I felt sure she was looking for some clue as to what happened to the people responsible for the break-in. But, while tempted to explain why they no longer worried me, I kept that bit of information to myself. I did, however, look forward to sharing it with Jinks.

~*~

My only scheduled photo shoot the following day commenced in the early afternoon: a touch football game featuring teams from the police department and the DFCS, otherwise known as the child welfare office. It seemed like a horrendous mismatch, until I learned husbands and wives were eligible to play, and the teams had agreed to field an equal number of players of either sex.

It turned out to be much more interesting than I'd expected. Best of all, Jinks joined me on the sidelines and even arranged some player poses for the benefit of my lens.

I secretly hoped Detective Weiner would be on the cops' roster, since there were a couple of beefy players on the defensive line for the welfare workers. Having one of them flatten his righteous ass would have made my day. Sadly, he didn't show.

"He's probably investigating the break-in at your trailer," Jinks said. The players had all trotted off the field for halftime, and I was eager to tell her what I'd learned from Zeke. It was the first opportunity we'd had to chat out of earshot from contestants and spectators.

"If Weiner really did go there to investigate, he's probably not looking for the jerks who wrecked the place." When she didn't respond, I continued. "I'm guessing they were hunting for Tats' ledger. I 'spect he'd be looking for it, too."

"Where is it?" she asked.

"Zeke hid it for me. It's somewhere in Hyde's burrow."

Jinks chuckled. "Wouldn't you love to see those hoods crawl in there to look for it?"

"Only if they never came out." I couldn't help but smile.

"Okay, why're you so happy?" Her eyebrows dipped down in puzzlement. "I'd have thought you'd be angry."

"Bear with me," I said, "you're gonna love this." I cleared my throat and gave her my best interpretation of the conversation I'd had with Zeke.

"So, Zeke was in the trailer when the thugs showed up?"

"He hid under the bed, and apparently it was the last place they searched. Poor Zeke had no idea what they were up to, but I believe he thought they were after him. One of the two grabbed him and dragged him out. Zeke retaliated in the only way he knew how."

"Which was?"

"To unleash the most vile-smelling gas you can imagine."

"Like... you know... a fart?" She made a face. "I've smelled his. They're awful."

"Trust me, this smelled much worse. But here's the thing, it wasn't just a bad smell, though it would put any self-respecting skunk to shame. No; this stuff also acted like knock-out gas."

She blinked in surprise. "Okay. And then what?"

"They both went down. Zeke called Hyde, and he hauled them outside. I have no idea if the stench bothered him, but I doubt it."

"Did Hyde sting them?" she asked.

"Zeke didn't say. It would probably have been better for them if he had. Can you imagine waking up, underground, with a gigantic—"

Jinks gently touched my lips with the tip of her index finger. "No. I do not want to imagine it, or hear about it." She remained quiet for just a moment too long, then added, "That's it, then. They must've been looking for the ledger."

"That's my guess."

"What are you going to do?"

I'd given the problem a good bit of thought, between worrying about everything else that seemed to have gone wrong in my life. Except Jinks, of course. "I think I'm going to turn it over to the cops."

"*To Detective Weiner?* I thought you didn't trust him."

"I don't, and I certainly don't want to admit to anyone that I have it. That would tie me to Tats' disappearance, and I've already done that dance with Weiner too many times."

"So," she asked, "how will you do it?"

"I'll mail it. I'm going to write a note as if it came from Tats. I've got his wallet and ID, so I know what his real name is. I'll say something like, 'I'm tired of beating people up for a living. Here's a list of victims my boss has sent me to harass. As for me, I'm going where no one will ever find me, including the Cossack.'"

"You think that'll work?"

I shrugged. "Let's hope so. Maybe it'll give the cops something to work with. I sure don't need it."

"You know who might?" she asked, then answered her own question. "Regina Hornsby."

"You're right! I'll make a copy for her before I mail it to the police."

"Good thinking." She smiled at me in a way that made me more than just proud.

"We make a pretty good team, you and I."

Just as the players were coming off the benches and back out onto the playing field, Jinks had a sudden thought. "What did you do with the car—the one those guys who trashed your trailer drove? And please, don't tell me you aren't able to drive it."

"I did drive it, just not very far. There's an old logging road fairly close to the trailer park that goes into the nature preserve. I parked it there, out of sight from the road, and walked back. It didn't take long."

She uttered tsks as she shook her head. "I don't think you should leave it there. It's too close to Shady Grove."

"I know, but it'll be okay there for a while, long enough for me to figure out what to do with it." I tried to reassure her with a smile. "I've got an idea or two."

She shook her head once more, still tsking.

The following Monday morning came early. I hadn't slept well, most likely due to worrying about the Cossack's next move, to say nothing of the three handguns under my pillow. They're lumpy, by the way, impossible to sleep on. So, I probably didn't fall asleep until much later than usual.

Despite that, I couldn't wait to get to the office. I not only needed to photocopy the ledger, I wanted to see if Regina had found out who owned the spiffy sportscar I'd seen next to Wanda's trailer. Regina was sitting at her desk, coffee in hand, a look of satisfaction plastered on her face.

"You're not going to believe what I found out," she said. "The car tag photo you sent me turned up some very interesting data."

"Like what?" I tried not to squirm, but I'm sure I looked like I needed to pee.

"That tag identifies a one-year-old Lamborghini Countach."

"A what?"

"A Lamborghini. It's Italian, obviously. And in case you wanted to get one for yourself, they sell for around the same price as a new, three-bedroom, two-bath home." She paused, then added, "In a really nice neighborhood."

I whistled. "I guess crime does pay after all. So, who owns it?"

"That's the odd part," she said. "The owner's name, according to the DMV, is Stanislav Doobin. I did a little digging and discovered Mr. Doobin changed his last name several years ago. It used to be Dubinski."

"*Doobin?* Are you sure?"

"Yes. Do you know him?"

"The only Doobin I know is Jinks' high school cross-country coach," I said. "And he drives a goofy little Fiat. If he had something fancy, I'm sure he'd show it off, especially since he has something going on with a teacher there who is... well, let's just say she's way out of his league. Anyway, that was months ago. I haven't seen him since, but Jinks has."

Regina eased back in her chair, apparently mulling over what I'd said. Finally, she scribbled something on a scrap of paper and handed it to me. "Here's the address listed with it, and it's out in the countryside somewhere. If you have some time, you might want to see if you can find it."

I slipped the note in my pocket and leaned back against the edge of her desk. "There's a little something else," I said as I pulled the photocopied pages of the Cossack's ledger from my back pocket. "We're both journalists, right?"

She nodded. "Well... Yes, sure. You're a photojournalist."

"So, you know the code of ethics about not revealing sources."

"Of course."

"Then you'll understand why I can't tell you where I got this." I waved the folded pages in front of me.

"What's that?" she asked.

It was my turn to smile as I told her what I had. She looked utterly shocked.

"But... But how... Where did you—"

I raised my hand, palm toward her. "We already discussed that part, remember? I don't have to reveal my sources, to you or anyone else."

I extended the pages toward her, and she reached for them with a trembling hand.

"I assume these might help you," I said.

After quickly glancing through the data, she looked back at me. "I'm pretty sure all these addresses are in Granville or neighboring counties."

"The Cossack's home turf."

"And you have the original copy?"

I shook my head and stretched the truth just a little bit. "Actually no. The cops have it. Or, they will soon. It's in the mail."

"Does anyone else know who had the original?"

"No. And it's best we keep it that way."

"No kidding. If the Cossack were to find out...."

"If the cops follow up on it, we won't have to worry about that."

She cast a worried glance in my direction. "And if they don't?"

Chapter Twenty-five

"It's not what happens to you, but how you react to it that matters." –Epictetus

Finally allowed to return to work, AARPA Field Agent Jonathon Fitzgerald's first stop was the headquarters of the Granville Police Department for an interview with their sole detective.

Jon tried to keep his expression neutral and his opinion about Detective Wiener's professional abilities to himself. The man's desk revealed a worker with no interest in organization, let alone sanitation. The contents of several files littered the surface of the gunmetal gray workstation, suggesting too many cases going unsolved. A file cabinet played host to paper cups and empty bags from a variety of fast-food joints. Jon recognized one from Babe's Burgers, the place where he'd first met Malindi.

"You're welcome, by the way," Weiner said.

"For what?"

"I located your car, your wallet, and your badge. Oh, yeah, and your suitcase."

"And my gun?"

"Geez." Weiner shook his head in disgust. "You people are never satisfied."

"Sorry," Jon said. "I didn't mean to sound ungrateful."

"Whatever."

"By the way, where was my car located?"

"We found it at your hotel. Parked in the back with all your stuff in it." The detective shrugged. "Weird, huh?"

"My parents said it was stolen."

"The hotel manager claims it just showed up one day while you were laid up."

"Just showed up? Like, maybe, it drove itself there?"

Weiner merely shrugged again.

Jon felt sure the man knew more than he admitted. A change of tactics seemed in order. "How come you never bothered to mention a guy by the name of Denver Stow when we talked before?"

Wiener's expression bespoke disdain. "It

didn't strike me as particularly relevant."

"You've had your eye on someone you think is responsible, or at least involved, in the disappearance of two people. But when I approach you for information on three more missing persons, you don't see any connection? Seriously?"

"You Feds..." Wiener paused, cleared his throat, and started over. "You've got a lotta nerve second guessing me. I'm on the scene. I know what's going on in this town and in this county. You cruise in here, spend a half hour lookin' around, and then assume you've got things all figured out. Well, lemme tell ya, you ain't got shit. If you'd told me everything you knew about your missing people, I might've been able to help. But no, you gave me next to nothing and then expected me to make connections."

He turned his head to the side and snorted.

Jon refused to let Weiner get under his skin. He'd been warned when in training that locals often resent the presence of federal agents. Treading softly, according to his instructors, was the best way to proceed.

"When it comes to national security issues, we're limited in the amount of information we can share," Jon said. "It's not a matter of disrespect."

"Yeah, sure."

"Tell me about this suspect of yours," Jon said. "I understand he's just a kid."

"In my opinion, a little asshole is what he is.

The thing is, I haven't got any solid evidence that ties him to the two missing guys, the Boeheim brothers."

Jon collected the particulars on the two who went missing and got the contact information for Denver Stow as well. He figured it likely wouldn't amount to anything, but since he had few leads to follow, a chat with the young man couldn't hurt.

"One last thing," Jon said as he prepared to leave. "Do you know anything about a woman named Dawn Popkin?"

Wiener made a face then exhaled as if disgusted. "Yeah, I know her. She's a real highbrow; thinks she's smarter than everyone else. Nadine, my ex-wife, used to play bridge with her 'til she lit out when her husband died and headed west. Oregon maybe, or Utah. I dunno; they're all the same to me. Nadine said Dawn decided to move there, but she had to come back here to pack up and sell her house."

"So, she's in town now?"

"Far as I know, yeah."

The return trip to Dawn Popkin's home went much faster the second time; Jon knew what to look for, if not exactly what to expect.

An older woman, slim and stern-faced, answered when he knocked on the door. "Yes?"

"Miss Popkin?" Jon flashed his badge. "I'm from the Advanced Alternative Re—"

"AARPA," she said as she lowered her brows and examined his credentials. "Haven't you people done enough already?"

"I'm merely trying to find out what happened to the team we sent to close out the—"

"You mean the brutes who wrecked our lab, grabbed our research, and killed our lab animals? The ones who destroyed three decades of work? Who caused my husband to have a coronary? *That team?*"

"Your husband also had a heart attack?" Jon blinked. "I had no idea."

"What do you mean, 'also?' He was the only one."

Jon couldn't hide his confusion. "Well, I... Uhm... Did Mr. Popkin—"

"Mr. Popkin was my late father. My *husband* was Dr. William Bledsoe. I chose not to adopt his last name; I already had a perfectly good one."

"I apologize. I didn't know—"

"Of course, you didn't know. That would've required that you study our project before you came 'round with your questions and demands. Just like that trio of cut-throats your Ms. Burnside sent. They barged into our facility without so much as a howdy do and dismantled our entire operation—the lab, the offices, the animal housing—everything! They forced us to leave. Gave us a few minutes to gather our personal belongings. Thirty-plus years' worth of personal belongings!"

"Ms. Pop—"

"It's *Doctor* Popkin. I have a PhD. Two of them, actually."

"Of course. Again, I apologize. It's just—"

"What the hell do you want? Or is your intent to waste as much of my precious time as you can?"

Jon shook his head. "I don't want to waste anyone's time—yours or mine. Nor have I meant any offense. I lack knowledge of your project because I wasn't given access to any records, reports, or operational details. That's all been restricted."

"By this Burnside person?"

"Yes."

"What gives her the right or the power to terminate any program, let alone ours? A program which, I might add, has made astonishing advances in a number of scientific arenas."

"Burnside's position gives her leverage, but just between you and me, that's derived from politics not skill or intellect."

Popkin squinted at him again, as if she could read his heart by examining his face. "You don't like her, do you?"

He shook his head, no. "She wants me to fail. It'll give her a reason to fire me."

The scientist mulled over his words for a bit before her lips stretched into a thin smile, and she spoke. "How can I help you disappoint this woman?"

Jon felt like cheering. "I'd dearly like to know about your research. I'm hoping it may provide me with some leads into the disappearance of our staff."

Popkin's smile dissolved. "Hmpf. Can't say I'm too upset to hear about those hooligans going missing."

"They were contract employees, not regular federal workers," Jon said. "I'm sorry they treated you so badly. I can't imagine how or why that happened. It's disgraceful, and I'll be sure to make that clear in my report."

Popkin nodded. "Thank you."

"So, would it be possible for you to give me a little run-down on Live Canary?"

"Isn't that the silliest name?" She shook her head. "It's based on an old coal mining practice. The workers would take a canary into the mine shafts with them. If there were any dangerous gasses in the air, the bird would die and serve as a warning for the miners to get back to the surface."

"So, your work involved birds? Canaries?"

"Oh, heavens no," she said. "Our mission was to create a way to clear tunnels without risking the lives of our troops. It started back during the Korean conflict, but didn't really get ramped up until Vietnam. The Viet Cong were notorious for digging tunnels for all sorts of things, not the least of which included the means to sneak up on our people."

"I've heard about the Vietnam tunnel rats," Jon

said. "Our guys crawled into the holes the Viet Cong dug and either rooted them out or destroyed them and anything they stockpiled. Must've been scary as hell."

"I'm sure it was. But the need to clear tunnels didn't end when we pulled out of southeast Asia. Now it's the drug cartels and human traffickers who create underground routes to avoid Customs and the Border Patrol."

"Okay, so you did what, train dogs?"

Popkin laughed. "That would've been far too easy. My husband's sponsor wanted something no one else on Earth could create. And he knew my Billy was the only one who might be able to do it."

"Do what, exactly?" Jon asked.

"Why don't you come inside?" She stepped back from the door which she held open. "I've got iced tea and a shady porch where we can drink it. I like mine with a splash of rum."

"That sounds wonderful."

Jon followed her through the house which was littered with partially filled moving boxes and out to a deck overlooking the woods beyond. She poured him a glass of iced tea and added two fingers of dark rum.

Once they were comfortably settled in side-by-side deck chairs, Popkin continued. "The trick, you see, was to come up with an animal considerably smarter than a dog, but one which appeared so innocent, so utterly harmless, that it could examine a tunnel without causing alarm. If something was going on that needed to be stopped, the animal could initiate stronger measures."

"You mean, like call in reinforcements?"

"Something like that, yes." She took a sip of her tea before she went on. "Let's assume a battlefield scenario, all right? Imagine the enemy has dug a tunnel under our fortifications, and our furry little friend finds it. How do we dispose of the enemy without suffering any casualties or damage?"

Jon shrugged. "I don't know. Gas?"

"My husband found a more interesting solution."

"Which was...."

"He created a second animal, an insect actually, and a truly nasty one. Billy's great ambition was to genetically engineer creatures capable of high-level interaction with humans. He succeeded beyond his wildest dreams with his first creation. With the second, he succeeded beyond his worst nightmare. And yet, the two creatures are interdependent, like darkness and light; one is useless without the other. They need each other to survive."

He wasn't sure if it was the rum or the conversation which had begun to make his head swim. "He *created* an insect? I know many people get freaked out by bugs, but seriously, how frightening can one bug be?"

Popkin laughed. "You'd have to see one to truly understand. Our bio-creations evolved over three decades, and that allowed us to generate mutations developed over many generations. There were countless genetic adaptations among our experimental animals, the vast majority of which didn't survive. Of those which did, only one proved to have the intellectual capacity we sought. And only one other had an appropriately scary form."

"Appropriately *scary?* I don't get it. What's the point of making something scary?"

"Imagine you're the one who just dug a tunnel. You crawl into it, ready to mount an attack when you're confronted by a scorpion that weighs nearly as much as you. It has massive pincers and a wickedly barbed stinger at the end of its tail. Oh, and it's racing straight toward you."

Incredulous, Jon sputtered, "A one-hundred and seventy-five-pound *scorpion?*"

She smiled. "That would get your attention, wouldn't it?"

"I should think so!"

"And would it change your thinking about the advisability of tunneling as a means of attack or of avoiding federal officials?"

"But they could be shot and killed, couldn't they?"

"Of course. Although firing a weapon would likely give away the location of the tunnel. Besides that, these things lay a prodigious number of eggs. Very large, beautiful eggs, actually. They look quite a bit like moonstones."

"You actually developed these things? Giant scorpions?"

"Technically, they aren't scorpions, although they share much of the genetic structure. The biggest difference, other than their size, is the fact they lay eggs. Normally, scorpions give live births, and the females care for the young and carry them around on their backs. That's not the case with ours. In fact, one of the primary tasks of his pleasant little partner is egg collection. We can't just leave them lying around. Even a newly hatched Hie-Duff is deadly."

"High Duff?"

Popkin waved her hand in the air. "We had to give them a name that was less cumbersome than the laboratory designation. We referred to our scorpion-like creatures as Hie-Duffs in a salute to the two geneticists who provided early strains of their DNA. The friendlier ones, which Billy evolved from Australian quokkas, we simply called seekers."

"Quokkas?" Jon shook his head. "Never heard of 'em."

"They're delightful little fellows. We managed to maintain that characteristic in ours, though we added a genetic wrinkle or two, and they're significantly larger. They're quite charming. Well, unless you try to harm them, in which case they have a highly effective means of defense. Think skunk, only much, much more powerful."

"I'm sure they are," Jon said, trying to square her bizarre claims with his own version of reality. They didn't seem to occupy the same universe.

"Y'know? I think I need another drink."

Chapter Twenty-six

*"I'm from Indiana. I know what you're thinking,
Indiana... Mafia. But in Indiana it's not like New York
where everyone's like, 'We're from New York and we're
the best' or 'We're from Texas and we like things big' it's
more like 'We're from Indiana and we're gonna move.'."*
–Jim Gaffigan

Since my schedule was based largely on when
other people wanted the *Gazetteer* to cover publicity
stuff, I had little to do with where and when I needed
to make myself available. Fortunately, Monday
afternoons tended to be slow, so I took advantage of
the free time to track down the address Regina gave
me.

What she described as "countryside" could
more accurately be described as "gentile, rural

ranchland." The homes were all situated on sizeable chunks of acreage, and most of them had beautifully fenced pastures surrounding hilltop homes. The house styles ranged from feudal manor to Old South mansion. Every one of them shouted, "Money!"

I located the address Regina gave me and parked to gander at the property spread out in front of me. There was no way anyone lived there on a high school coach's salary. Coach Doobin might occupy a guest house or a nifty little room in a stable, but in the manse proper? No freaking way.

I drove up to the gated entrance and got out for a closer look. A pair of well-fed rottweilers immediately appeared, neither of which seemed interested in compromising the estate's security. I backed away slowly, smiling, and offering my most sincere apologies for interrupting them. They didn't seem to care. Vicious guard dogs tend to be like that.

A cautious walk outside the homestead's pristine fence provided a reasonable view of the place. Sitting atop a hill, it sported a three-car garage, antebellum columns flanking a double-door entry, and a clear view of a lake in the middle of the front acreage. A pair of swans drifted lazily atop the water.

I didn't see anything that looked like a sports car. After briefly entertaining thoughts of how I might break into the garage, I decided instead to head over to the high school and simply follow Coach Doobin home. That, I felt sure, would solve the mystery.

But first, I had to visit Wanda Vickers and pay the rent on my trailer. Doing so every week proved to be a major pain. Making payments to a variety of mouth-breathing thugs for my crappy car was worse.

Wanda responded to my knock with characteristic disdain. Rather than say anything after opening the door, she merely held out her hand.

"I need your help," I said.

She eyed me suspiciously, said, "Yeah?" and took a drag on her ever-present cigarette.

"Right. I need to pay off my car, and I'd prefer to avoid the guys who've been coming around recently to collect my payments."

"I don't know nuthin' about your car or your car payments." The lie actually caused her to smile, sort of.

"We both know you're just as connected as Ivo was. Why can't you help me out?"

"Don't be stupid. Just pay 'em what they say you owe, and they'll leave. Don't make waves. Now gimme your rent money and go the hell away."

"Fine." I handed over the cash. "Y'know, there could be a lot of blow-back on you and Shady Grove if...."

"If what?" She stared at me so hard, I could almost feel it.

"Never mind," I said and left. Waving a red flag in front of one of the Cossacks' bulls didn't make any sense. But I couldn't shake the feeling I needed to push back a bit. All I had to do was figure out how.

~*~

I knew Jinks had cross-country practice right after school, so Coach Doobin would likely be on campus, if not out running with the team. Ordinarily, I'd give Jinks a ride home and give her a break from her carpool, but this time I had a different mission in mind.

Many of the juniors and seniors at H3 drove to school, but by the time I arrived most of their cars were gone. The football and cross-country teams were practicing, but that still left quite a few spots open in the parking lot. I found an empty one in the shade that gave me a good view of Coach Doobin's pathetic little Fiat.

I only waited a few minutes before student athletes streamed out of the sports building and headed home. Doobin would likely be one of the last to leave; someone had to lock up.

Eventually he strolled out to his car, got in, and drove off. I followed at a discreet distance and tried not to be too obvious. As usual, my efforts were based on TV cop shows and spy movies. I'm no James Bond, but Doobin didn't seem to notice as I followed him through town and out into the county's most expensive neighborhood.

Not surprisingly, he pulled up to the gated entrance of the estate I'd viewed previously. The two dogs that gave me an unwelcome greeting seemed to know the cross-country coach well. They wagged their abbreviated tails at his approach and appeared joyful, the exact opposite of how I felt.

As the gates closed behind him, Doobin motored up the hill toward the three-car garage. One of the doors opened at his approach and appeared to swallow him and the dogs before closing.

I leaped to the assumption that either Doobin was the Cossack, or he was directly related to him. Nobody gets to choose their parents. Mine were far from perfect, though I doubt they were aware of it. Mom even sent me a card on my birthday along with a check for twenty dollars and a reminder to send her a copy of my report card. She claimed that as a parental right since she paid my college tuition. I doubt my father even knew where I was.

They may not have been the best parents, but as far as I knew, neither of them made a living as a criminal. But, then again, who knows?

Doobin apparently lived in what I assumed was the Cossack's house. How could he not be aware of the dirty dealings going on? How could he pretend to be a caring person, a coach, and a mentor to young people?

On the other hand, maybe I was being too hard on him. It's not like you can fold the hand you're dealt in genetic poker and hope the next deal will work out better. I would definitely have to share the news about Doobin with Jinks and Regina.

~*~

Jinks' 18th birthday was only a few days away—a week or so before Halloween, and I had yet to find the perfect gift for her. During the arduous process of finding that one indefinable thing that would have the most impact and prove my undying love, I discovered a new word: perseveration. According to **Webster's** it meant the "continuation of something (such as an activity or thought) usually to an extreme degree or beyond a desired point."

In short, I was perseverating over my failure to find the perfect thing, whatever the hell it turned out to be.

I suppose that was a marginally better item to perseverate over than what I would do the next time one of the Cossack's goons hit me up for a car payment. Not having to worry about that would give me a great deal more time to worry about the birthday gift I couldn't find. I might as well have been searching for lost Aztec gold.

All this to say I was not in a good mood when someone pounded on my trailer door.

I growled a distinctly unhappy, "What?" as I yanked the door open.

"You Denver?"

The question came from somewhere within the confines of a hooded... hood. Dark glasses only added to the spectral appearance. I didn't care, so I demanded, "Who wants to know?"

By the time I finished asking my question, the thug in my doorway had produced a gun. My focus instantly shifted from my visitor to the muzzle of his weapon. My eyes locked on the huge, dark, circular opening which sat a few inches from my face.

"If you aren't him, tell me where he is."

"I'm him," I said, a little surprised to notice I had both of my arms raised high above my head. I had no idea this sort of thing was an involuntary reaction, like heartbeats and, I dunno, burps.

"Back up," he said.

I did.

"Car payment. Now," he said.

"Uhm, about that—"

He pressed the muzzle of the gun into my forehead. "What about it?"

I managed a shaky, "I want to pay the loan off. Completely." I still had most of the money I'd found in Tats' car, and this seemed like a great time to use some of it.

"Oh, yeah?"

"Absolutely! All you have to do is tell me the amount, and I'll pay you. In cash. Right now."

"That's a problem," he said.

"Why?"

"'Cause some asshole stole our ledger. So, I don't know exactly how much you owe."

"I can make an educated guess," I said. "I only agreed to six months of payments, and I've only got one more after this."

"And why the hell should I believe that?"

He had me there. "You only keep one set of records?"

"I don't keep track of shit," he said. "I collect. People pay. Or else."

"So, you don't really know how much I'm supposed to pay?" I intended it to be a statement, but my sphincter had already tightened into a pinhole, and my voice rose an octave despite my best efforts to prevent it.

"You bein' a smart ass?"

"What. Who, me? No. I... Listen, I'll be happy to pay what I owe." *He seriously didn't have a clue?* I couldn't let the moment pass and did a quick, self-serving recalculation of my debt. "I've been paying a hundred bucks a month. I've got one more month to go after today. So, that'd be... uhm—"

"Fine. Gimme the money."

"All of it? I mean, both months? That's like—"

He waved the gun in my face, again. "Just today's money. And I want it now. No more bullshit."

"You're gonna tell your boss you could have collected twice the normal amount and close the account? Nobody ever has to come back here?"

He appeared to be wavering. If he took me up on the offer, I'd save eight months of two-hundred-dollar payments. But he wouldn't know that, *couldn't* know that, unless the ledger showed up again. That didn't seem too likely. "Wait right there," I said. "I'll get you the rest of what I owe."

He started to protest.

"There's no need to thank me."

I hurried into my bedroom, hoping Zeke wouldn't make an unscheduled appearance. Fortunately, I'd prepared for this moment. I had two wads of cash available. The first would have covered what I actually owed. The second consisted of considerably more.

After grabbing the smaller stash, I removed a few twenties, smiled, and gave him the rest. "Here!"

He accepted it, though reluctantly.

"Are we good?"

He shook his head as if unsure. "We'd better be, or I swear, I'll come back here and shoot yer ass."

~*~

In a calmer moment, and without a gun pointed at my head, I had an epiphany—a blinding realization of what would be the perfect gift for Jinks: an engagement ring. What a grand solution! Just thinking about it made me feel much better, even confident.

I hopped into my dusty, red, '69 Ford Falcon and headed for downtown Granville in search of a jewelry store. The car was a bit over half my age, but handled like an octogenarian with a walker. But despite being old and cranky, much like a couple octogenarians I'd photographed, the little sedan got me where I needed to go.

Since I had already announced to Jinks that I wanted to take her to dinner at the Cascades the following week to celebrate her birthday, I had very little time to find the right ring. It boiled down to two requirements: it had to be pretty, and it had to be affordable.

A small, family-owned jewelry store in town had just the thing, a dainty but stunning, pear-shaped diamond mounted in a white gold setting. And, they offered to let me pay for it in installments. Having just extricated myself from one such plan, I wasn't eager to enter into another. But, they assured me they did their own financing, and they'd send me a tax form at the end of the year which would spell out how much interest I paid.

"That's not something crooks usually do," they told me. When I casually mentioned the Cossack, they claimed never to have heard of him.

Using the money I'd saved on my car payment, I made a down payment and walked away with the ring in a lovely little presentation box.

I couldn't wait to pop the question.

Chapter Twenty-seven

"No trait is more justified than revenge in the right time and place." –Meir Kahane

The Cascades restaurant, so named for its floor-to-ceiling murals of rambling mountain streams, hadn't changed since we dined there on prom night. Nor did it appear there had been any staff changes. The austere woman who showed us to our table clearly didn't remember us, and we didn't have my mother's efforts to pave the way.

Instead, the hostess seated us at a small table near the entrance, the least romantic spot possible. I apologized to Jinks for it, but she dismissed it as nothing. "I'm much happier with a small table," she said, reaching for my hands. "It means we're closer together."

Is it any wonder I fell in love with her?

We dined on food I didn't really taste; my focus was on Jinks, not the over-priced menu items. Nevertheless, we had multiple courses, and I wished her a happy birthday every time something else landed on the table. By the time we'd consumed everything but dessert, my heart was racing. Nervous tension caused my hands to tremble, and I had to make a conscious effort to keep my heels from bouncing off the floor.

Our waitress finally delivered the after-dinner treat I'd ordered ahead of time, a molten lava birthday cake. It arrived on a crystal plate surrounded by fresh berries all overseen by a stark white candle protruding from an artful glob of frosting.

Jinks' eyes grew wide, and she giggled as the waitress made the elaborate presentation which ended with the candle lighting. Once ignited, the taper cast a tiny burst of sparks. The liquid chocolate center of the cake provided the "lava" when we cut into it.

All but entranced by the dessert and Jinks' joyful reaction to it, I almost missed seeing a man wearing a hoodie enter the restaurant. Had we been seated farther from the door, I would not have seen him at all. I recognized him immediately as the goon with the gun who had come to my trailer to demand a car payment.

I know he saw me; his eyes narrowed briefly before he offered up a sinister grin and then left.

Much as I wanted to continue enjoying the dessert and my planned proposal, I couldn't rid my mind of the notion that the Cossack was shaking down a classy place like the Cascades. And if that was the case, why use the same small-time hood he used to collect money from me? It didn't make sense.

I tried to smile and remain chipper as we consumed the cake. A bit of drippy chocolate landed on my chin which Jinks deftly swept up with a pinkie finger. Then, giving me an anything-but-innocent look, she licked the digit clean.

That broke the spell. Pushing my chair back from the table, I reached into my pocket for the boxed ring. My hand may have trembled before, but now the action could be measured on the Richter scale. I hadn't been this nervous when a gun was pointed at me.

As I cleared my throat and prepared to move to her side of the table where I intended to kneel and ask the question, the hostess cruised into the dining area.

"Your attention, please, everyone. I apologize for this interruption, but we have a serious problem in the parking area." She looked down at a scrap of paper in her hand. "Will the owner of a red, Ford Falcon, license number BTT599, please come outside?"

I didn't recognize the license number, but I doubted any of the other Cascades patrons drove a crappy little car like mine.

When I stood up, so did Jinks. "Is it yours?" she asked.

"I think so."

"I'm coming with you."

"No, please. I'd rather you stay here, okay? Let me see what's going on." I hadn't mentioned the hoodlum I saw earlier, and I didn't want to take a chance on letting her go anywhere near him, assuming he had anything to do with whatever was going on outside.

She reluctantly agreed, and I sailed out the front entrance.

The cause for alarm became immediately apparent. My car was on fire.

I stumbled toward it only to be halted by a uniformed police officer who told me the fire department had been called, and he wasn't letting anyone go near the burning vehicle.

"But it's mine!" I exclaimed.

To his credit, he remained calm. "What're you gonna do, blow it out?" He shook his head and patted my chest with both hands. "Somebody smashed a window and poured gasoline in there. That's the only way a car would burn like that."

Though shaken, I took the time to survey the area to see if the hooded thug had stuck around. I told the cop, "I know who did this."

"Yeah? You saw it? What's his name?"

"There's a guy who's been after me to collect on a debt," I said. "He threatened me with a gun."

The cop appeared sympathetic and pulled out a small notepad and a pen, ready to take down any pertinent information. I didn't have much.

"He works for a guy who calls himself the Cossack," I said. "But I don't know his name."

"The Cossack's real name or the guy who threatened you?"

I knew I couldn't prove the Cossack's last name was Doobin, and I didn't want to associate myself with him any further, so I lied. "I, uhm, can't be sure of either one."

The cop put his pen and pad away. "Lemme know if you find out," he said.

I watched, mostly in shock, as a hook and ladder truck arrived and a handful of firemen attacked the flames with extinguishers. I felt a hand gently take mine. I knew it was Jinks without looking, but I didn't want her to see me being anything but happy and excited.

"It's just a car," she whispered. "We'll get another."

It no longer felt like the time or place to ask her to marry me. Instead, I apologized for spoiling her big night out.

She gave me a hug and said, "Don't be a dope. I love you."

~*~

A taxi dropped me off on the highway in front of Shady Grove; the driver refused to go on the gravel lanes leading to the trailers. Jinks wanted me to call her parents and have them pick us up at the Cascades, but I didn't want them to know what happened. Jinks promised not to tell them anything other than I'd had car trouble. I couldn't bear for them to know I'd gotten mixed up with the Cossack's gang.

Unfortunately, the destruction of my car wasn't the only surprise I faced that evening. As I walked up to my trailer I spotted the same hoodie-clad leg-breaker I'd dealt with the previous day. He had the same grin on his face, and I presumed he had the same gun in his pocket.

"Well," he said, chuckling, "look who's here. Have a nice walk?"

"I already gave you the money," I said, "now go away."

He shook his head. "What you gave me was a load of crap. You'll never guess what showed up today."

I tried to act like I didn't care. "I suck at guessing games."

He pulled the previously missing ledger from behind his back and held it in front of him. It looked suspiciously like the one I'd mailed to the Granville police. *Why couldn't I have sent it to the FBI?* I had to act not only indifferent, but innocent as well. "You win. What's that?"

"It's our list of who owes what." He tapped the book with a knuckle. "According to this, you're a liar."

"Let's not go overboard," I said. "I admit, I might have fudged a little, but can you blame me? Did you really have to go and torch my car?"

He laughed. "Somebody burned up your pretty little car? What a shame. I can't imagine who'd do something so gosh-all-mighty mean."

I tried to force myself to stay calm but firm. "I'll make good on the last payment, but that's it. I'm through with you and whoever you work for. The Cossack, right? Isn't that some kind of camel?"

"Ain't you the funny man. Now, the way this works is real simple. You screwed up, so you gotta pay a penalty."

"I did that already. With my car, remember?"

"Nah. That don't count." He tapped the ledger again. "Yer loan's been extended another year."

"You can't do that!"

He produced his gun in a quick and easy motion I'd have loved to copy—provided I had a gun handy, and knew how to use it. The three I had hidden away were useless at that point.

"You'll pay," he said, "or else."

"At the very least, you'll need to provide something I can file with my taxes showing the interest I've paid."

He just laughed. "I'll be back tomorrow to

279

collect. Be ready. If yer not, I'll let your girlfriend take up the slack."

"She doesn't have any money," I said.

"I ain't talking about money, dumbass." And then he laughed again, and kept laughing all the way to his car.

As I watched him drive off, my feelings of outrage and helplessness fed off each other. They fueled a ridiculous desire to even the score.

Stupid? Sure. But did I care?

Not a bit.

~*~

We were sitting in the glider, slowly swooping back and forth on the front porch at Jinks' house. Her parents weren't around. I'd brought her up to date on the latest visit of a Cossack creep and poured out my anger, my frustration, and my deep-seated desire to strike back.

Jinks was adamant. "You can't just run out and hurt someone in the name of revenge. That's what Buck Boeheim did, remember? And where did that get him?"

I hated to admit it, but I knew she was right. "I know; I know. It's just... Damn it! How come the bad guys get to do things the good guys can't?"

She smiled at me, something which normally calmed me down. "If you do the things bad guys do, then *you* become a bad guy. You don't want that, and

I sure as *hell* don't want that."

"It's not fair."

"Oh, please," she said. "How old are you, five? Didn't you get the 'Life's Not Fair' lecture?"

"There's another lecture, y'know. The one about standing up to bullies. Why doesn't that one apply?"

I think I stumped her, but only briefly. "The problem is," she said, "we don't really know who the Cossack is."

"It's gotta be the guy with the Lamber-genie, Doobin, or his dad. Maybe an uncle, maybe—"

"See? We don't know for sure. What if you do something mean or violent to someone who's innocent? What then?" When I didn't respond, she went on. "You get arrested, that's what. You go to prison. You break my heart. You—"

"Okay, okay. I get it."

"Good. Promise me you won't go off half-cocked and do something intensely dumb."

"Okay. At least, not until I'm sure of my target."

She sighed. "At least."

"So, how do we find out who the Cossack really is? If it's not a Doobin, who else could it be? A cop? Detective Weiner?" That thought had been bugging me a lot. "Someone on the police force gave that stupid ledger back."

"Maybe that's how we figure it out," Jinks said. "We need to be smart. We find out who opens the mail, and who decides what to do with it."

"That sounds great," I said, "but how do we manage that without exposing ourselves to whichever cop the Cossack has working for him?"

She thought about it for a long moment, then brightened. "We call in the cavalry."

"Your dad?" I didn't like that idea. "I told you, I don't want him to know how deeply I'm involved with—"

"We call in Regina Hornsby, Daddy's hot-shot reporter. She's got contacts everywhere. She probably already knows who she can trust in the Granville PD."

A bleak thought reignited my anxiety, and I voiced it, "What if Regina is the Cossack?"

Chapter Twenty-eight

"Mr. Lundberg: 'I asked you for your position on capital punishment.' Student: 'Prone.'"
–Kristin Hannah, ***The Things We Do for Love***

Between the flaming car incident and the discovery that the Cossack's ledger had been returned, I'd allowed myself to drift away from the idea of a marriage proposal. It wasn't that I'd somehow fallen out of love with Jinks; I couldn't imagine any possible way that might happen. I just let myself get overwhelmed—too much stimulation, and almost all of it negative.

I couldn't stop thinking about the most recent of the Cossack's bill collectors, a low-lifer who seemed all too eager to use his gun on me. I felt like smacking myself in the forehead when it occurred to me that he would most certainly know the Cossack's real identity.

All I had to do was figure out a way to pry it out of him.

He hadn't mentioned exactly when he would return, but he and the others had all come in the afternoon. Maybe they liked to sleep late. I didn't know, but I decided to take a chance and make some preparations for his arrival.

The weather had grown colder with the onset of fall, so I bundled up and hiked into the forest preserve to get the car left behind by the two hoodlums Zeke had knocked out. I prayed it remained where I left it after their untimely demise. Fortunately, it was, and better still, it revved to life the first time I tried to crank it.

I drove to Columbus, the home of Fort Benning, where there had to be at least a dozen Army/Navy surplus stores. I figured it would take longer to get there and back than it would to find the specialty items I needed. I was right.

I never dreamed I'd be doing early Christmas shopping at places selling government surplus *anything*. Crazy, right?

Zeke was curled up on my bed when I returned, and he woke up when I entered the trailer. He blinked at me a couple times, yawned, and then appeared to give me his attention.

"Is there a chance you could help me out with a bully?"

"Bull-leeze," he said, his voice dripping with disdain. "Zeke no like bull-leeze."

"Well, one's coming here later today," I said. "Now, I need you to be honest. If Hyde was here when the bully comes, could you control him? Could you keep Hyde from eating the bully?"

Apparently, Zeke found this to be a highly curious concept. "Have food; not eat?"

"Yes!" I said. "That's it exactly."

"Why?"

"I just want to scare him. I don't want him dead."

"Scare?"

"Yeah. When he gets here, I want him to see Hyde. It'll scare the pants off of him. Can you do that?"

Zeke appeared to process my request with some difficulty. "Not sleep? Not eat?"

"Right! Can you do that?"

"Hide-duh very busy now, hungry."

"I'll buy him a burger or two."

"Burr-gurr?"

"Okay, a ham. A big one." I glanced at my watch. "The Piggly Wiggly is just down the road. I'm sure they have some."

He looked doubtful.

"Okay, two. Two big 'ol hams. Smoked.

Yummy. Way better than... you know... humans."

"Hide-duh go fast. Hide-duh strong."

"Yes, yes, I know. But will he listen to you? If you say 'Stop,' will he stop?"

"Stop?"

"Yes! It's very important."

"No," he said. "Hide-duh hungry; Zeke find food. Hide-duh eat. No stop."

It wasn't what I wanted to hear and forced me to switch to Plan B. "Okay then, I need you to stay inside all afternoon. Under the bed, okay? Don't do anything unless I call you. Got that?"

"Zeke wait for bull-leeze under bed."

"Right. If I call you, I want you to use your sleep stink."

He nodded. At least, I think he nodded. It sure as hell looked like a nod. So much for Plan B.

Now, to be honest, I hadn't given a great deal of thought to Plan A, and even less to Plan B, but I had to do something. Though I hated to lean on her, I needed Jinks' help, or I'd never figure out who the Cossack was.

~*~

Once again, I had to use the car left behind by the unlucky pair of collectors who had spooked Zeke. Their car, unlike my Vespa, had a heater. Plus, doors and windows! I could drive it, pick up Jinks, and neither of us would freeze to death along the way, a concept with enormous appeal. Unfortunately, when I arrived at her house, she wasn't there. Then I remembered she'd said her parents would be out of town for a couple days, attending some sort of convention up in Atlanta. After a quick head slap, I zipped by H3 in case she hadn't finished cross-country practice, but the parking lot resembled a wind-swept prairie—no cars at all.

I cruised over to the library and popped in for a quick look around in case she'd gone there for something the H3 media center had banned, or more likely, lost. Again, I came up empty.

The idea of facing an armed thug on my own definitely had me on edge. Even Zeke's help— something I couldn't absolutely count on—failed to make me feel better. I just wanted to hold the bad guy at bay. If Jinks and I both held guns on him, he'd likely give up. That was Plan B. Zeke was my fallback in case everything else failed.

Knowing I was running late, I hurried back to Shady Grove. Avoiding the confrontation facing me would only make it worse later. If all else failed, I had the money they wanted, thanks to Tats.

When I reached the trailer, I got more bad news. The same car I'd seen parked there the day before had returned. The hooded hood was back. So much for Plan B and getting the drop on the bad guy *before* he arrived.

Did I mention Plan C was a might shaky?

What I *did* have, was a selection of weapons,

all provided posthumously by three of the Cossack's former associates. I grabbed one, racked a round into the chamber the way I'd seen it done on TV, and jammed the other two in my belt, praying that I didn't blow away any body parts. Thus armed, I walked into what I laughingly referred to as "home."

I was not at all prepared to see three people inside: two of the Cossack's henchmen, and Jinks. They had stuffed something in her mouth and tied her hands behind her back. One stood on either side of her, and both were smiling at me as I made my entrance.

Jinks' eyes were wide, terrorized. She cried out, but her words were garbled. One of the thugs elbowed her into silence.

Before I could even raise my stupid gun, they both had their weapons aimed at me. As a gunslinger, my career lasted about two seconds.

I quickly responded when told to disarm and set all three handguns on the card table beside the door. "What the hell's going on?" I asked, trying not to whine.

"It's called payback, asshole," said the one wearing a hoodie. Thug Two didn't open his mouth, but that did nothing to make him less scary. I tried, but failed, to ignore the Yankees ball cap perched atop his greasy mullet.

I summoned a bit of backbone from somewhere. "Let her go. She hasn't done anything."

"Yet," Hoodie said, then laughed. "Get it? *Yet.*

She hasn't done anything yet, but she will pretty soon. And you get to watch. Think of it as your interest payment." This struck them both as hilarious.

I've never cared much for comics who laugh at their own jokes.

Mr. Hoodie patted my frightened girlfriend's face. "Little Jinksie here is going to entertain us."

Jinksie? "How do you know her name?"

"Ah. See, the Cossack's got connections. He knows people. He can find out anything about anyone."

"Bullshit," I said. "He's not a magician. In fact, I'll bet he drives a fancy Italian sporty car to compensate for not having much of a dick."

The thug's eyes narrowed in suspicion.

I went on. "I've seen it. A Lamborghini, although he oughta call it a lamber-weenie."

"Shut the hell up," he growled.

Paydirt. I called Zeke's name.

Hoodie stepped toward me and stuck his gun in my face. "I said, 'shut up!'"

"Zeke! C'mon! Now!"

The thug poked me in the forehead with the muzzle of his gun. It hurt like hell. I kept waiting for Zeke to do his thing, but he may as well have been vacationing in outer space.

"Who's Zeke?" asked the second thug.

The pain in my forehead failed to make me shut my mouth. "*You can talk?* Amazing."

Hoodie threatened to poke me again. "Who's this Zeke character?"

I stared at the floor beneath my bed. "My watchdog. He's hiding under the bed."

Hoodie glanced at his pal. "Check it out. Shoot it if you need to."

"He's just a puppy," I said. "He won't hurt anybody. Go ahead, reach under there and pick him up."

Thug Two shoved Jinks down on the bed, then lowered himself to the floor for a quick inspection. "It's too dark. I don't see nothing."

"I know he's there," I said. "Want me to grab him?"

"I ain't stupid," Hoodie said as he pushed past me. "If there's a gun under that bed, you're dead. Don't move, or I'll shoot your girlfriend."

"Wait," said Thug Two reaching into the dark. "I do see something, but it don't look like no damn— *Geez!*"

Suddenly he was backing away from the bed and clawing at his face.

"What the hell?" Hoodie gasped as the toxic smell reached him. He tried to cover his nose, but his gun got in the way.

Thug Two, on his hands and knees, had slowed

down drastically, his head lolling from side to side.

Hoodie turned to look at me. "What'd you..." he began, then slumped to the floor beside his companion.

Jinks had been trying not to breathe, but she looked woozy. I couldn't hold my nose and carry her at the same time, so I turned to the door for one last, deep breath.

Zeke crawled out from under the bed and was working his way toward her. We arrived at about the same time; she'd nearly passed out. I scooped her up and carried her outside. Zeke trundled along too, and sat close to us as I removed the gag, untied her, and encouraged her to breathe unsullied air.

She slowly began to recover as I waved my hand over her nose to encourage oxygen molecules to pitch in and help. While Hoodie and Thug Two marinated in the anesthetic stink provided by Zeke, Jinks sat up.

After a mild round of coughing, she reached full consciousness. I didn't really expect her to thank me for sparing her the full effects of Zeke's gas attack, but her first words shocked me nonetheless.

"Do you still have a gun?"

"They're all in the trailer," I said.

She frowned. "Damn."

"Why? Those guys aren't going anywhere. At least, not anytime soon."

"I want to shoot them now before they wake up," she said. "They were going to—"

"I know," I said. "I wouldn't have let them."

"You couldn't have stopped them!" Her voice trembled every bit as much as her body.

"I want them dead, Denver. Dead as stones. Dead as... I don't know... dead. Sincerely dead."

"I picked up on that, sweetheart." I tried to smile. "But killing them—"

She finished my thought. "Makes us as bad as them? I don't think so."

"The law would probably disagree."

"Well, then, what are we going to do? Let 'em go? They'll just come back!" She reached for my shirt with both hands. "They came into my house and grabbed me. They tied me up and stuffed something nasty in my mouth. Then they forced me into their car and brought me here. That's kidnapping, isn't it? Can't we at least call the police?"

I hugged her, hoping desperately to calm her fears, but she kept shaking. "I don't think we can trust the cops. Especially after somebody on the force returned the Cossack's ledger." I looked at Hoodie's car. "I wonder if it's in there."

"So what if it is?" She shook her head. "I'm sure he's made a copy of it by now."

I smiled at her. "You're probably right. But that's not the point. I've got another idea."

She looked at me with apprehension, her lips moving but not forming words.

I forged on, "Now that we know where the Cossack lives, it's time to give him a taste of his own medicine."

"You're crazy," she said. And then she smiled. "I don't know what you have in mind, but I'm all in."

Chapter Twenty-nine

"Oddly enough, I think that everybody can relate to revenge, on some level. Everyone has wanted to exact it, at some point, and everybody has tampered with the idea, even if they didn't actually go through with it." –Emily VanCamp

Jinks remained angry, not that I blamed her. She described every element of her abduction by the two now unconscious punks in my trailer. It seemed as if each detail added to her disgust and her desire for payback.

I knew I should have been patient and understanding. I should have been not only consoling, but rational. Instead, I found myself growing just as angry as she was. There were no human beings in my trailer; they were something less, barely animal, perhaps just god-awful huge amoebas.

"I wish we could turn 'em over to the police," I said.

Jinks shook her head. "I'm more of a mind to go in there and shoot them."

"There's always Hyde," I suggested. "He'd not only kill them; he'd dispose of their bodies, too." The thought gave me a chill. "But that's... I dunno. Cold. Brutal."

Jinks shook her head. "Maybe, but it works for me."

"Shouldn't we at least give them a chance to get out of here alive?"

"Why?"

"We talked about this before," I said. "Do you want us to sink to their level?"

She thought about that for a while before responding. "How would we do that?"

"First, we drag them out of the trailer so I can turn the fan on and start airing the place out. Then we face them towards the woods and tell them they can make a run for it."

"And Hyde will be waiting for them?"

"More or less. There's a good chance one of them might make it to the trail. They'd both have to move fast to escape, but I think it's possible. Shoot, they might both make it. And if we really wanted to even the odds, we could tell Zeke to call Hyde only when they were both well into the woods."

She looked dubious. "You're gonna tell them about Hyde?"

"Good point, not that they'd believe me anyway. I'll just say there's a very dangerous animal out there, and they'll need to run like hell."

"You're way more generous than me," she said. After a long pause, she added, "But at least that way it wouldn't be outright murder."

"And once they've seen what sort of creature we've got on our side, I doubt they'll want to come back. That's the deal I want to make before we let them go."

"So how do we drag those guys out here without passing out ourselves?"

I couldn't help but feel a little pride for planning ahead. "I've already taken care of that. Check these out." With a bit of a flourish, I pulled out the matching gas masks I'd bought from the government surplus store in Columbus.

She reacted with surprise, and a bit of suspicion. "Do they really work?"

"The guy in the store said they would. There wasn't an easy way to test 'em. But he gave me a quick intro on how to use them. Watch."

I slipped the mask over my head and fiddled with the straps until I had centered it as comfortably as I could. After an experimental series of breaths in and out, I uttered a mask-muddled, "Ready to rock!"

"You look like something from outer space," she said.

I removed the mask. "Maybe if those jerks see us wearing these, it'll scare 'em."

Jinks squinted at the headgear. "I imagine having guns pointed at their heads will scare them enough. Let's not let anyone else see the masks for now."

I told Zeke to wait outside, handed one of the masks to Jinks, and helped her adjust the straps for a snug fit. Once I had mine on, we dragged my "guests" out of the trailer.

I have no idea what sort of gas Zeke used on the two thugs, but it had knocked them out quickly, and it took quite a while to wear off.

I could still see the anger simmering inside Jinks as she stared down at her assailants. "They had their filthy hands all over me," she said. "They stuffed a nasty rag in my mouth, and they taunted me. Told me over and over what they were going to do to me. They—" Suddenly, she re-donned her mask and bustled back into the trailer.

"What're you doing?" I asked. She didn't answer.

Moments later she reappeared holding my dirty clothes hamper which she deposited next to the thugs. She pulled off her mask and pointed at it. "For once, I'm glad you don't do laundry very often."

I still hadn't figured out what she was up to. "So?"

"I want you to dig out the two most disgusting bits of clothing you can find in there."

"Why?"

She pointed at Hoodie and Thug Two. "They need gags, and they need 'em in the worst way."

Though it struck me as totally gross, I liked the idea, except for one thing. "They won't be able to talk."

"Nope. But they'll be able to listen. We can yank out the gags if we need to hear them say something. Otherwise, they get to enjoy a little bit of what I went through."

Wasting no more time, I dumped out the contents of the hamper and dug through it. The best options boiled down to sweat socks and underwear.

"You wear tighty-whities?" she asked, then made a face. "Okay, sorta-whities?"

I nodded and put the socks back in the hamper.

With my dirty underwear suitably installed in the mouths of the intruders, we dragged them closer to the woods and propped them up with their backs against trees. It had to be uncomfortable since we also tied their hands behind them. Jinks and I each held one of their guns trained on them as we waited for them to fully wake up.

Though we'd relieved them of their wallets as well as their guns and car keys, I had no desire to inspect their IDs and learn their real names. Thinking of them as Hoodie and Thug Two seemed perfectly adequate.

Hoodie shook off the stink sleep a little quicker than his pal, so I addressed my remarks to him. "We talked about what to do with you two, and shooting you seemed like the best way to guarantee you won't come back."

He stared at the barrel of his own weapon, a view he'd probably never experienced before and tried to talk, so I yanked my Fruit of the Loom plug from his mouth.

"You wouldn't dare," he said, trying to work saliva back into his tongue.

"Maybe, maybe not. But then I'm not the one who got kidnapped. And while I'm still thoroughly pissed about it, my girlfriend is way more upset."

Jinks pulled back the slide on her weapon to chamber a round, something we'd practiced before the hoods woke up. She wasn't smiling, and Thug Two appeared ready to wet his pants. When he uttered a muffled mouthful, she removed the wad of underwear he'd been chewing on.

"We just wanted to scare you a little," he said, spitting, his voice unsteady.

"Oh, golly!" Jinks exclaimed. "That changes everything!" She let her momentarily animated smile dissolve before adding a decisive, "Not."

"You can't just kill us in cold blood," Hoodie said. "You'd go to jail, like... forever."

"That's assuming we got caught," Jinks said. "Ever heard of habeas corpus?"

Hoodie frowned. "That's some kinda legal shit ain't it?"

"It means 'show me the body,'" I added, flashing briefly on a conversation I once dreamed I'd had with Miss Lovingood. "Without a corpse, it's much harder to prove someone's been murdered."

"You can't—"

"Oh, but we can!" Jinks pointed her weapon from one hood to the other and repeated the word, "Bang!"

The two creeps looked distinctly worried, and I was content to let them stew for a while, just as they had left Jinks fretting over what they repeatedly told her they would do to her.

Jinks glanced at me. "I still think it would be simpler and easier to just shoot them now. That way we'll know for sure we'll never see them again."

"That's true," I said. "But we discussed this, remember? We decided that if they swore never to come back, we'd give them a chance to run for it."

"Oh, right," Hoodie said, his voice dripping sarcasm. "So you can shoot us in the back?"

"As long as you go through the woods, we

won't shoot," I said. "There's a trail about a hundred yards in. Once you get there, turn right; it's a mile or so, but it's the shortest way out. There's a road just outside the park. Go right again and after another mile, you'll reach a gas station. You can call someone from there to pick you up."

"The thing is," Jinks said, "there's a really nasty creature out there, and I guarantee he's going to come after you. If he catches you, you're dead."

Thug Two sneered, his bravado rekindled. "You got like a wolf or something out there? That's bullshit. You're just trying to scare us, and we don't scare easy."

I ignored his bluster. "Agree to our terms, and you can make a run for it. We'll drop your car off at the Cossack's house."

The two creeps exchanged looks. "How d'ya know we won't come back anyway?" Thug Two asked.

"Trust me," Jinks said, "Once you see what's protecting us, you'll be happy to stay away."

They looked at each other, smiled as if they'd won something, and agreed.

Jinks kept the weapons pointed at them while I had Hoodie stand and turn so I could untie his hands. The plan was to retie them in front, but I didn't get that far. He took a swing at me as soon as he could and grazed my chin. Though not terribly painful, it was enough to distract Jinks.

Thug Two, who was still on the ground, raised both legs and kicked Jinks in the stomach, propelling her backwards toward the woods. The guns fell from her hands.

Hoodie pounced on me and got in two quick punches to my face while Thug Two continued to kick at Jinks. With me woozy from blows to the head, Hoodie leaped for Jinks and pinned her on the ground.

"Go! Sit on him," Hoodie shouted at his partner.

I tried to get up, but my internal pinball mechanism continued to register *TILT!* I had just managed to roll over when Thug Two landed on me, crushing the air from my lungs.

I could hear Jinks groaning, but my senses were wrapped in gauze. Dazed and distracted, all I wanted to do was get the weight off my back. I had to get up. I had to help Jinks. But mostly, I had to breathe.

The two thugs shouted gleefully at each other before Hoodie settled into a gravelly monologue detailing what they would do to us. He took special care to detail what he had in store for Jinks.

Eventually, I sucked in enough air to convince myself I wasn't dead or dying. Hoodie's threats left Jinks crying, gasping, and sniffling between heart wrenching pleas for him to stop.

Turning my head to one side as I pulled my hands under my chest, hoping to throw Thug Two from his perch, I spied Zeke peering out at us from the brush at the edge of the woods.

"Zeke!" I yelled, though my volume wasn't near what I'd hoped for. "Get Hyde!"

"Bull-leeze," he squeaked, then raised his own voice. "High-duh! High-duh!"

Hoodie slapped Jinks into silence and kept a knee in the small of her back while he attacked the knot preventing Thug Two from throwing punches of his own.

I called out to Zeke again, urging him to bring Hyde, but Thug Two put an end to that by bouncing up and down on my back. He must have weighed half again as much as me.

Zeke ducked back into the woods, presumably to summon Hyde, but when he reappeared, the great hulking scorpion was nowhere in sight.

Just then, Hoodie caught sight of our six-legged companion. "What the hell is that?" he asked as he finally finished untying his sidekick's hands.

"It's some kinda skunk thing," Thug Two responded. "Grab one of the guns and shoot it. Shoot it now!"

Chapter Thirty

"Man is the only creature that consumes without producing. He does not give milk; he does not lay eggs; he is too weak to pull the plough; he cannot run fast enough to catch rabbits. Yet he is lord of all the animals." –George Orwell

Jonathon left Dawn Popkin's home with serious doubts about the woman's claims. He suspected she had dreamed up the monster story hoping she could somehow discredit AARPA. She clearly had it in for the agency which had pulled the plug on the project she and her husband had labored over for years.

On the other hand, what if she was telling the truth? Figuring that out would most likely be the only way he'd ever solve the riddle of the missing cleaners.

Between Granville's Detective Weiner and Dr. Dawn Popkin, AARPA's former researcher, Jon had reached his limits. He and his physician had agreed on one essential: Jonathon Fitzgerald had not yet fully recovered from the assault he'd suffered in the parking lot at Sweet Dreamz. He tired easily, and the tale he'd heard from Popkin continued to bounce around in his head. It was time for some R&R, maybe an early dinner at Babe's Burgers. And with any luck, maybe he'd run into the blushin' Russian again.

The parking lot had fewer cars than usual when he pulled into a space near the entrance. Having arrived ahead of the dinner crowd, he found most of the tables and all the stools at the bar vacant. He chose a spot as far from the sound system speakers as he could get. It didn't help much. The music seemed to have been imported from the neighboring show bar; every tune had a heavy syncopated beat, wailing vocalists, and too much volume.

Hoping to ignore the din, he dug into his burger and beer and focused on the things he knew to be true about his investigation. It was a damned short list: the team had dismantled the research facility; they had likely been the root cause for Dr. Bledsoe's heart attack; Dawn Popkin was understandably angry; she was also a very smart woman, easily capable of plotting revenge. And finally, if what she said was true, she had access to a frightening biological arsenal with which to extract that revenge.

Two of those items didn't add up. If the team had dismantled the facility in what amounted to a surprise raid, Popkin wouldn't have had time to plan anything. Besides, her husband's death had almost certainly occupied her full attention. She might be smart, arrogant, and vengeful, but he seriously doubted she'd had the time to plan let alone execute the disappearance of the cleaners.

He doubted his boss, the irascible Augusta Burnside, had anything to do with it, aside from her decision to shut Live Canary down.

Who stood to gain from killing or kidnapping the cleaners? Not Popkin. Not Burnside. Not the kid Weiner told him about. It didn't make sense.

"Well, look who's here."

Jon twisted in his chair to see the speaker and was pleasantly surprised to see the smiling face of Malindi... *Damn!* He couldn't recall her last name, assuming he'd ever heard it. "Well, hey! This is my lucky day."

"May I join you?"

"Please do," he stood and waved her into the chair in front of him.

Malindi settled in quickly. "I was really hoping to see you here. Once you left the hospital I didn't really know how to get in touch."

"That's my fault," he said digging into his wallet for a business card. He scribbled his room number at the motel on the back. "I'm not sure how much longer I'll be in Granville, but I'll be staying next door until it's time to go. You can leave a message at the desk if I'm not there."

Her original bubbly nature dissipated, and she scanned the largely vacant room as if to make sure no one was watching her. Satisfied, she leaned closer and whispered, "This may not be the best place to talk."

"Oh?"

"When you finish your dinner, we should go outside."

"Is there a problem?"

"I think so, but— Not here, okay?"

He pushed his burger and beer aside and stood. "This'll keep. C'mon."

He led the way to a spot outside, well away from the entrance then turned and gave her his full attention. "Okay, what's up? Is Tats back?"

"Tats? No, he's not. I haven't seen that creep for a while. I hope he never comes back."

"Okay, then what's the problem?"

"You remember I mentioned a guy I know, Denver Stow? The cops kept after him about two brothers who went missing."

"I remember. I'm gonna look him up tomorrow. Why, what's the matter?"

"I've heard some talk at the club. In addition to

Tats, a bunch of our other regulars haven't been around lately. I didn't think much of it until I overheard a couple guys talking about it. One of 'em mentioned Denver's name. He said all the guys who've gone missing either worked near him or went to see him at the crappy trailer park where he lives."

"How many guys are we talking about?"

"I don't know exactly. Quite a few."

"And why would they need to go see him?" Jon asked.

Malindi looked distinctly uncomfortable. "Well, uhm... This is just between you and me, right?"

"Of course."

"I'm pretty sure they all work for the man who owns my club and the other businesses around here. I've never seen him; he never comes around, but a bunch of the guys who work for him spend a lot of time at the club. In fact, they even get a discount, and none of 'em tip worth a damn."

Jon struggled to put the pieces together. "So, what kind of work do these guys do?"

She pressed her lips together, inhaled deeply through her nose, then responded in a low voice. "I'm not exactly sure what they do, but I doubt it's legal. They're all pretty rough-lookin'. Street toughs. Most of 'em carry guns. They sure as hell aren't out sellin' insurance."

"Sounds like a gang," Jon said.

She didn't try to hide her sarcasm, "Well, if it walks like a duck—"

"It's probably not a zebra."

That earned him a snort of laughter. "Prob'ly not. What worries me is that one of the guys said something about making sure Denver couldn't do anything to anyone else. I'm afraid they're gonna kill him."

"Have you mentioned this to the police?"

She responded with a heartier laugh. "The last thing I need is for someone to see me talkin' to the cops about anything. That definitely wouldn't be healthy. But, you; you're a secret agent. I thought maybe—"

It was his turn to chuckle. "I'm an agent, but it's no secret."

"Still, you might know somebody who could... I dunno. Do something. You could at least warn him, couldn't you? It's not like I'm in love with him or anything. I just don't want to see him get hurt." She shook her head. "Denver. He... he's just a geek. He wouldn't— He *couldn't* hurt anybody."

Jon patted her arm. "I'll see what I can do."

"Tonight?"

"You think it's really that urgent?"

"Yes!"

He nodded. "Okay then. As soon as I finish my dinner, I'll try to find him."

Malindi frowned. "That burger of yours is probably cold by now. Maybe you oughta forget about it and go look for Denver now."

"Hey guys, looky who's here!"

Jon turned the sound of the voice and spied a trio of street toughs ambling through the parking lot.

"Aw, crap," Malindi whispered. "I gotta go, and so do you. Those guys are trouble."

"I'm not worried," Jon lied. His back and head still weren't one hundred percent, and the last thing he wanted was another encounter with some of Granville's least desirables.

"I bet yer that fed Tats told us about. You are, ain't ya? Lemme see yer fancy badge. Tats said you were eager to flash it in his face." He waved his hand in front of his mug. "C'mon, let's have it."

Jon attempted a confident smile, though he felt nothing of the kind. "I don't have a beef with you or your friends."

"Oh, now I don't know 'bout that. See, I saw you chattin' up our gal Natasha here." He waved for his accomplices to cut off the girl's retreat. "Stay right where you are, sweet thing, while I have a little talk with this here fed'ral agent."

"Okay, I talked to her. So what?" Jon wondered how long it might take him to pull his back-up weapon from the ankle holster he wore. His regular sidearm hadn't been returned with his car and other gear. If he needed a weapon, the little .380 would have to do, assuming he could get to it in time. He didn't doubt for a moment that all three of the men facing him were armed. "What gives you the right to determine who she talks to? Who anybody talks to for that matter."

"That's the thing, right there. I do have the right to say who she talks to. She works for the same people I work for, and they don't like havin' a snitch on the payroll."

"And what's she going to snitch about? How fast she can take off her clothes? What kind of music the customers like best?"

"You think yer pretty damn smart, doncha?"

Jon managed a shrug. Any answer he produced would only antagonize the redneck more.

"Jay Dee," the thug said, "you and Beaner keep an eye on her. Things between me and this piece o' fed'ral shit are gonna git—"

The sound of a switchblade clicking open triggered him. Jon punched the redneck in the throat, ending the conversation. The punk dropped to the pavement along with his knife. There had been no reason to wait for the attack Jon knew would be coming.

"Geez, Lonnie!" yelled one of the other two.

While they gawked at their comrade's sudden incapacitation, Jon squatted down next to him and pulled his back-up gun from its holster.

"Asshole!" yelled the second member of the pair as he pulled a gun from the waistband in the back of his pants.

Jon fired a round into his thigh, spinning him around.

The third member of the trio had his weapon out, too, but Jon fired first, hitting him a good bit closer to his groin. Both men went down, though only one of them managed to hang onto his gun. Jon stepped on his arm, pinning it to the asphalt.

As the first thug struggled to breathe and simultaneously pull his gun, Jon aimed his weapon at the man's forehead. "If you want to live, don't move."

The jerk got the message.

Jon looked at Malindi who appeared to be in or near a state of shock.

"You shot them."

"Yep."

"Damn. What now?"

"We call the cops," Jon said. "Let them sort things out. It was three on one, right? Self-defense?"

"I guess," she said.

"This ought to slow down any efforts to find your friend Denver, don't you think?"

She shook her head. "I doubt it. The Cossack's got a lot of guys workin' for him. And you just pissed 'em all off."

Jon had Malindi call the police while he kept an eye on his attackers, moving his gun in a wide arc that brought each of them into the range of a kill shot.

Eventually two squad cars and a third, unmarked vehicle cruised into the parking lot. Jon was less than pleased to see detective Weiner slide out from behind the wheel of the unmarked car. "What've you done now?" he barked.

It was going to be a long evening and a long while before he located Denver Stow.

Chapter Thirty-one

"The world is in a constant conspiracy against the brave. It's the age-old struggle: the roar of the crowd on the one side, and the voice of your conscience on the other." –Douglas MacArthur

Jinks continued to struggle despite being pinned by Hoodie's knee. That didn't keep her from trying to hit him, though her blows were ineffective. But they did distract him, and when he finished untying Thug Two's hands, he returned to her with a vengeance. "Shoot the damned thing yourself," he shouted at his creepy companion. "I'm a little busy."

Muttering a curse, Thug Two rolled off me. Rather than waste time standing, he scrambled on hands and knees toward the guns Jinks dropped when the attack began.

Zeke seemed to be weighing his options while Jinks and I were being mauled. "Get Hyde!" I screamed at him.

"High-duh... busy," Zeke called back in a vowel-heavy squeak.

Busy? Seriously?

Angered by Hyde's indifference to our plight, I reached out and grabbed one of Thug Two's legs hoping to keep him away from the firearms. Meanwhile, Zeke decided to join the party.

Fairly sure I knew what he had in mind, I called out to Jinks to get ready.

She managed a fear-strangled, "What?"

"Zeke's coming!" I yelled back. I would have held my nose to get the point across, but I didn't want to give up my hold on Thug Two. The aforementioned asshole had shifted his position to kick me the way he'd kicked Jinks in an effort to free his leg. I wasn't about to give in or give up, not with Zeke on the move.

I just had to hold on a little longer.

And hold my breath, as well.

As an all too familiar aroma wafted through the air, I took in as much air as I could.

And promptly passed out.

~*~

Freezing.

I didn't think I'd be able to hear my own teeth

chattering, but I could sure as hell feel 'em. *Who can sleep like that?* I remembered hearing Regina say something about an early cold snap; I didn't expect it to be like this. It almost never snows in Granville.

I opened an eye, wondering why my back hurt, why it was dark, and why I was lying on the ground outside my trailer. A slow, pillow-less turn of my head brought Jinks into view.

"Hey, girl. Are you okay?" The events from the immediate past worked their arduous way back into my forebrain, quite a journey.

"Denver?" she groaned, her voice as shivery as her body. "What happened? What time is it? Where are...."

We both sat up slowly and looked around. I expected Hoodie and Thug Two to be sitting near us, guns in hand, gloating in the dim light.

But they weren't.

I helped Jinks to her feet, and she leaned against me for warmth as we scanned the area for clues. "It had to be Hyde," I said.

"I never saw him." She pointed a shaky finger at the thug's car parked nearby. "I don't think they're gone."

I tried, unsuccessfully, not to growl. "I'm guessing Hyde finally finished up whatever in hell was keeping him busy. Zeke bought us time. He probably saved our lives."

Jinks disengaged herself from my sheltering

arms and stepped away. "Does it seem a little odd to you that nobody showed up while we were dealing with those two jerks?" She spun around and looked at me. "I mean, there was a lot of cussing and shouting going on, and these crappy trailers aren't exactly sound-proof. If you heard someone screaming, wouldn't you at least stick your head out a window to see what was going on?"

"I've seen several people I think live here," I said. "But I've never actually met any of them. Well, except for the three in Ivo's trailer." I nodded at the wreckage still sitting beside my trailer. "Oh, and Wanda—Wicked Wanda Vickers, the lovely rent collector. She's such a sweetheart; reminds me of the witch from Oz, only skinnier."

"Please don't tell me I remind you of Dorothy," she said.

"Nah. You're way prettier. Besides, Dorothy wore pigtails and a smock. You've got a ponytail and wear jeans. Really, uhm… tight jeans."

"Thanks, I think," she said wiping bits of debris from her clothing. "But what are we doing here? We need to go. Now."

"Denvurr!"

I turned at the sound of Zeke's strained voice and said, "There you are! What happened to—"

"Need cage," he said.

That's when I noticed he had a double armload of shiny, blueish-white… *zucchini?*

317

"Zeke? What are you talking about?"

"High-duh eggs. Put in cage. Now!"

"What kind of cage?" Jinks asked.

Lord, how I wish I could think like that! "It doesn't matter," I said. "I don't have any kind of cage."

"Put eggs in cage," Zeke said. "Hurry, hurry!"

They were the strangest looking eggs I'd ever seen. They weren't just huge—zucchini-sized, like they appeared to me at first—they looked more like some sort of fancy gem stones than garden veggies.

"Do you have a box or something?" Jinks asked, still on task, and still shivering.

I shook my head, no.

"How 'bout a suitcase?"

"Nope." I thought for a moment. "But I've got a gym bag."

"Get it," she said moving toward Zeke. "I'll give him a hand."

I held my breath as best I could while rummaging around in the trailer in search of my old gym bag. Though cheap and worn, it was still serviceable. By the time I got back outside, Zeke was gone, and Jinks was cradling a half dozen of the weird eggs in her arms.

"Where's Zeke?"

"He went back for more," she said. "I guess Hyde's been busy."

"No kidding."

I put the bag on the ground and unzipped it. Jinks immediately off-loaded the eggs and arranged them as neatly as she could. Shortly after she finished, Zeke returned with still more. He hustled toward us with a disapproving look on his usually happy face.

"Not cage," he decreed and piled his four eggs on top of the others. "Lock now. Hurry!"

I zipped it shut. "It doesn't lock, but I doubt the eggs will try to escape."

Jinks frowned at me. "Can't you be serious for once? Obviously, it's what's inside the eggs we need to contain. Unless, of course, you're okay with a bunch of mini-Hydes running around looking for people to eat."

"Keep dark," Zeke said as he turned to leave.

Jinks stared at him. "Where are you going?"

"And where are the two guys who were here with us?" I asked. "The bullies."

"High-duh take bull-eeze. Food for little High-duhs."

Jinks beat me to the question, "Is Hyde coming back?"

"No," he said. "High-duh... sick."

"Sick?" we asked in unison.

Zeke's expression didn't change. "High-duh die soon."

"We can't stay here," Jinks said. "Someone will come looking for the two jerks who grabbed me. Besides, I'm freezing."

"You're right it's not safe here." I turned her toward Hoodie's car since I still had the keys. We took two steps in that direction when two vehicles I didn't recognize roared into the trailer park. We both stopped and watched as the cars pulled up next to my trailer.

"The woods! Quick!" I whispered, but Jinks was already moving in that direction.

Fortunately, the car's headlights weren't aimed at us, and we used the darkness and the vegetation at the edge of the preserve to hide.

Three men exited the first car, followed by two more from the second. "They sent five guys after me?" I whispered. "They've got me confused with Spiderman."

Jinks shushed me.

All five walked directly toward my trailer. The guy in front, presumably their leader, paused at the threshold and made some remark. It had to be related to the Zeke stink from earlier in the day. There were several responses, none of which I could hear clearly.

When the last of them entered the trailer, I stood up.

"What's the matter with you?" Jinks demanded. "Stay down!"

"Stay there," I said, keeping my voice low. "I'm

going closer so I can hear what they say."

"Who *cares* what they say!" She sounded on the verge of tears.

I pointed to myself and hurried to the back of the trailer. I'd left the windows open so it would air out, which made it much easier to eavesdrop on the intruders. They had already begun to trash my place a second time, not that there was much left to destroy.

To my knowledge, I'd never seen any of them before, so I had no idea who said what, and frankly, I couldn't have cared less.

"I can't believe anyone would live in a shit hole like this."

<Sounds of drawers being yanked out and dumped on the floor.>

"Must be some badass if he took out Tats and all those other guys. Two of their cars are still sittin' outside!"

"Way I heard it, he kilt two dealers right here in the trailer park. Musta dumped their bodies in the woods."

<Sounds of furniture being overturned.>

"Who sez it was this Denny kid?"

"Not the boss. He don't care. It was his cop."

"No shit? Which one?"

"You know which one, dipshit. But we don't

talk about him. It's s'posed to be a secret. Geez."

"Hey, guys—come check this shit out!"

<Sounds of people moving around, then silence.>

"Damn!"

"What are they? Pearls?"

"I dunno, but I'll bet they're worth sumpthin'."

"Anybody know a jeweler?"

"You crazy? If the Cossack finds out we found some diamonds—"

"They ain't diamonds, you idiot."

"Then what the hell are they?"

"Doesn't matter. If they're worth something, then they now belong to the boss."

"But—"

"But nothin'. We take these to the Cossack's cop and tell 'im the kid ain't here. Now, let's go."

"I'll drive Beaver's car."

"You got the keys?"

"Shit. Hadn't thought of that. Anybody know how to hot-wire a car?"

"Just leave it. We'll come back for it later."

I crouched low enough to look under the trailer and watched as the five of them sauntered out, climbed into their cars, and drove off.

Jinks stayed hidden until both cars were out of sight, then she joined me. We climbed into Hoodie's car, cranked up the heater, and took off.

~*~

Jonathon Fitzgerald had a vague idea about what would happen after he'd disabled the trio who tried to attack him. He had counted on Malindi to back up his version of events and she did, though reluctantly. The three being treated at County General had cooked up an entirely different scenario, and Detective Weiner seemed unable to decide which story to believe.

After her interview, Malindi approached Jon in a hallway of the Granville PD headquarters. "I'm scared," she whispered.

"Why?"

"Because of the Cossack. When he finds out I didn't stand up for his guys, he'll send 'em after me."

Jon scratched his still sore head. "Who's the Cossack?"

"He owns the club where I work. And a bunch of other places, too. It's... He's like a gang leader or something. He knows people everywhere." She cast furtive glances toward each end of the hall. "He probably has someone working for him in here."

Jon tried to sound reassuring, "The only way he might find out what you said is—"

"Is if that dumb detective tells him," she said.

"You think Weiner's being paid off?"

"It wouldn't surprise me."

"Then you shouldn't go back to the club."

"I won't," she said, looking distinctly unhappy about it. "I make good money there, even if the Cossack's men don't tip worth shit." She exhaled and crossed her arms on her chest. "Could you get me into that witness protection thing the government has?"

"I don't know. Maybe. Assaulting a federal officer is a federal crime, and if your testimony is needed to prosecute those three idiots, then you'd probably qualify. We'd need evidence of a direct threat against you."

"Can you look into it? I mean, after you've made sure Denver's okay?" She glanced at a clock on the wall. "It might be too late already."

"I'll get on it as soon as I can. That's pretty much up to Weiner. I've gotta cooperate with them."

"Well, I'm gettin' outta here now," she said. "It's just not safe."

"Where will you go?" he asked. "How will I get in touch with you if I need to?"

"I've got your card. I'll call when I get where I'm going."

"And where's that?"

She dropped her voice back down to a whisper. "My grandparents live up north in a little town called Canton. It's about the same size as

Granville, but it doesn't have the Cossack's footprint all over it."

She gave him a quick kiss on the cheek before scurrying down the hallway toward the exit. "Thanks for looking out for Denver," she said over her shoulder.

And then she was gone.

After a lengthy discussion between Weiner, an AARPA lawyer on a speaker phone, and the Granville DA over the criminal records of the wounded men, Jon was finally allowed to leave. Weiner actually grinned at him when commenting that the three hoods would be out on bail before the night was done.

Jon climbed into his car and checked his watch. Several hours had been wasted at the police station, hours which he could have used to locate and interview Denver Stow. And, if Malindi's fears were valid, Jon might well need to defend the young man from an attack by the Cossack, whoever in hell he was.

His first stop would be the easiest—Stow's home in the Shady Grove Mobile Home Park.

Chapter Thirty-two

"Time is too slow for those who wait, too swift for those who fear, too long for those who grieve, too short for those who rejoice, but for those who love, time is eternity." –Henry Van Dyke

Thankfully, Hoodie's car heated up quickly. Neither of us had prepared for cold weather since it usually didn't start until much later. December was still a good month away, but it felt like winter had already set in.

"Could you hear those guys where you were?"

"Yeah. It wasn't too hard. They weren't whispering," I said.

"What were they doing?"

"Other than looking for me?" I exhaled in a

whoosh. "They trashed my place. Again. But then...."

"What?" She looked alarmed.

"They stole the gym bag full of Hyde's eggs." I couldn't help but laugh. "Can you imagine the looks on their faces if— No. *When* those things hatch?"

"I only wish I could be there to see it." She leaned against the car window. "What time is it?"

I pointed to a clock built into the dashboard. "Two-thirty. You feel like breakfast?"

She gave me a look that would've turned a lesser man to stone. "Just kidding," I said and twisted the knob on the heater, which eventually flooded the front seats with blessed warmth.

Finally able to relax, Jinks suggested we go to a cabin her parents owned. It made perfect sense to me; we didn't have any other options that felt safe, especially since the Cossack's men knew where she lived. She insisted on driving since she knew the way, and that gave me the freedom to process what we'd been through, and where we might be headed next.

The drive was relatively short. The cabin looked old, dark, and peaceful. Just what we needed. Jinks parked the car next to the building, shut off the engine, and shrank back into the seat. "This car stinks," she said.

A glance at the overflowing ashtray on the console explained the aroma, one we were both eager to leave behind. "Let's go inside," I said. "Is this place locked?"

Jinks nodded. "But I know where there's a key."

I followed her out into the early morning darkness. Without a flashlight, Jinks left the car's headlights on and made her way toward a dormant flower bed beside the front door. A laughing garden gnome, hands on hips and head tilted back, seemed to be in charge of the plot. Jinks tipped him to one side and extracted a key from beneath his chunky feet.

I killed the headlights, pocketed the car keys, and we both slipped into the darkness of the little cabin in the woods.

"It's no palace," Jinks said, "but it's nice, and nobody will know we're here." She gave me a tentative smile. "We *will* be safe here, won't we?"

"I think so," I said, "but, not a palace? Are you kidding? Compared to my place, it's the Taj freakin' Mahal."

Jinks spread her arms and turned in a slow circle to present the place as if it really was something exotic. "There are two bedrooms. That's Mom and Dad's room over there. It's got a big bed. My room is over here. It's got twin beds. Mom said I could have a friend over whenever I wanted to, but... Well, that never happened. I suck at making friends."

"Sometimes," I said, "making friends can be hard. I don't have many, either." The look on her face suggested something, but I couldn't quite identify it. "Are you tired?"

"Not really," she said. "Zeke made sure we got

some sleep. Now I'm just cold."

I pointed at the fireplace behind her. "We could build a nice fire in that, couldn't we?"

"We could if there were any firewood, but Dad used it all up the last time we were here."

"Oh. Right." I wasn't sure what to suggest next, but I took a chance. "We could always snuggle."

"Like, in bed? Under the covers?"

"Sure." I slipped off my shoes and socks, then sat on one of the twin beds.

"There's way more room in Mom and Dad's room." She reached for my hand, pulled me to a standing position, and led me into the other bedroom.

"Are you sure you're okay with this? I mean... You know... In bed, together? After what we've been through?"

"I need to feel safe," she said. "And warm. And loved."

I watched, trying not to appear stunned, as she slipped out of her shoes, socks, and jeans and climbed into the bed wearing only a t-shirt and panties.

"Come on. Turn off the lights and join me." She patted the bedspread with the flat of her hand. "Really," she said, her voice soft and low. "I'm cold."

Jinks looked anything but cold with her long, dark hair and smooth, tanned legs. And her dimpled smile had me entranced. To say I'd dreamed of a moment like this would be the biggest understatement of all time. Ever since I met Jinks, thoughts of making love to her occupied a massive chunk of my grey matter. It's why I wanted her to marry me, though I had yet to ask her. I never really believed—despite my idiotic fantasies—that we'd ever get a head start on the benefits that came with marriage.

"Are you going to join me, or not?" she asked. "These sheets are freezing!"

"Yes!" It came out more like a yelp than a declaration, and I scrambled toward her.

"Not like that," she said, pantomiming the removal of my slacks. "Take 'em off."

I did as instructed, then added my long-sleeved t-shirt to the clothing scattered on the floor.

"That's better," she said as she scooted those beautiful bare legs to one side and beckoned me closer.

I climbed in beside her, and she pulled the covers up over both of us. She turned her back to me, and we lay like spoons, close together, warm, sensual....

She pointed to the ceiling. "You left the light on."

Dang it! "Want me to—"

"No!" she whispered. "Don't you dare let go of me."

I was totally out of my element, utterly

incapable of saying something suave, or cool, or romantically casual. All I could focus on was the soft, warm body pressed against me. I shifted a little to keep my stiffening response from being all too obvious.

"It's okay," she said. "You don't need to move. I... Uhm... I kinda like it—like that you'd react that way. You know... to me."

I'd entered uncharted territory. I adored this girl, this incredibly desirable... *woman*, and yet I teetered at the edge of a cliff overlooking cataclysmic failure. I knew I'd do something stupid, and this amazing dream would spiral into the real world, a world of rejection, a world where—

"I'll get the light," she said, slipping out of my grasp. I heard a click and the room went dark, but Jinks didn't get back in bed right away.

"Hey," I said, "are you okay?"

"Oh, yeah," she murmured as she once again crawled into the bed next to me.

I put my arms around her and discovered her t-shirt had disappeared, along with what little else she'd been wearing. I felt her tug at my underwear and automatically assisted in its removal.

"Much better," she whispered.

"Are you sure?" I asked, silently berating myself for saying anything which might alter the direction of events.

"Yes," she said. "We almost died today, Denver. And somewhere along the way I realized I didn't want my life to end without ever having made love to someone."

"*Someone?*"

"You," she said. "Without having made love... to you."

I have no idea how I did it, but I somehow doused the erotic fireworks in my head long enough to put one coherent thought into words. "I so want to make love with you, but—" I swallowed. "I have to ask you one question first."

She rolled over and faced me. In the dim light I made out the dip of her eyebrow and the tiny frown above her perfect chin.

"You want to ask me a *question?*"

"Yes," I said. "It'll just take a sec—"

"Are you serious? I just—"

I touched my index finger to her lips as lightly as I could to silence her then scrambled back out of bed and dropped to the floor in search of my pants. I prayed the engagement ring I'd intended to give her at the Cascades was still in my pocket. If so, this seemed like the most supremely likely moment I'd ever have to offer it to her. I took the ring out of the gift box.

"What are you doing?" she asked, a note of irritation in her voice.

And then I found it. "Hang on," I said. "I'll be right there."

I heard her exhale in exasperation as I got back in the bed beside her. "What was that all about?" she asked.

"Just this." I pressed the ring into her palm.

"What is it?"

"A ring," I said. "It's not a very exp—"

"A *ring?*" Her voice shot up an octave.

"Yeah. I wanted... I mean, I thought—"

Jinks' voice came out in a rush, "Are you asking me to *marry* you?"

"Actually, yes. That's exactly what I'm trying to ask you. Because I'm in love with you, and all I can think of are stupid song lyrics. And now, tonight, in here, with you in my arms, I just, you know...."

"Shut up, Denver," she said, laughing. "Of course, I'll marry you. I don't know when or how, but I know why. It's because I love you, too." And then she slipped the ring on her finger.

"Oh. My. God," I said. "Jinks—"

It was her turn to shut me up and did so with her hand to my mouth. "Are you going to make love to me, or not?"

It was the most bizarre day of my life.

And the most amazing.

Up until that point, anyway.

~*~

Jon found the approximate location of Denver Stow's trailer on the map he'd obtained from the local Chamber of Commerce. Including the word "park" in the name of the place had surely been intended as a joke. Shady Grove would have to up its game just to be considered a slum. With gravel driveways.

He found mobile home number 103 without difficulty. Its most distinctive feature was an open door. That did not bode well, so he parked a few doors further down, then returned to Stow's trailer with his gun drawn. He didn't relish another go-round with Weiner if he had to shoot someone, but it would be far better than taking a bullet himself.

Kneeling, he took a quick peek inside, noting an unpleasant odor emanating from within. *How could anyone live is such a smelly place?*

He quickly realized the smell wasn't the trailer's only unpleasant aspect. It had been completely trashed. Furniture was tossed about; clothing was shredded; drawers had been dumped on the floor and their contents scattered.

The only positive thing he noted, was a complete lack of bloodstains. That, he hoped, meant that Stow had managed to avoid whoever had been sent to hurt him. He wished he had a way to update Malindi.

His next step, finding out where Stow had gone, would be more challenging. This late in the evening, no one would be on duty at the newspaper where Stow worked, but Jon had no other leads. He certainly wouldn't go back to Weiner for input, in case Malindi was right, and the detective was in league with the Cossack.

AARPA maintained an information service staffed by people quite skilled at digging up details on pretty much anyone, if given enough time. Waiting a week or so while they did their research wasn't an option. His only choice was to contact the people Stow worked with at the newspaper. But that would have to wait until morning.

Jon went back to his motel room and prepared for a sleepless night. He hoped Denver Stow fared better.

As he lay in bed, mentally reviewing the events of the day, he kept coming back to something he'd noticed but not fully understood. An odd comment from Dawn Popkin during their chat on her patio finally broke through the haze.

"Think skunk," he said out loud, quoting her. *"Only much, much worse."*

And suddenly a great many things began to make sense.

He sat straight up and put his palms to either side of his head as it sank in.

"Oh... Shit!"

Chapter Thirty-three

"We hope that, when the insects take over the world, they will remember with gratitude how we took them along on all our picnics." –Bill Vaughan

We slept in, and I do mean slept. The previous day's events left us exhausted, though I'd guess it was more emotional than physical. The bedtime events from the previous evening went unmentioned once we crawled out from under the sheets in the cabin that morning.

"We need food," I said.

Jinks sniffed. "You need a bath."

"Actually, we both do," I said. "There's a shower here, isn't there?"

"Yeah, but neither of us has any clean clothes."

"Hm. Okay. Anyway, I think hunger trumps hygiene."

We straightened up the bed, climbed back into Hoodie's car, and left. I was still intent on finding something to eat, but it didn't work out that way.

"We need to go back to your trailer and check on Zeke," Jinks said.

"To see if he's found any more eggs?"

"Yes. And to see what he can tell us about them. He wanted us to put them in a cage, remember? And he said to keep them in the dark."

"There's not a whole lot we can do about that now," I said.

"True. But we need to know as much as we can."

"Why? I thought we were both happy that the Cossack was in for a big surprise."

"Hopefully a fatal surprise."

I gave that a snort of laughter. "I'm all choked up. Especially after what he tried to do to us. And besides, would that be so terrible? It feels like poetic justice to me."

"You don't think something like that would spark an investigation? An unknown species of gigantic scorpion attacks someone in their home, and you think nobody's going to be curious?"

"*Gigantic?* They would've just hatched."

"Well, maybe not gigantic—at first, but still pretty damned big."

"Okay," I said. "We'll swing by the trailer, and if none of the Cossack's goons are waiting for me—"

"Us," she said.

"Right. Us. If it's all clear, we'll look for Zeke. I can grab some clothes, assuming they don't smell too bad, and then we'll get something to eat."

Jinks delivered a light punch to my shoulder. "I need clean clothes, too, y'know."

"Fair enough. We'll swing by your house as well." I had a sudden epiphany. "We could bathe *together*. Think of the time we'd save!" *Think of the fun we—*

"Oh, that's absolutely brilliant," she said. "I can see it now: Mom and Dad get home from their conference just in time to catch us soaping each other up in the shower. I'd be grounded for life, and you'd bleed out in the bathtub. Dad's a good shot; he wouldn't miss. And he wouldn't mind having to find a new photographer."

"So, separate showers then?"

"Duh!"

"You realize it'll be suppertime before we're done."

That earned me another slug on the shoulder, but I could see she felt better knowing we had a plan.

That alone can make life a lot easier, even if the plan is vague. Sometimes, vague is good. Vague was especially good when it had anything to do with Zeke's insect pals.

~*~

Jon called his office the following morning and checked in with Cecelia Martin, Augusta Burnside's oft belittled AA. Bureaucratic legend suggested that some administrative aides were so loyal they'd take a bullet for their boss. When Cecelia put him on a brief hold, he ruminated about whether she'd do that for Burnside. Probably, he decided. *I sure as hell wouldn't. Cecelia's definitely a better person than I am.*

"Hey, stranger," she said when she came back on the line. "I'm glad to hear you're still alive."

"Gee, thanks."

"Now, what's this we hear about you shootin' some folks in a parking lot? That really got your boss's knickers in a knot. I could hear her carryin' on even though her office door was closed."

Jon explained the situation, filling in particulars that probably weren't included in whatever report was sent to Burnside. Cecelia seemed satisfied with that.

"Question: is there a set of encyclopedias in the research room?"

"I think so," she said. "I only go in there if I'm looking for someone. Why?"

"I was hoping you could look something up for me. Ever heard of a quokka?"

"A crock of what?"

He chuckled, then spelled it for her. "It's an animal. From Australia."

"Well, of course it is."

He imagined her shaking her head.

"What do you need to know about them?" she asked.

"I need to know if they're carnivorous."

"Seriously? What on Earth—"

"Trust me. It's important. I'll explain later."

"You'd better."

"Thanks, Cecelia. You're the best."

"And you're still full of shit."

"Aw, you say the sweetest things."

"You want me to go check now, while you wait, or call you back?"

"Now would be nice, but if you're terribly busy—"

"Hang on," she said.

He heard the phone hit her desk and her footsteps fading away. He checked his watch, saw that it was nearly lunchtime, and hoped Regina Hornsby, his contact at the local paper, would be on the job. He still needed to connect with Denver Stow, assuming he remained alive. Cecelia returned within minutes.

"You owe me," she said.

"What'd you find out?"

"Seriously, Jon. I wouldn't do this for just anybody."

"I know." He grinned, even though she couldn't see him. "How 'bout I take you out for dinner somewhere? You choose the place."

"You've got a deal, and don't be thinkin' I'll be satisfied with a burger. Now, you ready for the answer to your quokka question?"

"Yes!"

"They're herbivores."

"Okay; that's a huge relief," he said, then wondered if Dawn Popkin and her hubby had upgraded their version of the critter to something that preferred meat, preferably raw.

~*~

By the time Jinks and I got cleaned up and wolfed down a couple peanut butter and jelly sandwiches, I realized my daily check-in at the Granville *Gazette* was overdue. I prayed no one had found something for me to photograph.

Since Jinks' dad wasn't back in the office yet, I called Regina. She sounded out of breath when she answered. "Denver—thank God! I've been trying to reach you."

"Because I'm getting a raise?"

"Fat chance. Listen, I need you to take some photos."

"Imagine that." I hoped she didn't hear me sigh.

"I just listened to the weirdest call on the police scanner. Something very, *very* strange happened at the home of... Well, our mutual friend, if you get my drift."

Though I had a good idea what and who she was talking about, I played dumb. "You mean the Cossack?"

"Yeah."

"And the weird part?" *Please don't be anything about baby Hydes!*

"It was in response to a 911 call. Apparently, some people were hurt by..." She paused, probably for dramatic effect.

"By what?"

"Giant spiders."

Damn! "Giant spiders? You're kidding, right?"

"Spiders. Tarantulas. Something like that. I'm heading that way now. Can you meet me there?"

"I'll have to swing by the trailer and grab my camera."

"I thought you never left home without it."

"Yeah, well—"

"Just get there as soon as you can."

~*~

Jon opened the front door to the Granville *Gazette* building just as a slender woman with dark hair, a notepad, a purse, and a determined look on her face emerged.

"Thanks," she mumbled as she dug frantically in her handbag for something. He suspected keys.

"Hey!" he called out before she got too far away. "Do you know if Regina Hornsby is working today?"

The woman paused and turned toward him, her expression having shifted from resolute to suspicious. "Who wants to know?"

Jon flashed his badge and introduced himself.

"I'm Regina," she said. "But I'm in a huge hurry. Can this wait?"

"I really need to talk, and it shouldn't take long. I'm trying to find a guy you work with."

Regina checked her watch. "Seriously, this is a really bad time. Can't we—"

"This could be a life-or-death situation," Jon said. "I'm not kidding."

She aimed both eyes skyward and took a deep breath, then looked at him again. "Fine. Who're you looking for?"

"Denver Stow."

"Our staff photographer?"

"That's my understanding," Jon said.

"I just got off the phone with him. He didn't sound the least bit worried. Why should he? Is he in some kind of trouble?"

"It's kind of a long story. Do you know where he is?"

"No," she said. "But I know where he'll be." She gave him the address which he jotted down on his palm.

"What's the big rush, if you don't mind my asking."

She appeared to be debating whether to say anything, so Jon reminded her of his status as an agent of the federal government. "I think you'll be safe telling me."

"I got a report of people being hurt under really bizarre circumstances. I'm going to check it out, and I asked Denver to join me with his camera."

"Define 'bizarre,'" Jon said.

She continued to look indecisive, but only for a moment. "It involves insects. Very large insects."

Jon felt his pulse quicken. He had to find Dawn Popkin, fast. But he also had to reach out to Denver Stow. "Go," he said, raising his palm and pointing at it. "I'll catch up with you here."

"Whatever," the woman said, once again scurrying toward a row of parked cars. "Try not to get in the way."

~*~

"C'mon, Jinks—we've gotta go!" I felt pretty sure all females were born with a dawdle gene, instantly activated by the need to go someplace quickly. Jinks proved it.

"What's the hurry? Zeke isn't going anywhere," she said.

"First, I need to get my camera. Then we need to find him. After that, we've got to head over to the Cossack's house."

She looked at me as if I'd sprouted antlers and a rhino horn. "What the hell for? Haven't we had enough of that butthead and his creepy stormtroopers?"

"Yes and no," I said.

She squinted at me. "Sometimes, Denver, you drive me absolutely—"

"I think Hyde's eggs hatched. Regina told me. She wants photos. She—"

Jinks didn't wait to hear any more; she was already jogging toward the car. Hoodie's car.

"Wait!" I yelled after her.

"What? I thought you were in a hurry."

"I am. It's just— What'll happen if someone there recognizes Hoodie's car?"

"I dunno," she said. "Tell 'em we borrowed it?"

"Hoodie's dead."

She shrugged. "Well then, he can't object, can he?"

In the face of such unassailable truth, I caved. Between grabbing my Nikon and luring Zeke out of the woods, I figured I had maybe twenty minutes to come up with an alternative.

Jinks put her hand on my arm as I started the car. "Hold on a sec," she said and opened the passenger-side door.

"Where are you going?" I asked.

"I'm not going anywhere near the Cossack's house without a king size can of bug spray."

Chapter Thirty-four

"There may be more poetry in justice than justice in poetry." –George Will

After a short drive to Shady Grove, Jinks and I scoured the area for anything that might signal the presence of an arm-breaker or two. Or ten. Who knew? At the last go-round, there were four.

"Looks clear to me," Jinks said.

I agreed and parked as close to my trailer as I could get. We got out and parted ways; I went to dig out my camera while Jinks went in search of Zeke. We should have stayed together. Zeke was in the trailer watching a Spanish soap opera with the sound off. He barely looked up when I walked in.

"Find any more of Hyde's eggs?" I asked.

He pointed toward the tiny space which represented my bedroom. "In box," he said.

I didn't immediately remember having any boxes in there and put off investigating until I'd let Jinks know I'd connected with Zeke. I stuck my head outside and called her. She responded right away, and I headed for the bedroom.

The only thing even vaguely box-like was my clothes hamper. I couldn't help but laugh at the memory of Jinks dumping out the contents so she could look for something suitably nasty to use as gags on Hoodie and Thug Two.

But who brought it back inside? I certainly hadn't, and I doubted Jinks had, either. I carried it into the main room and set it down beside Zeke. "This box?" I asked.

"Keep closed. Keep eggs dark."

Since I'd hidden my camera in it, I began to lift the lid to get it out. Zeke suddenly became agitated. "No! No open!"

Zeke only raised his voice in dire circumstances, so I put my hands on the lid, palms flat. "No problem. I can tie it in place if it'll make you feel better."

I'm not sure he understood my words, but when I hooked a couple belts together and cinched them tight around the hamper, he seemed satisfied. Jinks arrived as I secured the buckle.

"Geez! How many eggs did he find?" she asked.

It didn't feel heavy when I brought it in. I looked at Zeke. "Is this full of eggs?"

He gave me a puzzled look, which wasn't all that unusual.

"I don't think he knows how to count," Jinks said.

"Will you please take him out to the car? I'll get my camera out once he can't see me. And I'll count the eggs, too."

She put her hands on her hips and aimed pouty lips at me. "He can hear us talking, y'know."

"He's more interested in the TV." As if to confirm it, I pointed at the screen where a voluptuous brunette was busy throwing dishes at some guy who'd obviously stepped over the line, and into something stinky. *Poor schlub.*

Jinks dragged Zeke away from the TV set and out to the car. When the coast was clear, I retrieved my Nikon and took note of the two slipper-sized eggs nestled in my dirty laundry.

I resecured the belts, carried the hamper out to the car, and put it in the back seat with Zeke.

"Time to go," I said.

Jinks put her hand on my arm. "Is this smart? I mean, taking Zeke with us?"

I smiled and replied as honestly as I knew how. "God, I sure hope so."

~*~

Jon went straight to Dawn Popkin's rural home, praying that she had not yet packed up everything and moved. He didn't relish the thought of trying to track her down without the benefit of a forwarding address.

Much to his relief, she was outside, loading boxes into the back of a van. He turned into the long drive and cruised up to a spot just behind her vehicle.

She watched him while he parked and walked toward her. She looked distinctly unhappy. "I told you everything I know. So why don't you just leave me alone?"

"I'm thinking—hoping really—that you left something out when we last spoke. Maybe the rum in our tea had something to do with it."

"Are you implying that I drugged you?" she asked.

"No, of course not. It's just— I couldn't get over what you said about your husband somehow creating huge bugs."

"Scorpions. Mostly," she said, like a grade school teacher correcting a wayward pupil. "Similar in overall appearance, but definitely not the same."

"Right. So, what if some of them got loose?"

"Impossible." She shook her head in a firm no. "We were more than careful. Bobby was positively manic when it came to securing our specimens. Besides, we only had one that was still alive at the time."

"I see. And how careful were the cleaners?"

"How should I know? They chased us out, remember? Didn't bother to ask about our security protocols, our experiments in progress, or anything else. They flashed a copy of that damned letter from your boss, Bridgeburner—"

"Burnside."

"Whatever. But if your hired stormtroopers let anything escape, that's on them, not me."

Jon nodded. "I'm thinking that's exactly what happened. They not only let one of your creations escape, they were killed by it and...."

"And what?"

"Eaten," he said. "Is that even possible?"

Her expression shifted from bitterness to concern, and her cheeks betrayed a thin flush of red. She gave him a slight nod. "That's possible. Well, actually, it's...."

"Go on," he said.

"Quite likely."

Jon mulled over her response. He'd suspected a connection between the missing cleaners and the bug attack Regina Hornsby told him about. Popkin's remarks felt like a confirmation. Of sorts.

She eyed him with doubt. "What is it *you're* not telling me?"

"There's been an incident near here. I'm told a

number of very large insects invaded a home and hurt several people." He hoped for a reaction of some kind, but she maintained a neutral look, so he continued. "You said there was only one of the big scorpions alive when the cleaners came. Was it pregnant at the time?"

She shook her head. "It's doubtful."

"Then how could it reproduce? How could it have gotten pregnant and generated a bunch of slightly smaller monsters?"

That scored a reaction: the return of the disdainful educator. "Have you ever heard of parthenogenesis?"

"Maybe. In high school. But I can guess what it means." He started back toward his car. "I'd like you to come with me. I can't force you, but I'd love to have an expert with me when I inspect the bug carnage."

"Without a seeker to control the creatures, there's not much I could do," she said.

Jon smiled. "Give me a break. You know more about them than anyone else on the planet. I suspect you'll have some thoughts on what to do. Or would you rather see more people get hurt?"

Popkin appeared hesitant, then wheeled around and shut the doors of her van. "Let me get my purse. Then I'll join you."

Finally, thought Jon. *Progress.*

~*~

Jinks and I arrived at the Cossack's spacious lake estate but decided not to pull into the driveway. We just didn't want to chance having someone recognize Hoodie's car. Instead, we parked on the road leading up to the estate and walked the rest of the way.

The two rottweilers that greeted me the last time I was there seemed to have gone on vacation. In their place we found two ambulances, three cop cars, and a firetruck. No one seemed to be doing anything.

I spotted Regina talking to an EMT and taking notes. At Jinks' prodding, we ambled over to her. By the time we got there, the EMT was walking away, shaking his head.

"I've got good news and bad news," she said.

"Bad first," Jinks said. "Dad says it's best to get it out of the way so we can appreciate the good news."

Regina frowned, but nodded. "The cops don't think anyone survived, although one of the firemen said he thinks there's a safe room inside. They haven't figured out how to tell if anyone's in it. I only have a vague understanding of how they work, but I'm not leaving here until somebody figures it out."

"How many people were in the house?" I asked.

"We don't know yet. The police are calling it an active crime scene, meaning whoever or whatever did the killing is still inside. They've called in some specialists. They found three bodies outside, however. Two of them were dogs, big ones."

"And the good news?" I asked.

"It looks like this could be the end of the Cossack's gang."

Jinks narrowed her eyes at Regina. "They got him, too? Are you sure?"

"No. Once the bodies are recovered, they'll begin the process of having them identified. But there's one that's already been recognized, and that came as a complete surprise. Well, a surprise to some folks."

Jinks and I simply stared at her, waiting for more, but she turned away at the sound of a gurney being wheeled toward one of the ambulances. The body wasn't completely covered, and I got a bit of a shock.

"Oh, geez," I breathed. "It's Weiner."

"Can't say as I'm terribly surprised," said Regina. "I had my suspicions about him."

Quite unexpectedly, one of the three garage doors opened, and the Cossack's Lamborghini rumbled through. People scattered to get out of the way, and two of the cops pulled their guns, as if bullets could stop a speeding sportscar.

Jinks and I were standing far to one side, away from most of the uniforms, but I instinctively stepped in front of her. Human shield, right?

The scream of the car's engine suggested the

driver had jammed the accelerator to the floor, and it looked certain to smash into the fire truck. But then it veered sharply toward the lake.

Instead of standing back and watching, like Regina, Jinks, and I, the firemen and EMTs rushed after the car as it careened into the water.

We would have joined them, but just then a car we hadn't seen before cruised up the drive from the main road. Regina recognized at least one of the occupants when they got out and waved for the couple to join us, away from the rescue efforts by the lake. By that time, the car was largely submerged.

Regina addressed the man and pointed at me. "This is Denver Stow, the young man you were looking to find because his life was in danger. He doesn't appear particularly threatened to me."

The man introduced himself and his companion, Dawn Popkin, a woman old enough to be his grandmother. Jinks and I exchanged looks; we had no idea why anybody other than the Cossack's hoods would be looking for me.

While the man—some kind of federal agent— told me about Malindi Moore's concerns for my well-being, Regina and the Popkin woman engaged in a conversation of their own. I'm pretty sure Jinks tried to follow both chats simultaneously, though once she heard Malindi's name mentioned she ignored the two women.

"I'm no longer worried about being the victim of a gangland slaying," I told the man. "From what I hear, the gang in question is most likely out of business."

"Permanently," added Jinks. "They just haven't brought all the bodies out yet."

"I see," he said. "Listen, don't go away. I need to speak with whoever's in charge, but I'll be back."

I pointed toward the lake. "Just about everybody is down there, but they don't look like they're doing anything."

Agent Fitzgerald gestured toward all of us. "Please. Stay here. I'll be back as quick as I can."

We waited, mostly in silence, while he conversed with a few of the first responders gathered near the spot where the Lamborghini went into the lake. When he returned, we gathered close to hear what he had to say.

"They've decided not to do anything more until they have a tow truck to haul the car out of the water and someone from an industrial pest control company who can take care of the bugs in the house."

"That's ridiculous," said Popkin. "Half of those men are armed. The bugs aren't bulletproof. But if they're going to spray, they damn well better use a flamethrower."

"How do you know all this?" Jinks asked.

The woman smiled at her. "Because my husband and I created them."

"And what about whoever is in the car in the

lake?" I asked.

The agent responded. "One of the fire and rescue guys dove in and checked on him shortly after the car sank. He said the man behind the wheel was already dead. The doors were locked, otherwise he'd have dragged him out."

"I'm going down to the lake and interview some of those guys," Regina said, looking directly at me. "Get any photos you can. I'll touch base with you in a little while."

"Well, I'm not waiting around," Popkin said. She grabbed the agent's arm. "Get your gun out, podnuh. We're goin' in."

Chapter Thirty-five

"Life will be interesting only when there is an element of surprise in it." –Hamsalekha

"When we get in there," Popkin told the agent. "Shoot anything bug-like that's bigger than a shot glass."

"My aim's not that good," he said.

"Unless I'm seriously mistaken, you'll only have to hit one, and it'll be plenty big enough. Just make sure you aim to kill."

Jinks stepped in front of them. "How do you know there's only going to be one? There were a lot of eggs—"

"Jinks!" I yelped, but it was too late; the cat—

okay, the *eggs*—were out of the bag.

Popkin stared at Jinks as if she could read her mind. "How do you know there were a lot of eggs?"

The agent gave me the same mind-reader look. "We're not going anywhere until you two fess up."

"It's not really a long story," I lied. "We just sorta found 'em, and then some of the Cossack's guys stole them. They must've taken them to their boss." I stabbed a thumb in the direction of the house. "In there."

"*Where* did you find them?" Popkin asked. "And this is critical: are there any more?"

"That we haven't found? I doubt it," Jinks said, adroitly dodging the question. "But that's beside the point. What makes you think there's only one scorpion inside the building?"

"Hie-Duffs are carnivorous; they're also driven by self-interest. It's the only way I can express it. When they hatch, unless it's under tightly controlled circumstances including low light and cool temperatures, they come out not just hungry, but ravenous. Then, once their initial appetite is satisfied, they turn on each other until there's only one left alive—the alpha."

The agent then asked her, "Have they had enough time to reach that stage?"

"Probably," she said. "But, there's only one way to find out. I just wish we had a seeker. It would make the search much less dangerous."

"The quokka-thing?" asked the agent.

"Yes. Well, the quokka *derivative*."

"A quacker?" Jinks asked, ignoring my elbow in her ribs. "So, a duck?"

Popkin chuckled. "They're mammals dear, not birds. And they're adorable, despite the job they were designed to do."

"Which is what, exactly?" I asked.

"Suffice it to say they work in conjunction with a Hie-Duff. Beyond that, they're dependent on each other. The seekers select food for the Hie-Duff; in turn, the Hie-Duff feeds the seeker. In fact, what the Hie-Duff dispenses is the only thing a seeker can properly digest."

Jinks and I shared a look, and I nodded. "Do they, by any chance, have six legs?" she asked.

The question stunned Popkin at first, but then she reached out and gripped Jinks by the shoulders. "You've *seen* one!"

I put a restraining hand on the woman's arm. "He's in the car."

Her eyes went wide. "Go get him," she said. "*Now!*"

We passed a cop on our way back to the car. He had a determined look on his face as he marched toward Popkin and Fitzgerald, the federal agent.

"This could solve our problems, you know?"

Jinks frowned. "If you mean giving up Zeke to somebody we don't know anything about, then yeah, I guess it does. But who's going to take care of him? Protect him? Some bozo from the government?"

I pondered those questions as we continued toward the car. Somewhere in the back of my mind I hoped Zeke might actually answer them for us. Though I was slightly winded when we reached our destination, Jinks didn't seem the least bit out of breath. At least, not until she pulled the car door open and looked inside.

"He's gone," she said.

I caught up with her and did my own inspection. "Crap! Where could he be?"

She shrugged. "Good question. And here's another one: what'll we tell those two back at the house?"

~*~

"I don't have a good feeling about this," Jon said. "We don't know anything about those kids. We don't know if they're lying. We don't know—"

Popkin shushed him. "We know everything we need to know. If they've got a seeker, none of the rest matters. We can—"

"Agent Fitzgerald?"

Jon and Popkin turned to face a cop. Overweight and winded from his walk up the hill to the house, he paused to catch his breath before speaking. "I called the chief and told him you intended to enter the house before we've cleared it. He didn't like the idea at all. Not one little bit. He put me on hold while he called your office and spoke to some woman in charge up there in Nashville."

"Augusta Burnside," Jon said. *Oh, just great. Just freakin' fabulous. Burnside's going to screw up everything.*

"Burnside, yeah. I believe that's what he said."

"And?"

"He told her about the situation here, with the bugs and bodies and all. After that, she told the chief you were free to do whatever in hell needed doin' to wrap up your investigation, but she didn't say anything specific about what you were lookin' into. The chief didn't like it, but he told me to give you the go-ahead."

Jon reined in his surprise, until he put the warped pieces of Burnside's logic together. *If the bugs made the cleaners disappear, she's probably betting they'll do the same to me.*

"There's another thing," the cop said. "One of the fire and rescue guys thought there was a safe room in the house. We didn't know if anyone was in it or not until someone called 911 from inside a little while ago. They refused to come out until the coast was clear. The 911 operator told him it would be a while."

Jon thanked him for the update and watched him head back down the hill. "Look who's coming back," he said. "Denver and the girl— What's her name?"

"Jinks, I think," Popkin said.

"Yeah. They're hiking back up the drive, but I don't see them carrying anything. Do you?"

Popkin grimaced. "No, damn it."

When the empty-handed teens finally arrived, Jon made no effort to hide his displeasure. "So, where's the quokka?"

"Seeker," Popkin interjected.

"We don't know," the boy said. "We left him in the car and told him to stay there."

"You *told* him to stay there? Like you expected him to understand you?"

"Seekers are incredibly smart," Popkin said. "Billy thought they were on the verge of communicating with us."

"How?"

"Verbally."

"Zeke's not much of a conversationalist," the boy said. "But, yeah, he can talk."

"Well, did he leave you a note saying where we might bump into him? You know, in case someone needed his help?" Jon couldn't keep the snarky tone out of his voice, nor did he care.

The girl responded in kind. "Nobody ever told us we were supposed to teach him to read and write."

"We've got to find him," Popkin said. "If what these two say is true, it's more important than ever. This could be the scientific breakthrough of the century."

"Let's not get ahead of ourselves," Jon said.

"You're right." She nodded at the house. "Hie-Duff. You ready?"

Jon pulled his sidearm and jacked a shell into the chamber. "You kids stay here."

"Change of plan," Popkin said, laying a hand on his arm. "If there's a Hie-Duff still alive, you can't shoot it."

Jon gawked at her. "Are you crazy? Of course I'll shoot it. Like you said, 'anything bigger than a shot glass.'"

"No, you can't! That's all changed now. I need it to feed the seeker."

"His name's Zeke," the boy said.

"Don't you dare shoot him either," said the girl.

"If he does, honey," Popkin said, pointing at Jon. "I'll shoot him!"

"I'm going with you," said the boy. "They pay me to get photos."

"They don't pay you to get killed," the girl said.

"She's right," said Jon. "But I wouldn't let you go in there under any circumstances." He turned toward the lake. "Look, the tow truck's here. Why not go and take pictures of the car, or whoever's in it?"

~*~

Jinks did her best to pacify me as we walked down the drive toward the lake. I had multiple questions spinning around in my head along with the names of people I'd just met—people who simply assumed they could take charge. They acted as if they knew better about everything, and yet they had to ask Jinks and I questions because they damn sure *didn't* know everything.

"Come on, Denver," yelled Regina, surrounded by first responders. "I need you and your camera down here, now!"

"I'm coming," I shouted back, then glanced at Jinks. "I suppose you think that FBI guy and the old lady are right."

"I don't think they're completely wrong," she said. "I just don't want to see you get hurt."

"And what about Zeke?"

"We feel the same way about him. You know that, so don't make me out to be the bad guy here. The thing is, we may not be able to take care of him. He needs Hyde, or one of Hyde's babies in order to survive. We can't feed him ourselves. And even if we could, are you ready to spend the rest of your life hiding them from the world?"

I was too busy wallowing in my own—what? Self-righteousness? Pity? Anger? I didn't want to admit she might be right. But damn it, Zeke was a part of *our* world, an important part. If not for him, Jinks and I would never have gotten together. Wasn't that worth something? Wasn't that worth protecting? Maintaining?

Not if the secret agent and his scientist lady friend had anything to do with it.

"Denver!" Regina yelled again. "Today!"

"I'm coming. Geez. Hold your horses."

"She's just doing her job," Jinks said.

"Well, it sounds like she's trying to do mine."

"Just take the dadburn pictures, okay?" She followed that with a light shove, and then jogged ahead, forcing me to try and keep up.

We reached the shore of the picturesque pond as the tow truck pulled the Lamborghini out. Once they had it on shore, the same cop who'd talked to the agent leaned down and peered into the interior of the car. He shook his head, turned to those around him and said, "The bug's dead, too. Looks like he got squished between the driver and the steerin' wheel."

One of the first responders then attacked the driver-side door with a crowbar, a terrible thing to do to a fancy car like that. Lake water gushed out as the rescue worker finally got the door open, and a trio of EMTs stepped forward to remove the body of the man behind the wheel and the bug that killed him.

I moved in as close as I could without getting in their way and managed to get a couple decent shots of them in action. Once they got the body clear, they placed it on a stretcher and prepared to carry it up to the pavement.

That's when I got my first good look at him, and recognition lit me up.

"No, no, no, no!" I screamed.

Jinks grabbed me with both arms. "What is it? What's the matter?"

I struggled to find the words. Stupid, simple words. "It's... He's my father!"

Chapter Thirty-six

"I'm an optimistic believer in good deeds, surprise endings, and the pleasant twists of life." –Josh Walker

As Jon and Dawn Popkin approached the house, he began to sweat. "This is absolutely the dumbest damned thing I've ever done. And that's saying a lot. I have no idea how we're going to capture this bug of yours. So don't be surprised if I end up shooting it after all. I'm not willing to sacrifice either of us because you think you've discovered something spiffy."

"Spiffy?"

Jon could almost feel her disdain.

"We should enter via the garage," she said.

"Why?"

"Because there's a lake out there. And a dock. And a boat. I'm guessing if the owner of this place went to all the trouble of having a lake installed, since they don't occur naturally in these parts, then he's probably stocked it with fish."

"Okay," Jon said. "But, so what?"

"Fishermen usually have nets. My husband did, and he kept them in the garage."

A mixture of relief and embarrassment coursed through him as he searched the three-car garage for fishing gear. He found it in a cabinet emblazoned with a huge decal of a rainbow trout.

"Clever hiding place, no?" observed Popkin.

Jon ignored her and plucked two large fishing nets out of the cabinet and handed one to her. "Think these will do?"

"They should. We have the advantage. The Hie-Duff doesn't know we're coming. Normally, he attacks with the element of surprise. Now, it's just the reverse."

"You're still assuming there's only one."

"True. But it wouldn't be the first time I was wrong. So, we'd best proceed with caution."

Jon made a modest show of his handgun. "If one of us gets jumped," he said, "I'm not waiting to ask about his intentions."

"Cowboys," she muttered as she walked

toward the door into the house.

"Wait up," he called, but she didn't respond, or slow down. He hurried to catch up.

They entered the building's basement which housed an array of cardboard boxes and two, plain tables. The workspace was littered with tiny plastic bags both filled and empty, a pair of drug scales, and little else. Jon had expected to find bodies, and felt more than a little relief when there weren't any.

"There's little doubt what went on in here," he said. He walked past Popkin and led the way up the stairs to the main floor.

"Oh, my land," Popkin gasped when she stepped past him and got a good look at the carnage in the room.

Unlike the basement, the main floor had been tastefully decorated, but it wasn't the art or furniture which caught their eyes. It was the eight dead bodies scattered about the room. In addition to them, the remains of several shoe-sized scorpions dotted the floor. There were bullet holes everywhere, and Jon surmised that some of the dead may have fallen victim to friendly fire as shooters opened up in fear.

"I'm tempted to do body counts—people *and* bugs—but I have no idea how many of either were in the house." He toed the remains of a scorpion for emphasis.

"Neither of those two kids gave us a bug count," Popkin said. "My guess is they didn't know, so we need to count as we go. I'll tally the Hie-duffs."

They searched the rest of the house and found more bodies of both species, more bullet holes, and more evidence of a massive struggle. Or, more likely, evidence of chaos and panic.

When they ran out of places to search, Jon suggested they turn the scene over to the local authorities.

Popkin agreed. "My guess is the last Hie-Duff was after the man who tried to escape in the car." She waved her hand at the horrific scene in the house. "You can easily imagine how intense the battle was. Hie-Duffs don't give up."

"Hello?"

Both turned in surprise at the sound of a new voice. Jon had his gun raised, and his sights trained on a meek-looking individual who somehow appeared out of thin air.

"Who the hell are you?" Jon demanded, still keeping his gun aimed squarely at the newcomer's chest. "And where did you come from?"

"In there," the man said, moving a bookcase aside to reveal a hidden entryway. "I've been in the safe room."

~*~

Jinks and Regina guided me back up the drive to the front of the house where I sat on the broad steps under a portico. I was still in shock, unable to process anything either of them said to me. Jinks had my camera; I had no idea when or where I'd let go of it. The camera had always been my lifeline to reality and my freeway to escape when I needed it. Right then, it was just a chunk of expensive hardware I didn't know what to do with.

"You're sure it's your father?" Regina asked.

I nodded.

I felt Jinks' arm around my shoulder. She kept saying how sorry she was, as if she were somehow responsible.

"He can't be the Cossack," I blubbered, clutching Regina. "Remember? We found out that the car—the Lamborghini—was registered to somebody named Doobin, the same last name as Jinks' cross-country coach. D-o-o-b-i-n. Doobin. Not Stow!"

"We don't know for sure that he was the Cossack," Jinks said. "We shouldn't jump to conclusions."

"If he wasn't, why was he in the Cossack's car? Or the Cossack's garage? Or his house?"

Regina didn't add anything, and we sat there for what seemed forever though my time sense was shot to hell along with my ability to be rational. I knew I had to let my mother know, but I just wasn't ready. I had no idea how she would react. It wasn't that Dad and I were ever close. We weren't. I can't remember a time when we were. But still, he *was* my father. And if he was also the Cossack—something I still couldn't believe—then he was the one extorting me, and possibly the one who wanted me dead.

It was all too much to process, too much insanity all at once. I didn't need to add Mom's probable reaction to the mix. Not yet, anyway.

Eventually, the federal agent with whom I'd grown increasingly frustrated, and Popkin, his elderly scientist pal, exited the building. They walked on either side of a short, fat, pale man who looked as if he were on his way to the gallows.

The agent summoned the cop in charge and told him the house was safe to enter. As far as they could tell, there were no more giant bugs. He also took credit for "rescuing" the guy who'd holed up in the safe room. We scooted to the side of the steps as the EMTs, fire and rescue guys, and most of the cops, lined up and went through the front door.

Regina stood and walked over to the agent and Popkin, who continued to hold up the man from the safe room. She briefly chatted with them before motioning for me to join them.

She pointed at the little man. "Tell my young friends here what you just told us."

His lip trembled as if he were facing a monster. "I— I'm just an accountant. I worked for Mr. Stow. I kept the books, that's all. I never hurt anybody. I'm not like some of those guys." He nodded at the dead hoodlum two EMTs were busy removing from the house.

"So," Regina began, "you're saying Mr. Stow was the Cossack?"

"Yes. He made all the big deals—drugs and stuff."

"Then who the hell was Doobin?" I asked.

"Doobin?" The guy scratched his head. "Oh, him. He came around every once in a while to work on that fancy car. Stow bought it from Doobin's father or his uncle; I'm not sure which. Somebody said he was a coach of some kind at the high school. I think he was just trying to earn some tax-free cash. Stow had a lot of that; couldn't spend it fast enough."

"And Detective Weiner?" Regina asked. "What was he doing here?"

"He was in charge of collecting money from uhm... debtors. He kept his own books. Insisted on it. I had nothing to do with him."

I couldn't keep quiet. I had to stand up for my fellow debtors and all the other poor schlubs Weiner intimidated. "It never occurred to you to do something about him? About *all* of this? You couldn't have called the cops, or the FBI?"

"I didn't know anything about..." He shut up and took a deep breath. "I want a lawyer. I'm not saying another word. I know my rights. I know—"

I shouldn't have punched the little weasel, but I couldn't help myself. All my anger came out at once. He folded around my fist, which landed squarely in the middle of his soft, bulging belly. It felt like hitting an overstuffed pillow. And it felt really, really good.

Jinks pulled me away before I could hit him

again, and suddenly I felt drained, light-headed.

"Let's go look for Zeke," she whispered. "He's got to be around here somewhere."

"Yeah, sure," I mumbled. "Zeke. Fine. Okay. Let's go." And then I stopped. I looked back over my shoulder at the guy who needed help in order to stand. A cop had joined them and was busy putting handcuffs on him.

"You're not an accountant," I told him. "You're a gutless asshole. A stupid, chicken-shit, spineless, shadow of a human. I've stepped in dog crap worth more than you!"

That at least got a smile from the agent.

I let Jinks pull me away, back down the hill toward the car. Hoodie's car. And that made *me* smile. We got them, before they got us. Well, the mini-Hydes did, and that was fine by me.

"What d'you suppose they're doing?" Jinks asked. She was staring at a cop aiming his gun at something in a section of heavy shrubbery near the water's edge. "Oh, geez! I hope it's not Zeke."

We hurried toward the officer who looked up briefly at our approach.

"Stay back!" he cautioned, his voice loud and tense, "I think I spotted one of those big-ass roaches."

"It's probably not!" I yelled back. "We think it's—"

I stopped talking when he started shooting.

~*~

Jon and Dawn Popkin heard the gunshots and immediately turned their attention toward the lake, where the two teens argued with a police officer. All three were clearly angry.

"I've no idea what that's all about," Jon said, "but we probably ought to zip down there and investigate."

Popkin shook her head and moved quickly toward the agent's car. "I'm not in the mood to zip anywhere," she said. "So, get in and get going."

Jon backed down the drive and brought the car to a shuddering halt when they neared the confrontation beside the water. He jumped out of the vehicle and jogged toward the two livid teens and the blustering cop.

"I told you to get out of here," the cop yelled, though less than three feet separated his mouth from the boy's face. "It ain't safe here, damn it. Now git, before I put you in cuffs and throw your ass in jail."

"What's the problem, officer?" Jon asked.

"This here wise-ass kid is getting' in my way, tryin' to tell me how to do my damn job. I gotta good mind to—"

"Take a breath, officer," Jon said, his voice oddly calm amidst the chaos. "Denver here has been through a lot today. He lost a family member, and he's simply not quite himself. So, why don't you cut him a little slack?"

The cop took two steps back. "This here smart mouth didn't say nothin' about that. Just came racin' down here, yellin' at me to stop doin' my job." He pointed toward the thick brush. "There's somethin' pretty damned creepy in there, and I 'spect it's the same kinda critter that kilt everybody up in the house. I aim to shoot that sucker dead before it does any more damage."

He glared at the agent and pursed his lips. "Who the hell you think you are, anyway?"

"Show him your badge," Popkin said. "And then escort him away from here."

Thoroughly frustrated, the cop turned on her. "And who put you in charge? God? Nobody tells me nothin'!"

Jon gave him a reassuring smile along with a flash of his credentials, and waved him away from the water. "I'll explain up here," he said, though he had no idea what he was ready to reveal.

Chapter Thirty-seven

"Amateur bureaucrats are often even worse than professional bureaucrats." –John McCarthy

"Let's start over, shall we?" the old woman said. "It's Denver and Jinks, right?" She held out her hand and introduced herself. "There's no reason why we can't work together."

"I suppose," I said, but Jinks wasn't satisfied by my answer.

"This whole thing has gotten way out of hand," she said. "We need to tell her everything."

It wasn't what I wanted to hear, but I knew she was right. "Okay, I guess. But we need to find Zeke, or there'll be no point in saying anything."

"It's an interesting name you chose for the seeker," Popkin said.

"I didn't choose it," I said. "That's what he told me it was."

"He was talking when you found him?"

"Yes. But only a couple words. A handful, tops."

Jinks chimed in. "We spent most of the summer teaching him more words and how to put them together."

I stepped away and began searching the tall grass and undergrowth where the cop had been shooting. I dreaded what I might find. Jinks walked a few yards farther away and began her own search while Popkin stood back and watched.

"He's over here," Jinks said, her voice hushed.

"Is he okay?"

"I can't tell. He's all curled up. But he's alive. He's shivering."

Popkin reached her before I could, and the three of us knelt down in the boggy terrain, surrounding Zeke.

I swallowed hard just looking at the poor little guy. "Has he been shot?"

"I don't think so," Popkin said. "But let's get him out of here so I can look him over."

Jinks stayed our hands. "What about all the

people? The police and firemen? We can't let them see him. God only knows what they'd do. Shoot him, most likely. Maybe shoot us, too."

"Let's take him to the car," I said. "If I wrap him in my sweatshirt, no one will see what I'm carrying."

Popkin grimaced and appealed to Jinks. "Will you please help me up? I'm not as spry as you two."

We ambled toward the car, trying to appear nonchalant, as if I wasn't carrying an absolutely one-of-a-kind amazing creature. Zeke continued to tremble in my arms, and I whispered to him that he was going to be okay. "Don't worry," I said. "We'll take care of you. You'll be fine." I wanted to believe that. I most sincerely did.

Jinks got the back door of the car open and pushed the hamper out of the way. I gently lowered Zeke to the seat.

"Pardon me," Popkin said, pulling gently on my shoulder. She donned thick glasses and looked very serious. "I've worked with this seeker before. I think he trusts me."

After examining Zeke with what I thought were a few too many pokes and prods, she straightened up and pronounced him alive, if not entirely well. "He was clearly terrified by the gunshots, but I believe he's also suffering from a lack of food." She shook her head. "Sadly, there's not a thing we can do for him without a Hie-Duff."

"Nothing?"

She looked solemn. "I can prepare some nutrients that might tide him over for a while, feed him with an eyedropper. But eventually, unless he gets food from a Hie-Duff, he won't make it."

I could tell from the expression on Jinks' face that she shared my sorrow. We both knew what had to be done. "Miz Popkin, that hamper holds more than just my dirty clothes," I said. "There are a couple more eggs at the bottom of it."

Her eyes instantly grew wide, and she turned toward Jinks. "I thought you said—"

"I said I doubted there were any more that we hadn't found. I never said the Cossack's guys got 'em all."

"Then there's hope!"

Popkin's smile seemed authentic, but I still had reservations. "We're not going to give Zeke up just so some trigger-happy lawman can shoot him."

"Of course not, and I promise you, he'll be safe with me," she said. "He's going to love Wyoming."

We stared at her. "*Wyoming?* That's like—" I couldn't finish the thought.

But Jinks did. "—like on the other side of the world!"

"My family has owned a ranch out there for generations," she said. "And that's where I'm moving. Have you ever been to Wyoming?"

We admitted that neither of us had.

"Well then, when you come to visit the..." she paused. "When you come to visit *Zeke*, you'll be my guests. I have plenty of room. Hardly anyone lives in that state, and that's where Zeke will be safe with me. There's abundant wildlife, so the Hie-Duff won't be tempted to go after any people. No one, except the three of us, and Zeke of course, will even know he exists."

Suddenly I felt good, actually happy. Jinks had a smile on her face for the first time all day. And even though I'd lost my father and truly felt a measure of sadness, I couldn't forgive him for being a racketeer. I can't say I was choked up about the late Detective Weiner, either.

With the loss of their only detective, the local police chief asked if Jon could stay for a few days and assist his department with follow-up and everything connected to civil forfeiture laws. Though not well-versed in the area of government confiscation, Jon offered to do what he could to help. But his intentions weren't entirely noble. He welcomed additional time to finish his report and find a way to explain how government funds had been used to create monster insects which were accidentally released when the program was abandoned.

On the third day following the "Lake House Massacre," a designation coined by local reporter Regina Hornsby in the Granville *Gazetteer*, Jon received a call from Cecelia Martin.

Breathlessly she asked, "Heard the news?"

He laughed. "Anything in particular? This is pretty primitive territory, I admit, but the natives do still have access to the networks They even get Johnny Carson and the 'Tonight Show.'"

"I meant the news about Burnside."

The mere mention of the woman's name cast gloom. "No. What has our dear leader done now?"

"She got herself killed, that's what."

Burnside dead and gone? He had to work at not sounding gleeful. *"Dead?* That's... That's astonishing. What happened? Car wreck? Heart attack?" *Bludgeoned to death by ungrateful subordinates?*

"Bug bite," she said, then corrected herself, "bug *sting*, actually."

How the hell had one of Popkin's scorpions gotten to Nashville? As far as he knew, she was on her way to Wyoming. Had she stopped by the agency on her way?

"What kind of bug was it?" he asked, hoping she'd blame a hornet or a wasp.

"One of the guys here said he thought it was a scorpion. Then somebody else said, 'No, it can't be; it's too big.'"

"Where is it now? Did someone catch it?"

Cecilia snickered. "I caught it all right. Squashed him with an encyclopedia. It'd been sitting on my desk since you called and asked me to look up that crazy Australian animal. What was it again?"

"It's not important," he said. "Any idea how it got in her office?"

"It came air mail, special delivery, straight to her. The package had a warning label and a photo of the contents on the outside. When the Director saw the picture, she immediately unwrapped the thing and extracted what looked like a very pretty stone, 'bout the size of a big cucumber. Shaped that way, too. She said it reminded her of a moonstone, which I, frankly, had never heard of. Anyway, she put it on the shelf of her brag wall. You know, the one with all the photographs of her and the other bigwigs, her diplomas, citations, and what-not. She even adjusted the little spotlight she's got in the ceiling to highlight it."

"She put it on *display?*" He couldn't believe what he was hearing. "What about the warning notice?"

"I doubt she even read it. I'm tellin' you, once she saw the photo, she was all about getting her hands on the thing in the box."

"It must've been an egg."

"That's what the lab guys said, too." She exhaled. "Have you ever heard of anything so gosh darn bizarre?"

Jon just smiled. "No, Cecilia, can't say that I have."

When the call ended, Jon realized he had one more person he needed to contact. Malindi needed to know it was safe to come home. He wondered briefly what his mother would think if he started dating the blushin' Russian.

And then he realized, he couldn't care less.

Epilogue

"There are worse things in life than death. Have you ever spent an evening with an insurance agent?" –Woody Allen

Granville, Georgia—six months later.

Jinks and I have come to understand what "normal" means, but that understanding didn't come easy. Obviously, Zeke had a lot to do with it. Growing up had a lot to do with it, too.

There have been a great many changes—in Granville, and in our lives. Shady Grove no longer exists. It was bulldozed to make room for a strip mall. And speaking of stripping, the Sweet Dreamz Gentlemen's club has been converted into a car parts store.

The truck stop is still going strong, but both Babe's Burgers and the Sweet Dreams motel are operating under new management. I know because I covered the grand re-openings of each one.

But it wasn't because I needed the money. It turns out the one really decent thing my father did—other than get the old genetic ball rolling—was to make my mother and me beneficiaries of his life insurance policies. The double indemnity clauses were contested at first, but the insurance company gave in without much of a fight.

In other news, Coach Doobin quit H3 shortly after Miss Lovingood left him to work on her Master's Degree. He now runs an auto repair shop. Turns out he's a pretty decent guy, and he promised to help me keep my car running properly. It's a Lamborghini. I bought it when the county auctioned off some of Dad's property. (And Jinks taught me how to drive it!)

Jinks and I are still planning to get married, but we've decided to wait until she finishes college. She talked to Miss Lovingood who told her great things about Auburn. She applied, got accepted, and will be starting in the fall. I'll be joining her to begin my studies in cinematography.

We'll be spending some time in Wyoming this summer, too. Dawn Popkin wants us to come visit and check out her ranch. She said Zeke is doing well, but she thinks he spends way too much time watching soap operas on TV. She also said that since she doesn't have any heirs, she'd like to leave the ranch to Jinks and me when her time comes. But that's only if we fall in love with the place when we visit.

The nicest thing about our new version of "normal" is having enough time to think about things and enough money to do the ones we want to do.

Oh, and Zeke says hi!

About the Author

Josh Langston's fiction has been published in a variety of magazines and anthologies, and both his Christmas and Western short story collections have reached the Amazon Top 20 for genre fiction. His many novels are split primarily between historical fiction and contemporary fantasy.

Josh also loves to teach. His classes on novel writing, memoir, and independent publishing are  filled with students eager to learn and have their work perused by a pro. His textbooks on the craft of fiction, memoir, and novel writing provide a humorous and easy-to-understand approach to the subjects while imparting valuable tips and techniques. *Naked Notes!* is the fourth title in his textbook series. All of his books are available in both paperback and ebook formats.

If you are a member of a book club and would like to arrange a chat with Josh for your group, you may contact him at: **DruidJosh@gmail.com**. Be sure to visit his website, too: **JoshLangston.com**.

And now, turn the page for an added bonus:

Chapter One of **A Season Gone to the Dogs**, a story that shines new light on Santa Claus and the miracles he performs every year. Hint: he has plenty of help, and not just from elves and reindeer....

A Season Gone to the Dogs

Some
Things
You Never
Knew
About
Santa

Bestselling Author

JOSH
LANGSTON

Chapter One

"Sometimes an itch isn't just an itch. Sometimes, it means something." – Raymond Mays

Lawrence K. "Skeeter" Malone didn't care much for newspapers. Didn't care much for magazines, either. He owned a few comic books, but once he'd struggled through them the first time, a second reading held little appeal. So, it came as quite a shock to his mother, Gloria, when Skeeter brought her an article torn from the Casual Living section of the Sunday paper.

"We should do this, Mom," the ten-year-old announced, presenting the ragged newsprint for her inspection. The headline stood out like a warning beacon:

Pet Auditions Today

She gave him her best puzzled look. "What are the auditions for?"

"TV and movies," Skeeter said. "It doesn't say which ones. They wanna find cool new pets for commercials and stuff. We should take Tater. He could be a star!"

"You actually *read* the paper?" Gloria asked. Though pleased, she remained all too aware of Skeeter's evolving skill as a con artist.

"It's today!" he said eagerly. "Can we go?"

"Do you think Tater's up to it? He's not a puppy anymore." She didn't mention the obvious—Tater's missing leg—and assumed such a handicap would automatically put the aging pooch at a huge disadvantage. The missing limb never seemed to slow him down though. He'd even managed to learn to stand, albeit briefly, on one hind leg.

"Tater knows lots of tricks," Skeeter said. "He can do all kinds of stuff."

"I know. But let me read the article, okay? Then we'll talk about it."

Shaking her head in a mixture of wonder and puzzlement, Gloria quickly absorbed the details. There weren't many. A company called Leon Farms had put out the casting call and said they were interested in seeing any pets with "unusual talents." The article gave no specifics about what programs or films the casting was for, but made it clear that Leon Farms personnel would do any training required. They would need to keep any animals selected for several weeks. The audition was open to all non-aggressive species.

"How carefully did you read this, sweetie?"

He shrugged. "Pretty good, I guess."

"Would you be willing to give up Tater for a month or two if he's chosen?"

Skeeter's face clouded. "I dunno."

"That's part of the deal."

"Maybe I could visit him."

Gloria held out her hands, palms up. "We'd have to ask. The article doesn't say anything about that." *Or what the job might pay.*

The boy considered the issue for a moment longer. "We should go."

"You sure?"

"Yeah."

"It'll take an hour or so just to drive there, and we might have to stay a long time." She didn't mention that she'd planned to do some Christmas shopping despite the deficit they'd been operating under since the company she worked for had let her go due to budget cuts. This year, Christmas wasn't likely to be terribly jolly.

"It's important," Skeeter said. She wondered where he'd picked up the note of finality in his voice.

"Did Tater tell you that?"

"Aw, Mom." He managed to draw out the "Aw" to thrice its length. "I knew we'd have to talk first."

Gloria squinted at him, but the modified view did nothing to help her decide if the boy was serious or not. They both talked *to* the dog, but Skeeter often seemed to listen to him as well.

~*~

Maeve Blessing exhaled as if she'd finished a month's work and could finally take a much-needed break. "It just makes me angry," she said. "This is the last place in the world I'd expect to find a bully."

Artemis Maker, a co-worker, shook his head. "Don't you think you might be jumping to conclusions?"

"I certainly hope that's all it is." Maeve shook her head and sent a torrent of red curls swirling. "I hate it when things don't work out the way they're supposed to. Of all the auditions we've conducted, we've only found two possible candidates. By this time last year, we had to turn away lots of animals with way above average potential."

"That's a bit of an overstatement." Artemis smiled. "Some years it's easier, that's all. It doesn't mean there's a bully involved."

"You're not outside, meeting and greeting, like me. We made it very clear in the ads that people shouldn't bring mean animals. And yet, they keep showing up."

"Every time?"

"Well, no. Not every time, but often enough." She tried to bring her wild tresses under control. "There was this one lady who brought an alpaca, and—"

"Seriously? An alpaca?"

"Yes! An adorable creature with a smile that'd just melt your heart. It sure melted mine, and it would've made a superb hauler. Anyway, some jerk showed up with a monkey, or maybe it was a chimp. I'm no expert. Anyway, the monkey started throwing stones at the alpaca, and the owner couldn't, or wouldn't, get it to stop. Neither could I. It upset the alpaca so much she ran off. I presume her owner found her in one of the pastures, but she didn't bring her back. She just left. And I can't say I blame her."

"And the monkey?"

Maeve snorted. "Rejected. On the spot. I wouldn't give that little monster an audition if it cost me my job. I told his owner to leave and not come back. Ever."

"That sort of thing is bound to happen from time to time," Artemis said. "You can't always tell how an animal will react before it's been trained. And you shouldn't assume there's a bully to blame."

"Well, that monkey was certainly a bully."

"Perhaps. But you know what I meant. Bullies come in a variety of forms, and just because some critter acts like one—"

"Doesn't mean it is one, or worse, was sent by one. Yes, I know. I know. Still, it makes me wonder."

~*~

Leon Farms occupied several acres of rural land, most of it in pasture. In addition to a modest, one-story, wooden farmhouse, the property boasted several additional buildings. Of those, only a barn and a stable had obvious functions.

"Oh, cool!" Skeeter said when they arrived. He pointed at a swimming pool and some other equipment Gloria guessed was used for agility training—ladders, ramps, plastic tunnels, and jumps. She couldn't help but wonder how Tater would fare on such apparatus. Skeeter's enthusiasm only grew, while hers had rapidly begun to ebb.

"Hey there," said a smiling young woman with bright red hair. It contrasted well with the worn denim she'd dressed in from head to toe. The name tag on her shirt said, "Maeve." She held out a clipboard and pen for Gloria, then knelt to get acquainted with Skeeter and Tater.

"What kind of dog is he?" she asked.

"The best," Skeeter said without hesitation.

"Obviously," Maeve said. "And how old is he?"

"Ten. We're the same age."

Gloria couldn't help but frown. "Is that a problem?"

"Not necessarily," the girl replied. "We've taught new tricks to lots of old dogs."

"Tater's not old," Skeeter said, his tone adamant.

The girl merely smiled. "Once we've got Tater registered, you're free to wander around anywhere, except the barn. There's nothing dangerous or scary in there, but the insurance company says we have to keep it off limits." She stood and rubbed her palms then pointed at a squat, windowless building near the farmhouse. "We'll call you from over there when it's Tater's turn."

"What, exactly, would you like him to do?"

"We'll explain all that inside, but basically, we want to see if he obeys simple commands, and if he's comfortable in an unusual environment."

"He knows tricks," Skeeter said.

"Should we be rehearsing them?" Gloria asked.

"If you'd like," Maeve said. "Just don't wear him out."

For the next hour they wandered around the farm, waiting. A steady stream of pet owners filed into and out of the low building. Most of them brought dogs, but a handful had other animals. In addition to cats and birds, Gloria noticed a rabbit, an iguana, and a goat.

They found a spot of shade to wait in, and Skeeter tried to run Tater through his repertoire of tricks.

"I thought you wanted to do this," Skeeter said after the dog refused to sit, beg, or roll over on command. "We came all this way, and now you won't do anything. I'm disappointed in you."

The words sounded distressingly familiar to Gloria. She gazed at her son and his dog, wondering if the little canine would react like the boy did when he heard those same words.

Instead, Tater licked Skeeter's face.

"Maybe he needs to rest," Gloria said.

Skeeter wiped his face on his sleeve but didn't look convinced. "I just don't want him to mess up!"

Gloria didn't either, especially after reading a

note on the sign-up sheet that said pet owners would receive union scale wages for the entire time a contracted animal remained in the care of Leon Farms, Inc. She didn't know what "union scale" meant in dollars and cents, but whatever the amount, it would be a welcome and much-needed addition to her budget.

~*~

"Was it something I said?" The question Ormsby Ivanov asked hung in the air like the aroma from an overflowing sewer.

"I don't understand. You didn't—"

"Correct me if I'm wrong," Ormsby said from behind his expansive desk, "but I could have sworn I heard you laughing about a monkey and a llama."

"I think it was an alpaca."

"Whatever. The monkey annoyed the animal into running away, which is fine. But how many other pets did you manage to upset?"

The man's mouth opened, but no sounds came out. He cast about Ormsby's oversized office as if seeking an escape route.

Ormsby continued, "Your job was to prevent the best candidates from being selected. Surely the alpaca wasn't the only one in line."

"Well, no," the man began, "but—"

"But you were kicked off the property before you could proceed further, right?"

"I guess, but—"

"Another 'but?' Can't you tell I've heard enough of them?"

"I can explain! You don't know how hard it is to tell which ones will be good or bad."

Ormsby crossed his arms on his fat chest. "You said you could tell. Your words, as I recall, offered a guarantee."

"Yes, I know, but—"

"There it is. Another 'but.' Get out! You're done. Don't come back until you're called."

"Bu— Uh... I only did what you told me to do."

Ormsby stared down at the man whose worth paralleled that of some insignificant insect. "You failed."

Somehow the man summoned enough indignation to stiffen his spine. A sneer replaced his snivel, and he squinted back at his employer. "I'll bet the people responsible for that audition would like to know how much you paid me to cause trouble."

Ormsby shook his head and mimed a sad face. "The depth of your stupidity astonishes me. Such a pity. Fortunately, there's a cure." He signaled for Mordecai to take care of the miscreant who quickly backed up against a wall.

"Let's not get carried away," the man said.

"On the contrary," said Ormsby. "That's precisely what's going to happen."

Mordecai yanked the man away from the wall, wrapped his arms around him, and squeezed.

"You won't like doing penance," Ormsby said. "You won't care for the preparation either. Young Mordecai here is quite the wonder. I think of him as part man and part boa constrictor. Wouldn't you agree?"

Mordecai's prey opened his mouth to respond, but with little air in his lungs, he could only mouth the words. His eyes bulged, and reminded Ormsby of the toads he'd stepped on in his youth.

With one pitiful wheeze, the man went limp in Mordecai's arms.

"You know what to do with him," Ormsby said. "When he wakes up, explain what will happen to him if he says anything to anyone about his employment here."

"Yes, sir. Right away," Mordecai responded. He then hauled the unconscious body away as if it weighed nothing.

~*~

When they called for Tater, Gloria and Skeeter walked directly to the building where the audition would take place. The same smiling girl who had welcomed them to the try-outs met them at the door.

"Which of you will be taking Tater through his paces?" she asked.

"Me," Skeeter said, although his eagerness had clearly peaked a good half hour earlier.

"Great," said the effervescent girl. She smiled brightly at Gloria. "You can wait out here. We won't be long."

"But—"

The girl already had a sheltering arm around Skeeter's shoulders. "He'll be fine. We just need to eliminate as many uncontrollable elements as possible."

Uncontrollable element? "I'm his mother!"

"Indeed, you are," the girl said. "And judging from your son and his dog, an excellent one. We'll see you in a little while."

The door closed quietly but all too quickly, and Gloria stood on the wrong side of it. She told herself she had nothing to worry about. She had seen other people enter and leave the audition venue without incident. No one wept, or cursed, or in any other way suggested there might be a malevolent angle to the proceedings.

She pressed her ear to the door and strained to make out any voices or activity within the building, but the effort failed. When she stepped a few feet away and gave the structure a slow visual inspection, she decided it had an even uglier, squattier look than she'd previously thought. And, as everyone knew, ugly plus squatty equaled sinister.

Several minutes passed, and no one entered or left. Despite the denim-clad girl's pleasant demeanor and repeated assurances, Gloria's apprehension grew. After all, what did she really know about these people? The world was rife with gracious, friendly, serial killers just waiting for their chance to do unspeakable things to innocent little boys. *And* their dogs!

What was taking so long?

Oh, she ruminated, there was Tater. An outstanding pet, for sure, but that didn't make him much of a guard dog. As far as she knew, he liked everyone. He liked the *mailman* for crying out loud, and she didn't have much use for him at all. The sad truth was, anyone who dared knock on her door stood in far greater danger of being licked than mauled. Fat lot of good Tater would be if anyone tried to do anything to Skeeter. Clearly, he was doomed.

The longer she waited, the more agitated she became.

Suddenly, one short, sharp, bark escaped the squat building. She knew, instantly, that it had come from Tater. *What were they doing in there?*

Finally, she'd had enough. No one had the right to stand between a mother and her child. Pushing her sleeves up past her elbows, Gloria stalked toward the door. She was, by golly, one *uncontrollable element* they'd darn well better accommodate.

As if responding to her rage, the door popped open just before she reached it, and out marched Skeeter, Tater, and the still-smiling, denim-clad Maeve.

Both Skeeter and Tater appeared safe and unharmed. Tater mouthed a dog treat while his ten-year-old "handler" chatted with the ever-cheery redhead who seemed to be the only public face for Leon Farms.

Gloria throttled her apprehension and forced herself to generate a smile at least as wide as the girl's. "How'd it go?"

"They did great," the girl said.

"So, Tater gets the job?" Skeeter asked.

Not surprisingly, Maeve responded with her million-watt grin. "I can't say for sure. We'll have to wait until all the auditions are done." She put her hand on the boy's shoulder and pulled him a little closer. Her voice dropped into a barely audible register. "We really like Tater. I shouldn't say this, but I wouldn't be surprised if we offered him a contract."

"Us," Gloria said. "You wouldn't be surprised if they offered *us* a contract."

The girl dipped her head in Gloria's direction. "Exactly."

Gloria glanced, yet again, at the building and decided it didn't look nearly as sinister as it had a little while before.

"We'll be in touch soon," the girl said, and then she was gone.

Gloria gathered her two companions close and ushered them back to the car. Skeeter chose to sit in the back seat with Tater, and despite Gloria's best efforts to pry some details out of the boy, he consistently responded to all her questions about the audition with single syllable answers.

And none of them satisfied her need to know what went on in the squatty little building.

~*~

Ormsby Ivanov had looked forward to a victory celebration, something his enemies had denied him. But the long delay had taught him many things about them, not the least of which was their uncanny ability to bypass the roadblocks he strove to put in their way.

Though he had never met the Boss, he knew the man's reputations—one of which painted him as a saint. Another, the one Ormsby had every reason to believe was true, painted a picture of someone who fouled the very essence of the holiday he supposedly embraced.

According to the message Ormsby had just received, the Boss and his minions had completed their recruitment efforts and located enough animals to continue their plans. Once again, the Boss was poised to win. Was there no limit to the resources that sinister figure called upon?

Despite having a spy within his enemy's ranks, Ormsby continued to be outmaneuvered. He had lost count of his failures, and yet he remained dedicated to his objective. His resources were considerable, and he maintained a prominent place in worldwide financial markets, but he lacked the mystical elements his foe employed to achieve his ends. Yes, Ormsby's resources were substantial.

But were they enough?

After a great deal of concentrated prayer, Ormsby concluded that the solution called for a bolder plan and more direct action. That would undoubtedly require more effort from his informant in the Boss's organization.

~*~

A few days after Tater's audition, Gloria got a call from Michael Bell at Leon Farms.

"With your permission," Bell said, "we'd like to sign Tater to a short-term contract."

"You want to use Tater in a commercial?"

"We have several openings right now, and I can't say for sure exactly how we'll use him. All I can promise is that he'll be given extraordinary care while he's with us. Our handlers and trainers are the best in the business."

"Tater is my son's dog," Gloria said. "My husband picked him out at the pound." She didn't mention her husband's disappearance shortly thereafter. Though it had been five years, neither the police nor the private investigator she hired had turned up any trace of him.

"Then," said the man on the phone, "I need to talk to your son."

"He's in school right now," Gloria said. "But if you'll give me the details, I'll pass them along and call you with his answer."

Bell agreed and filled her in on the basics. She promised to call him back by the end of the business day.

"We'll be here around the clock for the next few days," he said. "Call any time."

When the school bus pulled up to the corner, Gloria was waiting for it. She gave Skeeter a hug, and the two walked back to their house. The rental wasn't much to look at, but it served their needs, and didn't take too big a chunk out of Gloria's limited income.

"So," Skeeter said, "they wanna make Tater a star! I told ya they would. I bet it's a movie. They're always looking for special dogs to be in the movies."

"The man didn't say what Tater would be doing.

Only that he was needed, and that they'd take good care of him."

The boy wrapped his arms around the dog, who licked his face as if someone had smeared it with peanut butter. Skeeter laughed, and the dog trundled off, his three-legged gait oddly natural.

"How long would he be gone?" he asked.

"About a month and a half. They'd pick him up before Thanksgiving and return him just after Christmas."

Skeeter pursed his lips. "That's a long time." He stretched out the word "long."

Gloria shrugged. "Five, six weeks. Give or take. But the holidays are so busy. You won't have time to miss him." *And we desperately need the money.*

"Could we visit him?"

"Sadly, no. They said he'd be on a very precise training schedule, and they couldn't take the chance that seeing his owner might distract him."

"What're they gonna teach him?" he asked.

"They wouldn't say."

Skeeter always frowned when deep in thought, a trait he shared with his Dad. Seeing that expression brought an on-going ache to Gloria's heart. *What had happened to their perfect little family?*

"I have to talk it over with Tater," Skeeter said.

Gloria shifted mental gears. "Sure. But give me your decision soon. I have to call them back, and—"

"Oh, you can call 'em now," Skeeter said. "I'm okay with it. Tater really needs to do this, and I think he knows that. I just need him to know I understand, too."

"I sure wish I did."

"It'll be okay, Mom. Trust me."

He smiled at her and triggered another memory, one of her husband waving goodbye as he left for work that fateful morning. "You're absolutely positive about this?"

"Yes," he said. "No problem."

But as she watched him walk away, she thought he looked anything but positive.

~*~

Maeve finally felt she could relax. While the efforts of the Georgia unit had only located a few potential recruits, two of the others had come through with enough candidates to promise a grand season.

"I told you not to worry," Artemis said.

"I know, but every year it seems to get harder and harder."

"You make it sound like you've been doing this forever."

She laughed. "Of course not. This is my first full season, but it's been eye-opening. I've seen so much, learned so much."

"And there's a lot more," Artemis said with a knowing smile. "You're just getting started." He paused and handed her a note from their supervisor, Michael

Bell. "Looks like you've got a pickup."

She brightened. "Which one?"

"Guess!"

"I don't know. Is it Buck? Augie? No, wait." She closed her eyes and made a wish. "Okay, tell me."

"It's Tater."

Maeve beamed. "Yes! He's going to be amazing."

"Maybe," Artemis said. "But don't get your hopes up. You only saw him in the audition. Things could change. Nothing's guaranteed."

~*~

The same girl they'd seen at the audition arrived a week to the day before Thanksgiving to pick up Tater. Gloria tried hard to keep her emotions in check as Skeeter accompanied his dog on the short walk to the girl's car. She opened the back door, and Tater jumped in. She put a padded harness on him and secured it to keep him safe in case of an accident, then turned to address Skeeter.

"You've done a wonderful job with him," she said. "We noticed that right away. Love is a lesson that never gets old."

Gloria smiled at that. Skeeter backed away from the car and leaned against her.

"Now, don't you worry about Tater," the girl said. "He's special. You can't begin to *imagine* how special. So, believe me when I say we'll take good care of him. And we'll have him back as soon as we can."

"The day after Christmas, right?" Skeeter said.

She nodded. "Around then, yes." She climbed behind the wheel of her shiny, little, red car and drove away.

Though he tried to maintain a brave front, Skeeter's stoic facade crumbled before they reached the front door.

"I can call them," Gloria said. "I'm sure they'd let us have him back. I could explain that it was all a mistake, that we—"

"No," he said, wiping his nose on his sleeve. "It's okay. This is important."

"If it's just the money you're worried about, I'm sure we can get by without it. We've managed so far."

Skeeter shook his head. "It doesn't have anything to do with money."

It doesn't? Gloria opted to change the subject. "How 'bout some hot chocolate?"

"No thanks," he said in a dead monotone. "I think I'll just go to my room."

Gloria swallowed hard and wondered if surviving the holidays could get any tougher. Three weeks later, it did.

~End of excerpt~

A Season Gone to the Dogs is available from Amazon.com in both paperback and ebook formats.

www.ingramcontent.com/pod-product-compliance
Lightning Source LLC
Chambersburg PA
CBHW051438260626
47162CB00001B/144